CRITICAL
CHERI SCOTCH'S
VOODOO MOON TRILOGY

"Highly entertaining…ingenious…the manic intensity
is evocative…"

—Edward Bryant, *Locus*

"Stunning…action-packed…for those lovers of the
unusual this is a must-read [trilogy]."

—Jill M. Smith, *Rave Reviews*

Reminiscent of Anne Rice's vampire stories."

—Peter Rubie, author of *Werewolf*

A unique interpretation of the complex and fascinat-
ng world of the werewolf."

—*Romantic Times*

HORROR AND DARK FANTASY
Published by ibooks, inc.:

THE WEREWOLF'S SIN

THE VOODOO MOON TRILOGY
BOOK 3

CHERI SCOTCH

ibooks
new york
www.ibooks.net

DISTRIBUTED BY SIMON & SCHUSTER, INC.

A Publication of ibooks, inc.

Copyright © 1994 by Cheri Scotch

An ibooks, inc. Book

ibooks, inc.
24 West 25th Street
New York, NY 10010

The ibooks World Wide Web Site Address is:
http://www.ibooks.net

ISBN 0-7434-7981-5
First ibooks, inc. printing January 2004
10 9 8 7 6 5 4 3 2 1

Printed in the U.S.A.

To all those terrific readers who not only bought the first two books, but took the time to write me actual letters or leave me E-mail saying they liked them. You can't imagine how welcome your words were.

So this one's for Teri and the Texas gang, Oberon, Carolyn, Chris the poet, Elizabeth, the GEnie geniuses, Linda Jo and her sexy "warlock," Glenna at *Talisman* and Jill at *Romantic Times* and ol' Joe Ed his ownself at *Locus* . . . and all of you who bask in the full moon and—just maybe—feel the secret stirrings of the loup-garou.

PREFACE

On the first Sunday in April after the first full moon, the Louisiana werewolves, the loups-garous, have their annual reunion on Bayou Goula.

But for the New Orleans werewolves, there is an earlier celebration, when they come together in revelry and magic and laughter in the streets of the old city.

And that is Mardi Gras Eve.

On that night, the loups-garous band together as the Krewe of Apollonius, their version of the traditional Mardi Gras krewes, named for one of the first of their kind, the philosopher and magician Apollonius of Tyana.

They dance in the streets, half-changed and awesome in their lupine grace, yet with a dangerous allure that draws humans into their seductive embraces. And sometimes the humans, willingly entrapped in the erotic web of the loups-garous, realize that they never want to escape.

Under the sultry southern skies, the loups-garous are raucous, rowdy, and exuberantly happy. Any pain or sorrow, any troubles, any difficulties, are put aside for this single, enchanted night. And every loup-garou, no matter how far away or how scattered to the winds of time and fortune, feels the call of the Krewe. And longs for home.

Moon, moon, gold-horned moon, check the flight of bullets, blunt the hunters' knives, break the shepherds' cudgels, cast wild fear upon all cattle, on men, on all creeping things, that they may not catch the gray wolf, that they may not rend his warm skin! My word is binding, more binding than sleep, more binding than the promise of a hero.

—*Old Russian charm to invoke the Moon Goddess's aid in becoming a werewolf*

THE
WEREWOLF'S
SIN

PART
ONE

†

The Lives of
the Werewolves

1

Sgt. Joe Ed Landry of the New Orleans Police Department approached the little house as apprehensively as he had ever approached a crisis crime situation. It looked pretty peaceful out here in Addis—hell, people in Addis took relaxation to a fine art form—but he knew it could blow up at any minute.

The house looked like somebody'd just gotten up and gone inside. A rocker, peeling its paint, moved back and forth on the long front porch. A half-full glass of lemonade, the sides still frosted with cold, sat on a little wicker table beside the rocker.

Joe Ed shivered. Shee-it. It was early February. Even down here in the South, it was still too chilly in the mornings to sit on the porch with lemonade.

The first gunshot sounded close by. Thirty years of training made Joe Ed hit the ground, his eyes scoping the area. The second gunshot sounded just as loud. It came from the same place. This time, Joe Ed heard the pinging of metal as a bullet connected.

After the third shot, Joe Ed heard a familiar voice.

"Ooo-*wee!*" the voice complained. "I think I done lost my touch."

Joe Ed stood up and dusted off his pants.

"Will you watch where you pointin' that thing?" he

yelled. "Ain't you never seen the po-lice films on firearm safety? What are you, a NRA or somethin'?"

Joe Ed walked around to the back of the house, where Captain Achille Broussard, also of the NOPD, was aiming a .38 Smith & Wesson at the top of his house. He didn't look much like a police captain: his long, dark hair, usually kept neatly in a ponytail, cascaded free down his back. His short-sleeved T-shirt emphasized his powerful arms and shoulders. And the little gold hoop earring wasn't what Joe Ed would call standard police issue.

"Hey, Joe Ed," Achille said without looking at him, "where y'at?"

Joe Ed, unable to resist, followed Achille's aim. On top of the house was a large metal weather vane shaped like a rooster. The rooster's metal tail feathers and a good part of the rear end were shot off.

"I hate that fucker," Achille explained. "The last tenants I had in here were from someplace up north, Kansas or one of them places; they put it up there to remind 'em of home."

Joe Ed nodded. To a New Orleans native, anyplace above Shreveport was "up north." And inconsequential.

"You ever thought of just climbin' up there and takin' it down?" Joe Ed suggested.

"Maybe I shoulda used the nine-millimeter, you think?"

"Hell, you woulda blown ya whole roof off. You never was that good a shot. I always meant to tell ya that, but the occasion just never came up."

Achille tore his attention away from the offensive weather vane and clapped Joe Ed on the shoulder. "Well, come on in. I got some red beans and rice left over from last night, and there's a couple of cold Dixies in there. I even got a few bottles of that Blackened Voodoo beer— somebody dishonest done lifted 'em from a crime scene and left 'em in my office one time.''

"You drinkin' the evidence?"

"Hell, they weren't evidence. They were in the refrigerator. The ol' boys who owned 'em weren't gonna drink 'em where they were going.''

Achille led Joe Ed into a comfortable country kitchen flooded with sunlight. Cooking implements hung from exposed, stained beams, yellow café curtains hung at the windows, and Joe Ed found himself seated at a big butcher-block table on a yellow painted chair. The place was immaculate.

"You got a cleaning lady comin' in, Achille?" Joe Ed said, impressed. "My wife don't keep our place this clean.''

"I got a lot of time on my hands these days," Achille said blandly.

That reminded Joe Ed painfully of why he was here. Nothing official was being done, but the NOPD wanted Achille back to work. The acting homicide officer, Lt. John Sullivan, was worried about Achille. "I don't begrudge him his mourning period," Sullivan had said, "but this isn't like him. He's changing, and it's not for the better. We gotta get the Cap back here; once he's in the mainstream, he'll recover. He's not living in Mae's house in the Quarter anymore; he's just holing up in that little house of his in Addis and going slowly nuts. Go see what you can find out.''

Sullivan had handed Joe Ed a folder with some photos and press clippings. "See what he thinks of these.''

Achille heated up the red beans. Joe Ed watched him carefully, with a professional's eye. Achille looked as good as ever—Joe Ed had never figured out how Achille stayed so young and good looking; good genes, he guessed—but there was something very old, very painful about the way

Achille moved. Achille had always been all energy, all authoritative motion and decisive action. Now he was slow and tentative, as if he were moving underwater, or just slightly behind the beat of life. It was as if he had lost part of himself somewhere, the part that moved him and gave him his drive.

Well, thought Joe Ed, perhaps he had. Achille had lost plenty in the past few months.

Joe Ed inadvertently thought of his wife. They'd been together for so long that they took each other for granted, but if he ever lost her . . . He gave a slight shudder.

Achille set a steaming plate of rice smothered in red beans and spicy chunks of andouille sausage before Joe Ed. A basket of crisp French bread broken into large pieces sat beside the plate. "Damn, this smells good," Joe Ed said.

"Us bayou boys know how to cook," Achille agreed. "But you didn't come all the way nearly to Baton Rouge for the cuisine." Achille took a long draft of his beer.

Joe Ed looked at his plate. "Yeah, you right," he said quietly.

"Am I fired?" Achille said. He didn't sound particularly concerned.

"No!" Joe Ed said, startled. "*Hell* no! But the Chief wants you back on the job, Achille. Sullivan's up to his ass without you; he can't even begin to fill your shoes, not even temporary, and he knows it. The chief reminds him of it at least once a week—he's on Sullivan's ass like a pit bull. It's been over a month already."

"That long?" Achille mused.

"Achille," Joe Ed's voice grew softer, "We all loved her. Mae Charteris was one of the finest women in New Orleans. The Voodoos loved her better than any queen they'd ever had since Marie Laveau. Personally, I'll never forget all she did for the department; hell, we got cases'd still be open if not for her aidin' the investigations. Shit, she knew everything went on in this town. But. . ."

"You about to tell me she wouldn't want to see me like this."

"You should know."

Achille sat back in his chair, balancing it on its two back legs. His long, curly black hair, streaked with a little gray, freed from its usual ponytail, hung over the chair's back. Almost unconsciously, he reached up to touch the small gold hoop in his ear.

She had put it there, so long ago. She said it would keep other women away from him. She had been wrong about that; women seemed more attracted to him than ever when he wore it. But she was entirely correct in assuming that Achille would want none of them. Only her. It had always been only her, from the moment he saw her, when she was sixteen and he was eighteen.

It wasn't that he couldn't believe she was dead. He believed it, all right. What amazed him was that he was still alive without her.

"It's too soon," Achille said.

"Too soon, hell," Joe Ed said. "Look, I'm gonna play hardball here." He tossed the folder on the table.

Achille looked at it, but didn't move. "And this is. . .?"

"This is, among other things, a two-day-old newspaper story about Reverend Eric Ely. The rev has just been granted another postponement, courtesy of his high-priced New York lawyer, Russell Berkman. I guess you heard'a him?"

Achille had. Berkman was every felon's dream, a grandstanding publicity hound who happened to also be a fine lawyer. He took media-intensive cases and made a reputation for winning the hard ones.

Achille still didn't move, but he looked interested.

"How's Ely affording Russell Berkman? I thought he was broke just posting bail."

"He'll never be broke as long as people are willin' to be duped in the name of the Lord," Landry said in disgust. "Them religious fanatics in his church posted his bail and now they're paying for his defense. Some of 'em even mortgaged their houses to do it."

Achille closed his eyes and seemed to stop breathing.

"Listen, Achille, you ain't been around," Landry said. "You ain't heard it all. This guy's become a celebrity, especially since Berkman took his case. He's got money pouring in from everywhere; even these TV preachers who'd rather see their mothers raped at high noon in Jackson Square than give up a nickel are yellin' about what a martyr he is, how he was only doin' the Lord's work when he..."

Joe Ed stopped just in time. Achille hadn't moved or opened his eyes, but his face was heating up, his skin becoming suffused with blood.

Joe Ed waited a few minutes before he spoke again.

"You think I like sayin' this? You think I don't know what it does to you? Well, I don't care, not if it gets you outta this house and back in New Orleans, where you belong. I don't care if you never speak to me again."

It was a long time before Achille moved or spoke.

"Joe Ed, you ever seen pictures of Jack the Ripper's victims?"

"No," Landry said, mystified. "I didn't know there *was* any. I thought they just had artists in those days."

"No. There were a few pictures taken at the scenes. I saw them when I was just a young cop, studying everything I could about police work. I saw pictures of, I think it was Mary Kelly. She hardly looked like a human being. In all my time in homicide, I never saw anything worse. Not until

the afternoon in the morgue when they unzipped that bag
and I had to identify Mae's body. You see what he did to
her, Joe Ed?''

Joe Ed squirmed in his chair. He wanted to cry. He'd
seen.

"Thirty-seven stab wounds," Achille said, "the first one
through the throat would have killed her, but he didn't stop
there. He was going good, the Lord was guiding his hand,
he said he was ridding New Orleans of this Voodoo ver-
min—although I hear that's gonna be inadmissible as a
confession when it comes to trial.

"You know what was strange, Joe Ed, was that she never
took him seriously. Just the day before, he'd grabbed her
on the street and said, 'I could kill you right now and my
God would forgive me because the blood of Jesus says that
thou shalt not suffer a Witch to live!'

"She never told me this, of course. I heard it later, from
the Voodoo woman who was with her at the time, Sister
Claudine. Claudine said that Mae just shrugged him off and
laughed. She told him she was real glad, then, that she was
a Voodoo and not a Witch. If I'd known about that, his ass
would have been in jail even if he got me later for unlawful
arrest. I think that it drove him right over the brink that she
thought he was a clown. He had this picture of himself as
a powerful preacher, maybe someday he was gonna be Jerry
Falwell or Pat Robertson with big TV shows and people
who'd do whatever he told 'em and enough money to buy
himself a few congressmen. Hell, now he's famous. Maybe
he'll have everything he wanted.''

Joe Ed felt an overwhelming sadness settle on him.

"Ya know what was the worst, Joe Ed?" Achille said.
"It took me almost twenty-five years to talk that woman
into marryin' me. She never would. She just said we were
too different. I told her that if I had to, I'd go to another

Voodoo woman and get some gris-gris that'd *make* her marry me, and she just looked at me with that wise expression of hers and said, 'Oh yeah? And maybe someday you'll get up in the night to pee and your dick'll fall off.' "

Joe Ed couldn't help but laugh. That sounded like Mae, all right.

"But I wore her down, and she gave in. She said she was gonna stay *beautiful* forever, but she wasn't gonna stay *young* forever and she might need somebody around someday to help her out of her walker or change her diapers," Achille said. "The day she died was our five-month anniversary."

"I didn't know that," Joe Ed said quietly.

"Yeah. Well."

They sat a moment in uneasy silence.

Achille opened his eyes and suddenly tilted forward in the chair, settling it down on all four legs. He looked frankly at Joe Ed, and the stark pain in his eyes made Joe Ed flinch inwardly.

"Hell, what does the department need me for? I can't do any more work on this case. They think I haven't done everything I could already?"

Joe Ed shook his head. "We don't want you back for that. Hell, we got other cases, ya know. It's just that . . . you're not doin' yourself or anybody else any good out here, Achille. You're just gettin' worse. You were never the kind of man who could stand doin' nothing."

"Who says I'm doing nothing?" Achille said enigmatically. Joe Ed expected him to elaborate, but he didn't volunteer any information.

"I could come back to New Orleans," Achille said, "but the next homicide you'd be investigating will be a lot closer to home. Because if I'm anywhere near Ely, even if he's in protective custody, even if you got him locked in a vault at the Whitney Bank with a round-the-clock SWAT team on his ass . . . I'll kill him. If I hadn't come out here, I'd of killed him already.''

Achille patted Joe Ed on the shoulder.

"So just eat your red beans and drink your Dixie, *cher ami*. You tried your best. Tell 'em I'll be back when I come back.''

After Joe Ed left, Achille sat for a long time in his house, looking at nothing, trying to think of nothing. It was no good. He could still see Mae's face as she laughed over morning coffee with him, or as she closed her eyes and gasped in passion when she lay beneath him. He could remember her flashes of anger as she recounted to him some act of violence done to one of her followers, a crime that would never even come to trial, and told him that the only way it could be made right was through the intervention of the loup-garou, the Louisiana werewolf, the last route to justice when human justice failed.

For the last thirty years, Achille had administered that justice.

Transformed, with supernatural strength and with a precise psychic power that gave him unquestioned proof as to the guilt or innocence of a man's conscience, Achille would stalk the night until he had seen to it that true justice was finally done, the balance of good and evil restored.

And now, when he himself had been violated in the most awful way, he was helpless. He was imprisoned in his own principles. He wanted to let his fury out, to let it swell and grow and burst until the corruption of it drained from his soul and made him a free man again.

Every day, every night, was a struggle against his anger. Each second that he let Ely live was actually a victory for him. But it was hollow, unsatisfying, a victory that stung like defeat.

Achille took up his Smith & Wesson and went back out-side, to vent a little of his venom on the unfortunate weather vane.

When Mae was killed, Achille wasn't as rational as he was with Joe Ed. At first, he was too stunned to mourn. He couldn't speak coherently or see anyone, he refused to go anywhere. He shut himself in the cocoon of Mae's house, the house he'd shared with her for so many years as her lover and for so brief a passage as her husband.

Even his friend Andrew Marley, who could usually get Achille to see the reason in anything, couldn't communicate with him. The Voodoos, and the heartbroken but strong young woman who was Mae's successor as queen, had given her a wonderful funeral in her faith. The young queen had performed the necessary and solemn rites for Mae, free-ing her soul to fly away in freedom. Achille couldn't bear to attend this ritual, but the Voodoos, dealing with their own pain and loss, had well understood.

Another tribute that Achille never saw was the requiem mass that Andrew, who was the Episcopal bishop of the diocese, had said for Mae. Andrew said that the Voodoo Queen had done so much for the city of New Orleans that she deserved as many memorials as the people who loved her wanted to have. Mae had been a good friend to Andrew and they rarely saw any conflicts in their respective reli-gions.

"We're all trying to be the best people we can be, to make the world a better place," Mae had told him once. "Doesn't really matter how it happens, so long as it hap-pens."

His closest friends, Apollonius and Zizi, tried to watch over Achille, fearing for his sanity and his physical health. Zizi once brought a big pot of gumbo over to Achille, and found him asleep in the middle of the afternoon, the silk scarf Mae used to wear tangled in his hands, its bright colors running with tears. Zizi merely left the gumbo in the kitchen and quietly left the house.

"He looked horrible," Zizi told Apollonius. "Even asleep. He's not eating, I can tell by how thin his face looks. And his eyes have dark circles. Just lying there, he looked tortured, as if he were screaming in his sleep."

"Did you try reading his dreams?" Apollonius was referring to the psychic bond common between werewolves.

She shook her head. "The kind of dreams he's having, I want no part of. I'm not even sure he's feeding at the full moon. He looks so *starved.*"

"He's feeding. He has to: if he wasn't, he'd be dead by now."

But that conversation left Apollonius worried. Usually, under stress, a loup-garou will ease the tension by transforming and running it out, until sheer exhaustion dropped him into a cleansing sleep. But it seemed that Achille, usually the most exuberant of loups-garous, exulting in the transformation and the chase, had not done that. There was something ominous about Achille's torpor, as if he were building up to something, and Apollonius was afraid he knew what that was.

"He's guarding his thoughts," Apollonius told Zizi, "trying not to let either of us see. That's a warning sign right there."

"It doesn't take a genius to figure out what he's going to do," Zizi said. "He's thinking of killing Ely. And he's going to do it at the full moon, when he has to kill anyway. I don't see what the problem is, Apollonius. If ever there was a kill for justice..."

"It doesn't work that way, and you know it," Apollonius said gently. "If it did, I would have killed the bastard myself. But human justice has to have failed. And Ely hasn't even been brought to trial yet. My God, he's going to be convicted, it's obvious. Look at the circumstances, look at the outrage in the black community. Just look at the crime itself. The authorities want to make a public example of Ely, and they're right."

"Oh, Apollonius," Zizi said in frustration, "you know that there are kills all the time that are . . . well, a little *premature*. Cases where the loup-garou kills to stop a serial murderer or a rapist or a child abuser from doing it again. They haven't been brought to human justice; we *are* the justice in these cases."

"Despite your being French, my dear, that's a very American attitude. A Judge Roy Bean approach to the law."

"It's realistic. Your view is *idealistic*. You're the only werewolf in the world, perhaps the only one in *history*, who has never killed for anything but justice. The rest of us have done it for other reasons on occasion, even the most disciplined of us."

"Perhaps I am, perhaps not," he said enigmatically. "But it still stands that I believe that the state will give the Reverend Ely what he deserves."

But Zizi had lived in America longer than Apollonius, who had spent most of his life roaming the world. She was the first loup-garou in America, arriving in 1722 as Marie-Thérèse de la Rochette, Duchesse de Marais. She had known Apollonius before that, while she lived in France. In fact, he was almost the only person now who called her by her proper name. Although he had not been the one who had made her a loup-garou, still she had learned about true lycanthropy from Apollonius. From her came the beginnings of the Louisiana werewolves, and she had taught them Apollonius's code of ethics. Over those centuries she had seen the workings of the American judicial system—in which the victim had no rights and the killer had the full protection of the law—long enough to have had the idealism burned right out of her. She would have been bitter, except that she knew that true justice, the justice of the gods, never fails. The loups-garous saw to that; it was the reason they existed.

Both of them knew that Achille had always been the foremost proponent of the loup-garou's code of justice, an almost fanatical devotee of their strict principles of ethics. His adherence to those ethics, his willingness to make sure that young loups-garous knew what they meant and how they operated, and his prominence as one of the leaders of the loup-garou community had guided many a werewolf to a fulfilling, productive life.

These were the ideals that Apollonius himself had set forth thousands of years ago and that Marie-Thérèse had passed on: that it was killing in the name of higher ideals that ennobled a loup-garou, that made him more than a murderous monster. Controlling the inbred impulse to kill took great dedication to those ideals, and if one wavered from them, one could well be lost.

Apollonius could see that Achille was just on the edge of the gulf.

So, as the full moon approached, Zizi and Apollonius sought help from Andrew Marley. There was a solid little cabin in the Honey Island swamps that had been in Andrew's family for years. Windowless, with one stout door, it could withstand an onslaught from within.

"It's no use being evasive with me and you know it," Apollonius told Achille. "You also know that you can't kill Ely."

"He deserves it," Achille said tonelessly, twisting Mae's scarf in his hands.

"He deserves to die, I'll grant you that. But not by your hand. Not yet, at any rate. If the state of Louisiana doesn't get him, I promise you, Achille, he's yours. You know that. But at this point, to take it into your own hands is wrong."

Achille stared at a bit of the sky beyond Apollonius, where he saw nothing except the ghastly pictures in his head. They were the same ones that kept running over and over, like bad movie clips: Mae's body on the autopsy table, Ely's gloating face covered with her blood, Mae's screams—the screams that he had never really heard in actuality but were almost ceaselessly with him now.

"The state will kill him quickly and painlessly," Achille said. "Want to know how I'd kill him, Apollonius?"

"Please don't do this, Achille."

Achille knew he didn't have to elaborate. "He might not even be convicted at all," Achille said. "An insanity plea would get him off. A couple of years of therapy, a team of smart lawyers. He'll be back, preaching what he considers the word of God. And there'll be people who'll believe him, who'll be convinced that God actually condones what Ely did because, after all, he let Ely get away with it. He can just pick up his life where he left off. Where am I going to pick up *my* life, Apollonius?"

"Pick it up right here, Achille. Start by leaving this house for a while. Come stay with me and Zizi; there's plenty of room and our place is too quiet these days."

Achille looked directly at Apollonius, and the bleakness of his eyes struck Apollonius's heart.

"What if it had been Zizi? What would you have done?"

Apollonius had asked himself that question a hundred times since Mae had been killed. "I would hope that you'd do for me what I'm trying to do for you. And I think you would."

Unexpectedly, Achille collapsed against Apollonius.

Waves of his anger and grief smashed against Apollonius's rocklike strength. His sobs were wild howls, great gasps of anguish that turned the air in his lungs to fire. Apollonius thought that he had heard few things as terrible in his long life.

At the full moon, Apollonius locked Achille into the Honey Island cabin, keeping him there until his murderous fever passed. Because a werewolf cannot survive without a kill at the full moon, Zizi brought him a victim.

The kill was a man whose financial machinations had brought ruin to hundreds of people. He had been caught, tried and fined, had served six months in a country-club prison, and was now out of jail, reunited with his millions. To the courts and the newspapers and the parole boards he was profusely apologetic, beating his breast and chanting his *mea culpas* in a loud voice. But privately, he bragged about his business savvy, he talked about his dirty deals and his "hostile takeovers" in terms appropriated from war, which was his only way of viewing the world. He regarded the people who tried and convicted him with scorn, and the people he had ruined as inconsequential serfs who had no reason to complain. They deserved it, he said often. They brought their destruction on themselves since they lacked the—as he put it—"go-for-the-throat instincts" that were his substitutes for human emotions. "If they couldn't run with the big dogs," he snorted, "they shouldn't have gotten off the porch."

Zizi knew he was vacationing in New Orleans. She caught him out that night, stunned him, and brought him swiftly to Honey Island. As she threw him through the door into the cabin, where Achille, transformed and terrifying, stalked like a caged and starving animal, he regained his senses.

"You'll certainly respect this gentleman," she told the

financier. "You're about to find out what 'going for the throat' really means. Meet one of the *real* big dogs."

And she closed the door on his screams with a satisfied smile.

That kill took some of the sharpness off Achille's vengeful edge, but he knew that if he stayed in New Orleans, where Mae's murder was going to be an emotional topic on the news and in the papers for months, his mindless anger would grow beyond his limits to control it.

He missed the police department. Achille had always loved his work. But with the investigation of Mae's murder still going on, it was impossible for him to be there. He wasn't involved in it, not officially, but the case was on everyone's agenda. He couldn't avoid the topic. He knew that going back to work would save him, would give his mind and body something concrete to do, but he just couldn't face the reminders of Mae.

He thought of quitting the NOPD, giving up his seniority, his pension, everything. He could get another job, in Port Allen or Lafayette or Baton Rouge.

But for the moment he decided to do nothing, knowing that his thought processes weren't the best and any decision would probably be the wrong one.

So he sat in his little house in Addis, cooking gumbo and drinking Dixies, going into town for new fishing lures and ignoring the admiring stares of the single ladies, taking target practice at the weather vane. He worked around the house. He did some fishing. His cooking improved since he had more time to devote to it, and he watched endless TV and rented movies in an effort to turn his mind off. He slept more hours than he needed, and his sleep became dreamless, his mind saving itself from destruction.

Sometimes he thought about what Joe Ed had said and whether he was right or wrong.

He figured the answer would come, but he was going to give it time.

2

When a man has lived five hundred years, he bores easily. Merely to make a change in his life is meaningless: for it to distract him at all, the change has to be dramatic.

John Luparo wanted a whole new incarnation this time, a complete upheaval. Pining for the snap of winter air, he decided to leave Los Angeles for Boston. Last week, he'd sold his custom Harley to another Hell's Angel who couldn't believe his good luck. When the man expressed astonishment that John would part with the machine, John just scratched his chest and eyed the Harley dispassionately.

"Well, ya know," John said in that soft Jimmy Stewart drawl he'd developed over the last few years, "it never was as good as *Easy Rider* and *The Wild One* made it out to be. Grit and bugs blowin' in your face. Smog chokin' ya. And I never got used to it when I'd climb offa that thing with my balls still vibratin'." He slapped the Angel absently on the shoulder and handed him the title and registration. "It's all yours now, amigo. I'm gonna try an' get my sperm count back up. See ya."

With the astonished Angel still staring after him, John slid behind the wheel of his new Volvo station wagon and took off.

He'd intended to stop and get his long hair cut, but this simple thing presented a problem. Was he getting it "cut" or "styled"? Was he having this great tonsorial event done in the fashionable salons of Rodeo Drive or in a local barbershop littered with raggedy *Sports Illustrated*s? He debated on the kind of life he wanted: Armani or Brooks Brothers? Armani would have needed a hairstyling job, preferably with a ponytail, a house in the hills, and a Porsche Carrera. He'd be back in the fast life. Granted, the Carrera meant fast and *rich* when what he'd just left was fast and *sleazy*, but still . . .

The Volvo was really the key here: he'd unconsciously picked his new life when he'd decided on the car. When he got to Boston, he'd settle in for a few days with his friend Georgiana Marley, then take a side trip up to Maine, to L.L. Bean. He smiled. Yeah, this was a good direction. L.L. Bean, a Volvo, the Sierra Club, the Society for the Preservation of New England Antiquities, a Tai Chi class, an antique house in Concord or maybe up in Danvers or Salem, a golden retriever named Max. Or perhaps a town house on Beacon Hill or on Union Park. He could definitely wear this persona for a while. He was pretty sure he could teach at Harvard. He'd taught at Yale, in the 1920s. After the first few hundred years of doing it, doctoring the necessary documents was never a problem. In the computer age, with nothing on paper anymore, it was even easier. His field was history, the irony of which never failed to crack him up. He wasn't so much a scholar as just a good observer and reporter. He didn't study history; he remembered it.

John had left the hot, purifying air of the desert behind, feeling it burn away his old life with the Hell's Angels. Out here, it was easy to forget that it was February. That was one thing that amused him about Southern California: the only way he could tell what season it was was by the change in the store displays. If you got back from the beach and Santa was in the window, it was December. He turned off the Volvo's air conditioning and cruised through New Mexico, arriving in Albuquerque just as the sun was rising. The sight was so astounding that he'd had to pull over. In just a little while, the city would be up and at it, the highways crawling with machinery. But right now, it was almost totally quiet; the air was still and cool, and the mountains rose purple against the rose-colored clouds. Jesus! John thought. So that's what that song means: "purple mountains' majesty." He shook his head slowly, appreciating once more the sight of nature doing what she does best. He started the car and drove on.

John loved long-distance driving, loved eating in odd roadside diners with paper place mats decorated with drawings of the local places of interest or coloring-book games to keep people's kids entertained until the food came. He liked alternating offbeat motels with Holiday Inns and sometimes posh four-star hotels. He liked driving at night, especially on roads with long stretches of dark between houses, and those houses lit with comfy-looking lights in the windows. He'd repeat the traveler's litany: "If I lived there, I'd be home now." Even driving through cities, he'd look up at the high-rise apartments with glass walls. The yellow light was the same as in the little farmhouses. Home is home, he'd think.

He often stopped at Stuckey's to buy peanut brittle and look over the touristy merchandise: plastic back-scratchers with "Souvenir of Denver" pressed into the handle, fragrant cedar jewelry boxes with tacky postcards, or tackier pictures of a WASP-y blue-eyed blond Jesus pasted on the lids and glossed over with heavy varnish, cheap water globes that swirled genuine plastic snow over any one of a dozen garishly painted scenes.

As often as he stopped in these places, he was aware that

they weren't actually part of his life, and that was the powerful attraction. Whose life *were* they part of? he wondered. People with kids and mortgages and imitation Izod shirts and two weeks' vacation from their jobs. Most of John's friends would sneer at the people who would cheerfully take these things home, but John found the objects, the artifacts of their lives, fascinating, as if they would give him the keys to the lives themselves.

It was February for real when he hit New England a few days later. The slushy remains of snow and the weak, dull sunshine through gray clouds told him that he might as well get over California. And then the oddest thing happened: somewhere along the Massachusetts Turnpike he began to notice a black Mercedes following him. Or, at least, he thought it was following him. It was staying awfully close. It only crossed his mind for a few minutes, though: on these freeways, you have a lot of cars that you see frequently, all traveling long ways and bound for similar destinations. At one point he lost the Mercedes for a while when he stopped for lunch, then it picked up his trail again outside Boston. Coming into the city, in that maze of twisty-turny, one-way streets that made up so much of Boston, he lost sight of the car again.

John remembered quite a lot of Boston from the old days. He'd been coming here, off and on, for a couple hundred years, and it always comforted him that, even though the city changed, there were parts of it that remained pretty much the same. The north end would always be the north end. Old North Church and Copps Hill Burying Ground, where he had a wife buried, were surrounded by change, but not really touched by it.

John thought about that wife with tenderness. Molly. What a sweet woman she'd been! And how it devastated him that she'd been carried off by typhoid fever, when it could have been avoided. He could have saved her, given her the precious gift that would have kept her by his side for hundreds of years. But she refused, horrified, and it was part of John's grief that his confession to Molly may have hastened her death. Confronted by the truth of John's existence, by what accounted for his apparent resistance to aging, disease, and death, Molly's mind simply wouldn't accept it. Did the shock of it weaken her? Did her bitterness kill the spirit, that part of her that might have fought harder against her fever if she had believed she had anything left to live for? For a hundred years, that question haunted John's nights.

He had been a widower before and since, three times in all, his weakness for loving human women overriding the common sense that told him that in his love there was the inevitable pain of loss. Only Molly had known his secret, and it was Molly's grave that he had never been able to visit.

He didn't even consider stopping there now. To think of Molly under the ground, the children they could have had, the *life* they could have had, was still painful and unreal.

To distract himself, John drove out of the north end, going south, past Boston Common and the Public Gardens, to Copley Square. The beautiful old Copley Plaza was one of his favorite hotels. He'd stay there for a week or so, call Georgiana for dinner, and give himself time to settle into the city rhythm. Tonight he'd visit one of his favorite seafood places in all the world, a restaurant with food so renowned that people gladly stood in line on the sidewalk for an hour, making friends and chatting about past culinary revelations. Then maybe he'd walk around, feel the energy, revisit some of his past.

He ended up doing none of those things. He and his luggage were shown to a quiet, spacious room overlooking

H. H. Richardson's magnificent Trinity Church. He turned on the water and stepped into the shower: the strong smell of chlorine and something nasty overcame him, as if the water had stood stagnant in the pipes for some time. He turned off the water, intending to call the front desk. Then he remembered. Ah yes. Boston water. This was normal; it was what you got used to after a short while but what always brought you up short when you were new to it. Even longtime Boston residents, arriving home after vacations, had to get used to the water all over again.

So the water sucked, John thought. Boston was worth it.

John turned the water back on, took a deep breath, and let the gloriously hot water do its job. Within a few minutes of toweling off, John was unable to resist the soft, warm bed. He was asleep almost instantly.

He woke up at nine, called room service for breakfast, thought better of it, and canceled the order. Instead, he called Georgiana.

She sounded cranky. John remembered with amusement that Geo liked to keep late hours. "It's the middle of the night," she said, less than conversationally.

"Nice greeting, sweetheart. Is that any way to talk to someone who wants to buy you breakfast?"

"Agh. The very thought turns my stomach. Who is this?"

He started to tell her. "Wait a minute..." she said, her voice waking up. John could just see her suddenly sitting up and removing her white satin sleep mask. "Don't tell me. I know this voice! You always sounded like Jimmy Stewart would if he'd swallowed sandpaper.... John Luparo! Where are you? What are you doing?"

"What a memory!" he said, impressed.

"Only forty or fifty years, John. That's a minute to us. Oh, gosh... it's good to hear you again!"

"I'm at the Copley. Wanna meet me?"

Her voice took on a different timbre. "Depends. In your room or in the restaurant? Shall I bother to dress or just throw my coat over my nightgown?"

He smiled into the phone. "*Stop* it."

"Just checking. I can't wait to hear what you've been doing. Why are you back in Boston? Are you taking on another incarnation?"

"Yep. And you have to help me make the transition. I'm trying to remember what polite speech sounds like—I still talk like a Hell's Angel."

She let out a roar of laughter. "John Luparo was a Hell's Angel? Are you kidding? Oh boy, I'm sorry I missed this one!"

"It wasn't really that interesting."

But she couldn't stop laughing. "Think of your colleagues at Yale! Think of the prissy boys in Rome! This is just too much! Did you ride your motorcycle here? How do you look? They must have *loved* it when you walked into the Copley—a Hell's Angel! Don't move—I'm coming *right* over!"

"You'll be disappointed. But I'm coming over to pick you up. You still live on Louisburg Square?"

"Always. I'll be ready. I'll run right out the door the minute I hear a motorcycle. Shall I wear something slutty? A tight leather skirt and no underpants?"

"Dress for a Volvo," he said, hanging up.

John was waiting for the parking attendant to bring his car around when he saw the black Mercedes again. Or—at least, *a* black Mercedes. They all looked alike. Strange how they kept crossing paths, if it was the same one. John was so happy with his life at that moment that he was caught completely off guard when the Mercedes pulled close to him and the tinted window rolled down.

The driver was looking right at John, directly into his eyes.

John staggered slightly, stepping back in an instinct of pure self-preservation. He actually felt the blood leave his face.

The man said nothing, although the car was close enough where John was standing on the curb so that John could have heard him without his having to raise his voice. The man simply smiled. John was immobile with shock.

The *first* time he saw this man, John was human. He was also Cesare Giovanni, Cardinal Orsini. And the man, not human at all, had been Pope Honorius V. By the time he left the papal palace, which was the *last* time he saw Honorius, he was exactly as Honorius was: a loup-garou; one of the charmed company of the werewolves of France.

Well, not *exactly* as Honorius. The pontiff, living in luxury in fourteenth-century Avignon with his court of French cardinals, his powerful friends, and his devastating mistress, was a man of far-reaching influence. The papacy was, for Honorius, simply another in a long line of incarnations, assumed to hide the fact that the man had been alive and well since the earliest days of Greece and Rome. His real name was Lycaon and he had been the first werewolf, a man of awe-inspiring intellect, made terrifying by the fact that he was perfectly charming, perfectly logical— and perfectly insane.

Lycaon didn't have to say a word to John. As John stood immobile with dread, Lycaon only smiled and pointed at John, as if to say they were not done with each other. And then the window rolled up over the handsome and terrifying face and the Mercedes moved on, leaving John breathless and dazed with the sure and certain knowledge of impending ruin.

If ever there was a man who personified everything evil

in this world, Lycaon was that man. His appearance now, after hundreds of years of silence, hundreds of years of speculation in the loup-garou communities of the world as to what had become of him, could mean many things.

None of them good.

John knew better than to try to stop Lycaon from whatever nastiness he was up to now. There was only one loup-garou who had so much as a prayer of doing anything about Lycaon, and it sure wasn't John. And that loup-garou sure wasn't in Boston.

So it was good-bye to the conservative life in New England, good-bye to the beautiful Georgiana, the Society for New England Antiquities, L.L. Bean, and the golden retriever. He'd have to break his breakfast date with Georgiana: he thought about explaining to her about Lycaon, then thought better of it. No reason to alarm her. He knew—just as Lycaon wanted him to know—that Lycaon's real destination wasn't Boston. Oh, he could do a little damage here if he wanted, but he wouldn't waste the energy. The Northeast was insignificant for him. If Lycaon wanted to strike at the real heart of the werewolves, he'd have to go to Louisiana.

John turned back to call Georgiana, check out of the Copley, gas up the car, and it was on down south to New Orleans for him.

And let the bad times roll.

3

It was Carnival time.

Festoons of bright ribbons floated from every ironwork balcony, billowing out in green, gold, and purple: the Mardi Gras colors. Shop windows were filled with masks, from simple half-face masks to fantasy creations of gold and silver and glittering stones, of towering feathers falling gracefully over bare shoulders, of ethereal colors born in dreams, not in nature. Maskers strutted in starry sequins, their bodies more revealed than concealed, conscious of their otherworldly beauty and radiant sensuality. On this night, the last night before Lent, anything you could imagine could come true, anyone you wanted, you could have. Behind the liberating masks, the night would be a passing homage to the delights of the flesh and the imagination.

Over it all presided the city, the queen of the South, her crescent river smiling placidly on the festivities, her ancient streets and houses and gardens blurring the lines of time. She had smiled on Mardi Gras for a hundred years and would smile for a hundred more, secure in the knowledge that, although there may be Carnivals elsewhere in the world, only American exuberance could produce a festival exactly like this one.

In the more polite circles, bred in the Garden District and in French Quarter houses owned by the same families since slave times, more civilized celebrations took place. The cream of that year's debutantes formed the court around the Queen of Carnival. She was elevated on a high scaffolding with the other maidens in attendance, like Guinevere in a tower, and waited for the Rex parade, for the first of her moments of glory on Mardi Gras. His great float stopped beneath her feet, a bottle of champagne burst its cork and fizzed liquid fireworks, and Rex toasted the young woman who would reign as Queen of Mardi Gras. That night, at Rex's ball, she would parade around the room, an impossibly heavy, jewel-encrusted robe trailing for yards behind her. In her bewitchment, she would hardly notice the weight, as if the glittering dress, the crown, and the robe were all fairy garments, weightless, vanishing in tomorrow's first light.

The Queen and her court, the fabulous parades, the air full of streamers and confetti and beads tossed high from dreamlike floats, the elegant balls, the private parties all over town, the bawdy music, and uninhibited maskers of Bourbon Street: these elements all blended in the alchemical crucible that made the magical gold of Mardi Gras.

And in the morning, with the first church bells, none of it ever happened. Among the Bourbon Street maskers, nothing would ever be acknowledged, even by the two or three or more people who spent the night together in unaccustomed abandon.

Last night's mermaid metamorphosed back into a secretary. The goat-footed Great God Pan reassumed his banker's pinstripes. Aphrodite, her beautiful body in chiffon drapery so lately worshiped by a pirate and a prelate, brewed the morning coffee and herded her kids to Lenten mass.

But the Queen . . . the crown would never leave her. In later years she would find herself paused in the middle of some mundane chore, and realize that she had been lost for a few minutes in a single evening that had already passed into dreams.

These visions of Carnival and New Orleans blinded Sylvie Drago to what was really going on around her. She forced herself out of her memories and back into reality.

She was actually sitting front row center at the Metropolitan Opera in New York City, watching her husband conduct *La Bohème*. The key word here, Sylvie thought wryly, was "watching," not "listening." *Bohème* wasn't one of her favorites, so the opera alone wasn't enough to get her out on a February night in New York. But watching Lucien conduct was irresistible, even after fifteen years of following him from city to city, orchestra to orchestra, sitting in theaters and concert halls and outdoor music amphitheaters where Puccini or Mozart rode on the night air and melded with the moon. Lucien was an instrument all by himself, a very physical conductor whose obvious passion for the music influenced his movements onstage. At first, Sylvie was hypnotized by the motions of his hands as they delineated the sounds he wanted and pulled them out of the equally enchanted musicians: they were the identical movements he used when he made love to her, when his hands coaxed out of her body exactly the reactions he wanted and gratified his sense of harmony and sensual pleasure.

She knew that Lucien was never a man to kid himself. He was a great, passionate conductor, a keen interpreter of the music and an inspired composer in his own right. But he realized that all this wouldn't have gotten him the kind of audiences he attracted now: a mix of sophisticated music lovers and star-struck fans. He and his publicists shrewdly exploited his good looks, his sea green eyes, and his thick blond hair. And they made good use of the publicity value of his beautiful wife, the southern belle who had once been Queen of Mardi Gras.

Sylvie sometimes thought that her life was killing her. Every day, upon awakening, she faced a long list of responsibilities, things that had to be done on schedule, people to call and arrangements to make. It wasn't that she couldn't get it all done, although she had plenty of help to do it, but it felt to Sylvie as if it were all getting away from her, that she was just on the edge of losing control of things. Somehow, this life wasn't her own. It had nothing to do with what *she* wanted.

She longed for just a few hours out of each day, or a few days at a time, where she'd wake up and think, What am I supposed to do today?, and the answer would be "Nothing." Then she'd stretch contentedly, nap selfishly for another hour or so, then spend the day reading or taking her ten-year-old daughter Claire to the beach or the country or the zoo, doing whatever struck their fancy at any given moment. No one would be waiting for her to decide on the flower arrangements or the seating arrangements or any arrangements whatsoever.

There would be only she and Lucien and Claire. The three of them together, like in the old days, when their lives had not gotten so complicated.

Sylvie smiled when she thought of Claire. Claire was so much a perfect miniature of Lucien. She not only had his physical beauty and his coloring, but she had acquired some of his traits. That all-encompassing scowl when he was deep in concentration was sexy on him, enchantingly funny on Claire. Sylvie thought that, even though her own life was somehow incomplete and stalled, perhaps it was enough that she had produced Claire.

It was only late at night that Sylvie would occasionally jolt out of a sound sleep with her skin prickling all over, suddenly wide awake. What's going to become of Claire? Sylvie would think. Is she going to be like me? And is that bad or good?

The first time this happened, when Claire was five, Sylvie told her fears to Lucien. He didn't quite understand the problem.

"Claire will be what she will be," he said philosophically, "and time will take care of everything when she's ready. Just let nature take its course, Sylvie."

"I want her to have a normal childhood!" Sylvie said, aware of the desperate note in her voice.

Lucien had held her close. "Why are you worried?" he said. "Few people except me and my mother would agree that I had a 'normal' childhood, but I loved it. Do you think I turned out so terribly?"

He was perfectly right; logically she knew that, but emotionally she wavered.

The complications of her life seemed insurmountable. She sometimes thought that without their special nights, the precious nights that she and Lucien kept sacrosanct, no matter what, she'd go crazy.

She found herself thinking of the plans she'd had, when she was seventeen and still living in New Orleans, when she'd first met Lucien. She'd had a blueprint for her life: she was graduating from high school, she'd been accepted at college, she was going to medical school, she was going to be a psychiatrist or work in neurobiology.

How did she ever become a celebrity wife, as much a decoration to Lucien as his gold records and his Grammy? She knew, with her analytical logic, that this wasn't Lucien's fault. He had been perfectly willing for her to get on with her life, even though he would have had to make some sacrifices. He had been well on his way to fame when he met Sylvie, and travel was becoming his way of life. But he'd urged Sylvie to stay in New Orleans, where their families were, finish her education, and they'd see each other between his engagements.

"With all the time we have ahead of us," he had told her, "a few years now isn't going to matter."

But it was her choice to follow him, and before she knew it, she had no time for herself. They spent more time in New York, London, Milan, Rome, and Vienna. They bought a huge co-op apartment in Manhattan and, when Claire was born, a country house in upstate New York.

No one, she thought now, should be locked into a decision they'd made at seventeen. But it just seemed like things happened so *fast*—just snowballed down the mountain and took her right with it.

The music ended and the applause snapped Sylvie back to the moment.

Lucien turned briefly in the orchestra pit and winked at her, his accustomed little gesture before he joined the singers onstage. Only she knew that the wink meant that he had done it, he had pulled it off, no one could tell what a nervous wreck he was inside.

Now, like so much of their lives, Sylvie suspected that he did it simply because he always did it. The magic had worn itself too thin. It wasn't that Lucien no longer loved her, or that she no longer loved him: that would never change. It was just that, in the past few years, things and events and circumstances and priorities had crowded in on them, leaving them no breathing room.

After the performance, Sylvie and Lucien were anxious to get away. They made a token appearance at the patrons' party, then slipped out to the car.

"Want to drive out to the country?" Lucien asked her. "Or would you rather do it here?"

She shook her head. The lights from Lincoln Center, receding behind them, left their last glints in her dark red hair. "Oh, no, Lucien! Not in the city again!"

"I was just thinking that it might be easier here."

"I know. But we have time, if we don't hit traffic. I know the city is always such a challenge to you, but . . ."

He gave her his sweetest smile, the one that kept his salary so outrageously high. "Then it's upstate for us, angel. I feel like a little fresh night air."

Within an hour they were near the New York–Connecticut line. Just outside New Salem, they drove slowly over a small bridge, stopping for just a moment in the middle.

"Isn't it fabulous?" she breathed.

The full moon lit the water in glittery ripples. There was still some light snow on the hills that enclosed the reservoir, frosting the ground and the trees. The moonlight touched everything with a pale light, the snow reflecting back ice blue. The light and the stillness transformed the panoramic view into sacred space.

"It's so quiet," Lucien whispered. "It seems almost a shame to break this silence."

"Not like Bayou Goula," she said wistfully.

This surprised him. She hadn't talked about Bayou Goula in months, maybe even longer. Funny, but when they first moved away from New Orleans, both of them were terribly homesick for Louisiana, and their fondest memories were of the rowdy, raucous nights on Bayou Goula.

"I know you miss it," he said. "I do, too. So many of us out there, laughing, joking, just enjoying being together. There'll never be anything like it."

Sylvie sighed and looked out at the moonlight, lost in her own thoughts.

They parked the big Mercedes just off the main road on a shadowed dirt path invisible to any traffic. Lucien opened the trunk. He removed his shoes, slipped the studs out of his cuffs and shirt front, folded his jacket and pants as he took them off and placed them neatly in the trunk. On top, he tossed his wedding ring and his Patek Phillipe watch. Naked, leaning against the fender, Lucien watched Sylvie shrug out of her green silk Carolina Herrera party dress, and laughed.

She looked up, bewildered. "What's so funny?"

"You," he said, shaking his head, "standing there stark naked except for all your jewels."

He moved quickly, holding her at arm's length, running his hands down her sides as if he had to reconfirm the body that had always so pleased and excited him, then around her to cup both buttocks, pulling her close to him. In a moment, with only one hand, he unclasped the sensational diamond and emerald necklace, and tasted the warmth of her skin. The night cold touched neither of them.

"Do you want to make love now?" he asked.

She shook her head. "Afterward."

He laughed again. "I've never understood that. For everyone else it's the other way around." He made no move to let go of her.

"Lucien," she said with a little impatience, "it's so late."

He moved back slightly, dropping her necklace on top of her dress in the trunk. Sylvie pulled off her rings and earrings, stepped out of her gilded shoes, and closed the trunk, uncaring that she had just locked half a million dollars in jewelry alone in a highly stealable Mercedes.

Naked, they concealed themselves in the shadows.

Sylvie and Lucien once again silently agreed to put aside their bewilderment over what was happening to their marriage. Concentrating only on the moment and the moon, they held tightly to each other, two drowning people counting on the other not to let go.

Simultaneously they felt the first beginnings of the change, their mental pain submerged beneath the more insistent demands of physical pain. Sylvie's fingers, her gilded nails stretching into powerful claws, sank into Lucien's shoulders as if she were making love. They felt the simmering of their blood to the surface, their breath catching in their throats. This was something for which they had no misunderstanding, no confusion; it was primitive and basic, their bodies demanding all their attention and wiping their minds clear of everything else. The real world was being washed away beneath a flood of pain that was transformed into pleasure.

Their bodies pulsated, mutated, changed with the shimmering silver light of the full moon, the only mistress to whom they owed complete obligation.

And when the last of the pain was over and forgotten in the twinkling of an eye, they stood upright, powerful and gorgeous, two magnificent werewolves who would live the rest of the night in perfect harmony and perfect freedom, united in a bond stronger even than love.

For now, for as long as the night lasted, they would be happy again.

"I want to go home," Sylvie told Lucien afterward.

He knew she meant New Orleans. It was the next question that gave him so much trouble. "With or without me, Sylvie?" he asked. His voice was much more straightforward than he felt.

She hadn't even thought of going without him until he asked; then she realized that it was a decision she had been keeping in the back of her mind so that she wouldn't have to think about it.

All of a sudden, the possibility of being away from Lucien was intolerable. She loved Lucien. More than that, they were bound together more completely than any human couple could have been. The werewolves' bond was more than sex and more than love; it was a complex intertwining of their lives. It was said that two mated werewolves actually melded into one soul, and no matter what time and fortune had in store for them, no matter if they were separated by circumstances, their shared karma would always draw them back together.

Lucien ran a hand through his thick blond hair and held on to it near the roots, something he always did when he was disturbed. "I don't know how to help you, Sylvie. I have no idea what's wrong, all I know is that something's badly out of sync here. And I can't make amends for a problem if I can't figure out what it is!"

She put her fingers lightly against his cheek. "Whatever it is, it isn't you. I don't want to go without you."

"Is it that we don't spend enough time together?"

"No. Lucien, really, it isn't anything like that. Nothing that you've done or didn't do, or anything that we've failed to do. I just . . ." She wanted so desperately to blurt out something, *anything,* in the hopes that it miraculously would be the right answer. But in truth she knew she had no answer at all, right or wrong. Her frustration made her want to scream.

"Sylvie, look," he said, "it isn't like I can't leave here for a while, at least after next week. I'm not on the schedule again at the Met for another two months, and I can easily cancel the Houston thing. I told them it was a maybe in the first place. So let's pack Claire up and go back home. Zizi and Apollonius will be thrilled to spoil her a little more, not to mention your parents . . ."

"Who probably still aren't speaking to me," she added bitterly.

"They love you," he said. "They just don't understand

a few things. Maybe this is a chance to settle it. And . . . Achille. We haven't seen him since Mae died."

The thought of Achille Broussard, who was like a second father to Sylvie and Lucien, made going home even more poignant.

"I'll be honest with you," he said, "I've been thinking a lot about New Orleans myself lately. It's almost been like an obsession, my wanting to go there. I've been homesick before, but *this* . . . the more I think about it, the more intense it gets." He ran his hand through his hair again and sighed. "Maybe I just need to talk to my father."

Yes, Sylvie thought, hope suddenly bubbling to the surface. Troubles always seemed to straighten themselves out when you told them to Apollonius.

"Hey," Lucien said, brightening, "you can sit around the Rex Room at Antoine's with all the ex-Queens and reminisce."

She laughed and threw her arms around his neck. "You told me that if I let you make me a loup-garou I'd never have to do that, remember?"

"I lied. Besides, you'll love it. They'll all hate you because they won't be able to figure out how you've managed not to age. They'll tell you to your face how good you look and then when you leave for the powder room, they'll all speculate on how much plastic surgery you've had and whether the flaming red hair on your head still matches the hair on your pretty twat. Now tell me *that* won't be a good time."

"You know, Lucien, it doesn't comfort me that you know so damned much about women," she said with mock suspicion.

"Besides, it's Mardi Gras time. And Claire's never been. You want our child to grow up deprived of cheap beads and plastic go-cups?"

4

Walter Marley II thought back on when his troubles first started. They weren't even his troubles, really. The problem rested with his family. Walt himself felt perfectly fine, reasonably happy with his life: it was in no way his fault that his family in New Orleans had decided to reject him. Still, his family's disapproval managed to stretch its way across half the continent, lurking just behind him like a ghost seen out of the corner of an eye.

It was too easy to say that the discord began on his nineteenth birthday. The real attraction to a different way of living had started long before that. It might even have been with him all his life and he just never realized it until certain cataclysmic events took place when he was ten years old.

One night, when he was ten, he watched as his seventeen-year-old sister, Sylvie, had her first transformation into a werewolf. He was unable to tear himself away from the sight of it. He knew he should be scared—every horror movie he'd ever seen told him so—but he was thrilled. He watched, unable to speak except for a few inadvertent mumbles, as Sylvie mutated into a powerful, flame-colored myth, half woman, half animal, graceful in her enormous strength and stature. As Walt had watched, he felt something in himself confirmed, something he'd known all along. This was what he wanted, what he'd always wanted: the power, the strength, the unquestioned freedom. He wanted to change under the moon with Sylvie, to run with her and her loup-garou lover, Lucien, to be part of the dark family of the night who shared bonds even stronger than love.

He didn't have a name for what he was feeling. He didn't know where the emotions came from, or the knowledge that what Sylvie was doing was perfect and right, that she was an instrument of a destiny and a purpose far more important than he could understand. All he knew was that this was what he was supposed to be, what he was supposed to do. To fulfill his own life, Walt had to be reborn in the same way his sister had been.

He wanted it more than he'd ever wanted anything. He had a sudden flash of maturity: that if the loup-garou's life was going to be his life, he had to learn now to prepare for the responsibility of it.

He also knew that no matter how deep and strong his yearning was, he was never going to be able to tell anyone. Not until he was much older. And he knew instinctively that someday he was going to suffer for his choice.

He could talk only to Sylvie. After that night, she was no longer the child of her mother and father; her human family was still important to her, but her real family had become Louisiana's tightly knit loup-garou community.

The Marley family tried hard to understand Sylvie's choice, but it was difficult for them. Walt's twelve-year-old sister, Geo, refused to speak to Sylvie and ignored her when she came to visit. Geo was exasperated with the whole family, and her attendance at a private boarding school in Virginia was a great relief to her. All Geo required of her family was a large allowance check every month to keep up her lifestyle and her horse: she discouraged visits and barely tolerated phone calls. She declined to speak to Sylvie at all. Walt, on the other extreme, accepted Sylvie completely and understood what her life had become.

Shortly after her transformation, Sylvie married her lover, Lucien Drago, who had initiated her into the mysteries of the loup-garou's life, and they went to live with Lucien's loup-garou parents in their house and shop on Royal Street. Walt sometimes dropped in to see Sylvie in the afternoons after school and on Saturdays. Sometimes Lucien was there, between concerts, and sometimes Sylvie had gone away with him, to far-flung cities that sounded remote and romantic to Walt. But there was always someone there to talk to him: Sylvie's husband had carried her off to a wonderful, mystical place when he took her to Royal Street, a place that was alive at all hours.

Sylvie's new home was Luna, the elegant antique and curio shop of Sylvie's mother-in-law, Zizi. It intrigued Walt that the dark-eyed, gold-haired Zizi, on whom he had a terrific crush, had actually lived in Louisiana while it was still a French colony. She had met Bienville and had danced with Lafayette. She had seen Jean Lafitte and his pirates selling their stolen swag on Bayou Barataria; had been friends with the Baroness Pontalba; had listened to Jenny Lind sing in the old French Opera House; had watched the gorgeous Marie Laveau dance to the Voodoo drums in Congo Square. He had even overheard (though he wasn't meant to hear it) Lucien and Zizi laughing over the days when Zizi kept a flashy, overpriced house of ill repute in Storyville.

Not that she looked old enough for even the most recent of these stories. Walt learned that loups-garous age only one year to a human's ten, and even with that, they sometimes looked younger.

For some reason, the antiquity of Zizi's husband, Apollonius, never fascinated Walt as much as Zizi did. The only thing Walt could figure was that Apollonius's immortality was simply too staggering for the mind to comprehend: Apollonius had been a contemporary of Christ.

Over the centuries Zizi had collected fantastic objects of art, all having to do with wolves and the moon, which she now kept in the shop. Luna was a lively, sophisticated place, made more so by the constant flow of the Louisiana loup-garou community dropping by to chat with whichever of the family was tending shop on that particular day. The shop fronted on Royal Street, and in the manner of so many French Quarter houses, was really a small complex comprised of the shop, a courtyard, a large house, and an old slave quarters. The slave quarters had been converted to guest rooms, then converted again into a spacious, airy apartment when Sylvie and Lucien married and moved in. Luna connected directly with a gathering room in the house, where the loups-garous were almost always in attendance, hanging out, talking shop, trading gossip, sometimes watching werewolf horror movies on the big-screen VCR and cracking up at the clichés, and just taking joy in being together. They were a clannish group, delighting in each other's company and mostly bored with the company of human beings, but they liked Walt and accepted him as a kind of mascot.

Walt asked Sylvie thousands of questions, technical and philosophical, but the only question he never asked was why she had done it. He knew why.

They had many discussions about death. "Does it bother you to kill people?" he asked her.

Sylvie had sighed and shook her head. Walt knew it was not an easy question, but he wasn't looking for easy answers.

"Loups-garous like us," she told him, "like me and Lucien and all the loups-garous of our community, kill because we have to. We have to feed, at least once a month at the full moon. We have no choice. This is the price we pay for our long lives, for our freedom. But we kill for higher reasons, Walt. Our kind of werewolf is dedicated to the goddess Hecate, patroness of things dark and secret, the goddess who metes out justice. We're her instruments. When human justice fails, the loup-garou succeeds. We know who's innocent and who's guilty, and as long as we have to kill by our very nature, we make the choice to kill selectively."

"But how do you know who's really guilty? I mean, couldn't somebody be framed and it looks like they're guilty, but they're not?"

"We know. Our psychic abilities tell us. You can't lie to a loup-garou."

Walt studied the pattern in the antique wallpaper, trying to put his thoughts in order, trying to form his next questions. Even though he and Sylvie—and sometimes Lucien or Zizi or Apollonius—had long discussions over dinner or at odd times when Walt dropped in, Walt still felt that the loups-garous were holding something back, that there was part of their lives that Walt would never know. And he felt that he *had* to know it, that whatever information was hidden there, just out of his range of vision, would clarify his life and his future.

"I want to be what you are!" he blurted.

She smiled and stroked his arm. "I know. But the time isn't right. And you're too young. Think about what's happened to me, Walt, what I've given up. Mother and Dad try not to show it, but they're disappointed in me. Geo ignores me."

"But you have Lucien and Zizi and Apollonius and all the others."

"It isn't the same. Everything in life is a trade-off, Walt. Make sure you really want something badly enough to give up something else. Something that might be more important to you in the long run, even if you don't think so now."

"You sound like you're sorry."

She ran one hand through her coppery hair. "I'm not sorry. But it was still hard for me to lose my family's trust."

"And what happens when I'm old enough and sure enough?"

"Then you come to me," she laughed, "and I'll take care of everything."

"This is in the nature of a promise?"

She took his hand in both of hers and said seriously, "It is. I promise you, I'll see to it that you have what you want. As soon as you and I are both sure you want it."

When Walt was fourteen, Sylvie and Lucien left New Orleans. Lucien had always had a good reputation as a rising young conductor and composer, but he was becoming so famous that he was hardly ever at home, and Sylvie's place, she said, was with him. It was easier for them to live in New York.

On the afternoon they left, Walt stood on the sidewalk in front of Luna, waving good-bye as Sylvie and Lucien drove off. Lucien's parents were there, and so were his own. Relations between the four older people were not hostile, not strained; in fact, they liked each other. Lucien's mother and Walt's father had known each other for over twenty years. But the differences in the way they lived, the human and the loup-garou, were always unspoken and always there. They had dinners together sometimes, and attended family holiday gatherings, but the conversations between them were kept to the superficial level, as if the things most central to their lives had to be kept in silence.

As Walt watched the car disappear down Royal Street and turn the corner, he felt a wrench, a sudden hollowness as if his soul were leaving him and following that receding car out of New Orleans. Surprising himself, he cried aloud in wordless anguish, more the desolate howl of an animal than the cry of a human. It sounded so shocking and so wrong there in the civilized borders of Royal Street that both sets of parents were immobile with confusion. Walt, hardly knowing what he was doing, blinded and stricken, threw his arms around Apollonius, burying his face against Apollonius's chest, and gasped out his pain.

Later, he would wonder, as did everyone present at the time, why he turned to Apollonius and not his own father. He knew it had hurt his father, and he wouldn't have hurt his father for the world, but like so much between them these days, it would remain unspoken. Besides, it seemed that everyone, in times of trouble, turned to Apollonius, so it was finally taken as simply a natural thing.

Walter went back to his old life. He went to school, he played sports, the faculty of his school chose him as editor of the school paper, and his slightly sarcastic wit infused the paper with a new energy. Sometimes he went too far and it got him in trouble, but Walt was everyone's golden child. He was handsome, with the Marley family looks: dark hair and turquoise eyes. He was smart and funny. He had always been a wiseass, even as a child, and he found that, judiciously applied, this would stand him in good stead. Teachers liked him because he was obviously destined for success; students liked him because he didn't take himself too seriously.

Walt was the first boy in four generations of Marleys ever to be educated outside of New Orleans. The Marley children always went to private school in the city and then to Tulane or Loyola. It was Sylvie, with her wider acquaintance with the world, who insisted that Walt be sent to Phillips Exeter for prep school and then to an Ivy League school. Walt had the grades and the family had the money, she told her father, and it was time that the Marleys started branching out beyond New Orleans. For generations, the family had been too parochial.

Walt's own enthusiasm overcame his family's faint objections, and he was shipped East to school. He was close enough to be with Sylvie and Lucien on long weekends, and sometimes with his aunt Georgiana, for whom his sister was named, in Boston. But as close as he was to Sylvie, their conversations about the loup-garou and lycanthropy in general were never resumed. When Walt brought up the subject, Sylvie evaded. At one point she said that she had told him everything on the subject that she had to say, and there was no point in repeating herself.

Something told Walt not to remind her of her promise, that she would either honor it or not, but that it was nothing he could force.

Walt graduated from Exeter and was accepted to Harvard. It was a time of both profound and superficial changes. On the superficial side, his parents had given him the money to buy a new car for a graduation present.

"Get rid of that rust-bucket," his mother had said firmly.

"It's an antique," Walt replied. "It has historical significance."

The car in question was a VW Microbus, of hippie-era-late-sixties/early-seventies vintage. It had been in mint condition when Walt acquired it, from an ex–draft dodger who had driven it to Montreal to avoid the Vietnam War and had immediately started driving a Jeep. But the aging hippie had kept his VW and had taken perfect care of it. Walt had lavished a lot of affection— not to mention money—on the VW, but time was taking its toll.

"The first time I got laid, it was in that bus," Walt told his mother reverently. He eyed the bus as if it were a holy relic.

But his mother, as always, was feisty and unshockable. "I don't care if you had Mother Theresa and Madonna in a three-way in there," she said, arching an eyebrow, "the thing's falling apart. Are you the only kid in the world who doesn't want a new car?"

"Okay," he said, reconciling himself, "but I want a new minivan. Customized."

"Far be it from me," his mother said, rolling her eyes, "to ask you to alter your mating habits."

He bought his new minivan, almost immediately parked it at his Aunt Georgiana's, and took the train to New York to be with Sylvie and Lucien. His nineteenth birthday was coming up in July and he wanted to spend it with his sister. It was time—he could feel it in every breath he took—for Sylvie to fulfill her promise.

As it turned out, he spent his birthday in quite a different way than he'd thought he would.

A week before Walt's birthday, Sylvie, Lucien, Claire, and most of the staff of the Manhattan place were going to the house in the country.

"We'll celebrate your birthday there," Lucien said. "We'll make it a pool party, barbecue kind of thing. How many people do you want to invite? Just remember, we only have room for about eight to stay over. Ten, if we use the spare room in the pool house."

"Lucien," Sylvie said, exasperated, "remember high school and college? Spring break? You stayed with as many people as could be crammed into a room."

"She always forgets," Lucien said confidentially to Walt, "that when I went to school, it was in 1868 at the Moscow Conservatory of Music." Lucien may have looked young, but he was a very old loup-garou. He had been born into the life at age eight, in the eighteenth century, initiated by his mother. Lucien's old-fashioned romantic, emotional musicianship was no accident: he had studied with Tchaikovsky.

Five-year-old Claire was ecstatic. "Party, party!" she said, clapping her hands and jumping up and down. "Cake and ice cream and presents!"

No matter whose birthday it was, Claire always got a present, too. She loved birthdays.

"Yeah, presents for *you,* Moosie," Walt said, picking her up. He often called her Moosie because she loved Bullwinkle cartoons, to which he had introduced her. "God, you *are* a moose! How big are you getting, anyway?" Claire, who was built along the lines of a fairy child, cackled with mischief as he put her down again. "Actually," he said to Sylvie and Lucien, "I thought I'd stay in town and come out Sunday for the party. I've got some things here I have to do." Walt hoped he sounded casual.

Sylvie gave him a look. Then she tossed it off. "Okay, but come out early. And remember, the cleaning lady's not coming this weekend, so wash your own dishes. Better yet, eat out." Walt's cooking was good, but it involved a lot of space and mess. She gave him a quick kiss, Lucien gave him a pat on the shoulder, and they were gone, Claire waving bye-bye.

Walt hated to lie to them but, in a way, he really hadn't. He did have things to do in town. One of them was Mathilde Grimaud.

At Walt's spring break just before his graduation from Exeter, Lucien had introduced Mathilde to Walt at one of the parties he and Sylvie gave for the opera people. Matty had been singing Violetta in *La Traviata* at the Met. She was perfect for it; a slender, girlish-looking brunette who could be almost any age onstage. Walt had been amazed that so much sound could come from that slight body, but when he met her backstage, he discovered her trade secret. Onstage, Matty looked wraithlike, able to blow away on a spring breeze. In person, she was all sinew and muscle. When Matty wasn't performing or working with her vocal coach, she was working out. A singer, he found out, needed strength. Singing opera was almost as physical as blocking for the New York Jets. The costumes alone could weigh forty or fifty pounds, the wigs were so heavy they could tilt the head back if you didn't have a strong neck, the lights were incredibly hot and the stage was dusty. Just singing was physically taxing: the lungs and abdomen alone had to be flexible and well developed, and the singers had to stand for long periods of time, which strained the legs and back. In Matty's case, in this particular opera, she was onstage most of the time. Even then, the position she had to maintain in order to sing but still appear to be lying limp and dying was strenuous. Matty loved singing Violetta, but it exhausted her.

"The woman's a *hooker*," Matty complained, "so how come she doesn't get to lie down until the last act?"

"She's a *courtesan*," Walt said. "They're on their feet more."

Walt started sleeping with Mathilde shortly after that, every weekend when he could get to New York or she could get to Boston. Every night, Walt closed his eyes and thanked God for the Boston–New York air shuttle. The only complication was that she was married. The saving grace was that her husband was divorcing her and they had been separated for six months. It was an amiable divorce and Matty didn't want to embarrass her husband, so Walt and Matty kept everything low key. Even though opera is a business that thrives on gossip and it's impossible to keep anything secret, at least the affair never became *public* knowledge and was never in the gossip columns.

Walt figured that Lucien knew about him and Matty, but that he might not have told Sylvie. In any case, it wasn't discussed, and the affair intensified over the summer.

Walt saw Matty on Monday and Tuesday night of that week. By Wednesday, she had worn him out and he decided to stay in the apartment, order Chinese take-out, and watch a movie on tape. He'd take a long soak in the Jacuzzi and go to bed early.

He never even got to the Chinese-take-out part of the evening.

Sylvie returned to the apartment just after dark.

Walt, lounging on the couch, phone and menu in hand, trying to decide between Szechuan beef and cold noodles in sesame sauce, was startled to hear the door open.

"It's only me," Sylvie called.

"Got bored out there in suburbia, huh? Want some moo shu pork? I'm about to order."

She smiled wickedly. "Forget the food. I came back to give you your birthday present."

She didn't seem to be holding anything.

"So. . . ," Walt said, not getting it at first, "where is it?"

Her face grew serious. "I made you a promise, Walter. So long ago that maybe you don't still want me to honor it."

The phone hung from Walt's hand, half-raised. He was aware of the phone company's loud recording telling him to hang up, but it seemed to have no relation to him at that moment.

"Are you joking?" he whispered.

He could see that she wasn't. "You've been thinking about it, Walt. It's all you've really been thinking about lately; whether you want to go to college or not, what you want to do when you get there. You still want the loup-garou's life, but you don't know how it will affect your future. You feel like everything you do is just marking time until you become what you've always wanted to be, and you're not sure that any decision you make now will be the right one, not until you *know* for sure what's going to happen. It's time to end that indecision. Now you can deal with life from what you are, not what you're waiting to become." She laughed slightly. "Put down the phone, Walt."

He looked at it like he'd never seen a phone before, and replaced the handset in the cradle. He could feel his face flush, his heartbeat quicken.

Sylvie stood up. "Come on. It's good you're wearing old clothes; you'll get dirty where we're going. I'm going to teach you the most difficult part first: how to kill in the city."

Too stunned to speak, Walter followed her out, and shut the door on his old life.

They were in one of the most beautiful and historic parts of the city, and one that no one ever sees. The subway station had been abandoned for fifty years, since the modern cars were much too long to stop there. The city had simply closed off the few stations like this one, but they still survived: unseen jewels glittering in the dark. One had come into the light at Grand Central Station, reincarnated as the Oyster Bar restaurant, its graceful arches and vaulted ceilings paved in mosaic tiles, its elegant solid brass chandeliers polished and lit, the inlaid golden bronze letters kept spotless and gleaming.

This particular station was just as splendid as that one,

only no one had set foot in it for years. Only the city employees saw it, infrequently and just as they were passing through. It was intact, but covered in dust and years: the brass chandeliers, gas jets shut off and clogged with dirt, still hung motionless; the arched ceiling, tiles intact, soared; the bronze letters, darkened with green verdigris, still spelled out the stop, "City Hall." The modern age had passed it over so completely that there was not even a touch of spray-painted graffiti anywhere. Even in the dark, even in the secret heart of the city, it was glorious Victorian opulence falling into picturesque ruin.

Walter really had no idea how they had gotten there. Sylvie seemed to be able to open doors that were not to be opened, following pitch black tunnels like it was daylight, leading him through a maze of filthy passageways filled with sounds that Walt dared not even contemplate. If he had been less dazed by what was going to happen to him, he would have been more apprehensive.

But she could read his mind. "Don't worry about it," she told him. "After tonight, nothing much is going to scare you, ever again."

He shivered on the platform, under the curved branches of the chandelier. "I'm just nervous, I guess," he said.

"Well, nervous is fine. Scared is unacceptable. If you're scared of this, you're not ready. But you're not scared, are you?"

He smiled. He didn't have to reassure her on that point. She was as sure as he was.

"This is one of Lucien's favorite places," she told Walt. She produced a key that opened a small, tiled door. You'd have to be looking for the keyhole, or know it was there, so perfectly did the tiles in the door align with the tiles in the wall. "Lucien took an impression and had the key made," she explained. Behind the door was a small, empty

storage closet, oddly clean. "Undress and leave your
clothes here," Sylvie said, starting to step out of her jeans.

Walt was so nervous that he was simply a robot at that
point. If she'd told him to lie down with his head on the
tracks, he would have. Mechanically, he pulled off his ratty
Exeter sweatshirt and pants and started to fold them neatly.
Sylvie, he noticed, just dropped her designer jeans and expensive cotton-knit sweater on the floor. It was a careless
gesture so like Sylvie that the very ordinariness of it erased
his nerves. "You're not at home, Syl," he said, indicating
her messy pile of clothes and shoes. "The maid's not going
to pick up after you."

She smiled and calmly shot him the finger, not looking
at him.

But he looked at her. Walt was, like his namesake grandfather, extremely appreciative of women. He had seen Sylvie naked before, or nearly so, several times during
childhood and a couple of times after she was grown. Sylvie's body was perfect, a work of art, pale marble tinted
with the fire of her flame-colored hair. For the first time,
he saw his sister as a woman, as she must appear to other
men, and he was proud of her. He could understand why
Lucien was so consumed with his wife and always had
been, from the first moment he saw her. Another thing Walt
learned: when two people are naked together, and there was
not even the slightest hint of sex, the exposure of each other
without the clothes that define us and bind us into our public facades constitutes a bond of trust.

It was like a cold shock to him to realize, too, that as
beautiful an example of a woman that she was, Sylvie was
not human. She was no longer exactly the sister he loved.
They were not just siblings any longer. Sylvie was showing
him only her human form, a form that was merely a con-
venience for her in that it let her pass in the world. What

she was about to share with him was her true soul, the soul of the werewolf. And he would become more than a brother to her, more than a brother-in-law to Lucien; he would share the heart and secret of their lives, they would at last become equals.

Walt was so happy, it made him dizzy.

He had seen her transform only once, her very first time, and then only by coincidence. Then, she had been uncertain and halting. Now, with the experience of years, she was in complete control of herself. She motioned him to sit cross-legged opposite her while she took a deep breath and closed her eyes.

She was so still that Walt thought nothing was happening. Then he saw the changes in her face, small at first, then becoming momentous. Her body contorted, and he knew it was painful for her, but Sylvie kept her calm composure as long as she could, which was almost until the last minute. Walt knew that each werewolf transforms at his own pace, in his own order: with Sylvie, the fangs grew out first, the bones of her head elongated and tilted, her face coated with a light sheen of red hair, the cheekbones standing out prominently, the eyes and brows swept back dramatically. The hair on her head burst forth in a shower of copper fireworks, settling into a long, thick mane flowing down her back, almost to her knees. Her hands and fingers elongated; three-inch claws, clear as crystal, erupted from her fingertips. She grew taller, her upper body more powerful, her shoulders wider, until she was seven or eight feet tall.

Under an enchantment, Walt watched without moving, without fear.

She opened her eyes. They were a bright turquoise blue, the Marley family trademark.

She stood up, towering over his mere six foot two inches,

and pulled him to his feet. One hand gently caressed his hair, like a mother strokes a much-beloved child. The other arm wound around his back and pulled him closer to her, lifting him slightly and arching his back.

Her voice was clear, slightly deeper, more sonorous.

"This is your gift, Walter. The werewolf's kiss. From Zizi to Lucien, from Lucien to me, and now from me to you."

She bit her own lip, and Walter could see a scarlet bead form under the razorlike fangs.

He felt more of a sting than a pain as the fangs went into his chest. He was a little surprised: he thought it would be a large wound. But all that was needed, he found, was a transfer of the genetic material from her saliva and blood into his body.

The instant it happened, he knew it. His eyes flew open wide and his breath caught in his throat as the rush of energy hit his blood and his brain. He was glad she had a firm grip on him or he would have fallen as his knees buckled with the unaccustomed power flowing into him. It was like, but not exactly like, getting an electric shock that jolted every part of his body at once.

He cried out, and the sound was like the same cry he made at orgasm, only no orgasm had ever been this intense.

She raised her head, the blood still on her lips and fangs. "Now, take control of it, Walt. It's best to try and learn this from the very first. Feel what's happening to your body and try to direct it. Picture in your mind what you're becoming, what's happening to you. Don't just let it wash over you; feel every part of your body as it changes."

With the greatest discipline he had ever mustered, Walt felt his body change. He tried to identify each mutation in each limb, in each organ. It was as if he, like Lucien, was a conductor, bringing all the instruments to life at their proper intervals.

"Now try to slow it down. Keep up with it." She lowered him to the floor.

The pain was just incredible, he knew, but somehow, he didn't feel completely *attached* to the pain, although he could see his body react. He was so amazed watching what happened that the pain was secondary to the astonishment.

And behind the astonishment, joy.

He looked at himself, then at Sylvie, and he laughed. It was wonderful!

With a gradual, but swift, subsiding of the pain, he was left aware only of the power, the new energy flooding him. He became calm, steady, sure of himself.

When he stood up, a lot of that steadiness left him.

Good God! he thought, she's seven or eight feet tall and I'm looking *down* at her from at least six inches!

He looked at himself, at his chestnut brown pelt, at his own claws, deep brown instead of her crystal. He felt something brush him from behind: his hair, grown into a supple cape over his shoulders and down his back.

He held his hand in front of his face and flexed the claws. He couldn't get over it. Another thing: he could *see*! Really see, as if the great chandelier had suddenly burst into light. He knew it was his new vision, sharpened for the night.

"You look okay, I guess," Sylvie said. He knew from her voice that he was *beautiful*! "Can you talk?"

He tried. His speech was incoherent, but his voice was a deep sonic boom.

"It will happen as your body adjusts. For once, I've got the edge on my smart-mouth brother."

The friendly jab he gave her arm would have broken a strong man in two. She didn't even flinch.

"Now I want you to stay very, very close to me," she

said. "We can't stay down here, we'll have to go up above. This is your first night and you have to feed, so I'm taking you to Central Park, where you can have a little more freedom. Stalking unobserved in the city is an expert's art, but if you're running flat out and don't stop, no one can see you, you'll be too fast. We're only going to slow down when we get to the park, but you're going to be distracted: nothing will look like you're used to seeing it. Your vision, your sense of smell, and your hearing are all magnified; that and your new height are going to disorient you. Before we go, I want you to take a deep breath."

He did, and was sorry. When he had walked in here as a human, it had smelled musty and unpleasant, but what hit him now was the reek of hell. He could smell a decaying rat that was probably a mile off. He could smell all the accumulated years of human and animal excrement, filth and garbage up above. There was an odor in every speck of dust.

At almost the same time, he was nearly knocked over by a wall of noise, a screaming, grating, banging cacophony that made him clap both hands over his ears.

"This is probably the worst city in the world to learn to smell and hear, but you might as well start out the hard way. You'll learn to shut it off selectively," she assured him, "the same way you'll learn to shut out sounds. But you need these new senses to survive. Try now to take control of it, the same way you did with your transformation. You did very well with that, by the way. Much better than I did, even after eight or ten tries."

Walt summoned the same discipline and awareness of his own body, and systematically shut down his senses. It was still awful, but bearable.

"Now the true test, little brother, and the true rewards. Let's let you find out how it feels to be free."

Taking his hand, she led him out of the tunnels, through the mazes, through unlocked doors. The same trip that had taken an hour now took only seconds. They slipped into the darkness on a deserted side street.

"Take a deep breath, Walt," Sylvie said, "and let's go!"

She had been right: it was all very distracting. The familiar world looked like a fairyland to him, with the colors enhanced, the details sharpened, the dark corners lighted, and from a new, taller perspective. The sounds, too, closed in on him and then were gone as he passed, but they were getting clearer and more distinct. He could isolate whole sentences spoken in a single voice, a separate sound of glass tinkling, or a taxi banging its way down Broadway. He shook it off, pleased, and stuck to Sylvie, moving like a flash of swamp fire just ahead of him. He caught a glimpse of people fanned by the wind the werewolves created, looking puzzled at the quick, passing breeze that blew their skirts or hair, and he laughed. His laugh, too, caught on the whirlwind, but before the humans could recognize it, it was gone.

They entered the park up near the Museo del Barrio and the Museum of the City of New York, near 104th Street, leaping easily over the gates. It was still early, only about eight or eight-thirty, and a few people were still in the park, jogging or power-walking along the paths.

"I know what you're thinking," Sylvie whispered. "What is anyone sane doing in the park at night?" She shrugged. New Yorkers, the shrug said, go figure.

A strong-looking man in red jogging shorts whizzed by. Sylvie, her attention caught, gazed after him. Her eyes narrowed as she concentrated.

"Him," she told Walt. "Let's follow him."

Walt obeyed, keeping to the shadows with Sylvie, but he was clueless as to why she'd picked that particular man.

He looked like a clean-cut, straight-arrow type, a lawyer or some kind of professional man, probably with a co-op on the Upper East Side or the park and a commute downtown to Wall Street. Walt knew enough of the loup-garou's principles to know that a kill for justice was what they were looking for. This guy looked like his most serious offense was taking an extra deduction for business lunches.

When the man stopped, taking a breather and stretching, Sylvie nudged Walt and whispered, "See if you can tell why he's your man. Try it. Pick up on his thoughts."

Walt wasn't sure how he did it, but he was conscious of concentrating his gaze on the man's forehead, so completely that his vision blurred. Other pictures began to form, pictures that had nothing to do with the reality he was in at the moment. Walt saw the man with a nylon stocking in his hands; he saw several young women, screaming, strangling, terrified, dying. And he saw the man, masturbating over their bodies and smiling, then walking away.

The pictures jolted Walt badly and he jerked back to reality, shaken and horrified.

"Do it quickly," Sylvie advised. "When you're killing in the city, it has to be done quickly and quietly. I think you know what to do. I can't help you physically, you have to do it yourself. It must be your kill, completely."

Walt took a deep breath. The man looked so harmless that Walt hesitated: could he have been wrong? Once more, he probed the man's mind, just for a flash of truth, and got the same nightmarish pictures. Anger took him, and before the man knew what was happening, Walt had pulled him into the darkest part of the park.

He knew what Sylvie had told him about speed, but he wanted this man to suffer. He wanted him to be afraid.

And he *was* afraid. The first thing Walt did was pin the man to the ground, standing over him, towering toward the sky, with one gigantic foot on the man's throat so that he couldn't scream. One step, one almost infinitesmal shifting of his weight, and the man would die. The scent of the man's fear exploded out of him and up to Walt's nostrils. Walt felt another sensational burst of energy and power, and he knew that it was the fear spurring the loup-garou's adrenaline rush. Sylvie had told him to expect this, and had even tried to describe it, but nothing had prepared him for it.

This was why a loup-garou loves to take its time with the kill, loves to toy with its prey: for the almost sexual flood of adrenal power. Walt could see at once how addictive it was.

But he knew that Sylvie was right: in the city, it just wouldn't do. He was taking too big a chance on being seen.

He leaned down, never moving his foot, until his face was only a few inches from the man's. "Don't even bother to kid yourself about why you deserve this," the loup-garou growled. He wasn't sure whether or not his words were clear or just gibberish to the man's ears, but Walt felt better having said it.

He straightened up, then brought almost his entire weight down on the man's throat.

Blood burst from the man's mouth, from his nose, even from his startled and still-staring eyes. He made a short, strangled sound, thrashed briefly, and died, with more mercy shown to him than he had shown to his victims.

Walt knew what he had to do now. With one claw, he slashed at the man's left side, ripping it inexpertly, but thoroughly, open. He broke aside the ribs and pulled out the heart. Tilting his head back, he let it slide down his throat like a ripe, raw oyster. He knew that, through this ritual act that sustains a werewolf's life, he would be nourished until the next moon cycle.

This wasn't even a full moon, the time when a loup-garou *must* change and feed, regardless of circumstances. This night was a special gift, his very first, a chance for him to learn to control the experience on his own. At the full moon, it would be out of his hands. Sylvie fed only at the full moon. Her transformation tonight was simply for the pleasure of it, and part of her gift to Walt.

"We can't leave him here," she said. "That's the bad part about killing in the city. It's not like it was in Louisiana, where the swamps took the bodies. Or if they were found, it was assumed that animals had done the damage. A killing like this would be on the front page of every tabloid."

"What can we do with him?" Walt said. His speech, he noticed, was becoming more distinct, but was still slurred.

"You have two choices. You can consume the entire body..."

"I don't want to have anything more to do with this doofus," Walt said with distaste. "Even his heart tasted vile."

"Then we're going back to the place we started, and we're bringing him. Let's go."

Walt slung the body casually and easily over his shoulder, as if it weighed nothing at all. The trip back to the tunnels was faster, because Walt was less distracted, more comfortable with his new senses. Very shortly, they were back on the ornate subway platform.

"Take him down the old tracks, that way." She pointed to an unused tunnel. "Just dump him there. And don't look back after you leave him."

Walt thought this was strange, but he did as he was told. The tunnels were black as the bolts of hell, but he could see well enough. He slung the man against a wall, wedged into a corner.

As he started off, there was an explosion of soft sound behind him, so curious a sound that he did exactly as Sylvie had warned him not to, and looked back.

The body was already aswarm with rats. The seething movement of their bodies over the skin and inside the exposed entrails imparted the illusion of life.

The next time Sylvie told him not to do something, he promised himself, gagging, he wouldn't do it.

On the platform, under the silent, dark chandelier, they transformed back into human form. They dressed without a word, but exchanging secret smiles full of shared knowledge, and left the tunnels the way they had come.

Outside, Walt was disappointed to see that everything looked normal again. But his senses were a little sharper, his body a little more powerful, his mind keener.

"It stays with you from now on," Sylvie said, squeezing his hand. "Was it what you wanted, Walt? Was it what you thought it would be?"

"It was . . . inexpressible," he said, shaking his head.

"I would rather it had been upstate, or back in Louisiana, where you could run for miles and never see another soul. You could have taken the kill slower there, you would have enjoyed it more. Although Lucien loves to run and kill in the city: it's a challenge to his skills. He doesn't even bother with the park, he's so good at it."

"I enjoyed it just fine," he assured her. "Getting that jerk off the face of the earth was the finest feeling I've ever known. I just wish I could have found him sooner." He shook his head with regret, remembering the look of the killer's victims. "And they call *us* monsters."

"There's nothing like killing in the cause of justice, Walt," she said. "Once you've done that, you never want to kill for any other reason, even if just out of necessity, because you have to feed."

"How do you find them, though?" he said. "The ones who deserve it? Do you just get lucky?"

She shook her head. "They're all around us. Everywhere. There are lots of bad people in the world, Walt, more than we can ever hope to handle. You'll learn to keep your radar open slightly, to pick up on the signals, to spot them. Then, when the time comes, it's easy to find them again."

They walked part of the way in the summer night, exhilarated, enjoying the sights and sounds of the city. It wasn't all dangerous and dirty, Walt knew. New York was a Jekyll-and-Hyde town, and the beauty was there when you went looking for it. They stopped at an ice cream parlor with tables outside and had hot fudge sundaes and lemonade, like when they were kids. They stopped talking because there was so much between them now that could never have been put into words. The loup-garou's psychic bond, Walt found, was also a bond of subtle emotions, not just of imparted information.

"I think," Sylvie said, unable to conceal a knowing, maddening smile, "that you should pay a surprise visit to that pretty singer."

He was shocked. "How did you . . . ?" He didn't have to ask. He knew how she knew. "Damn. I'm never going to have any secrets again, am I?"

"Oh, you'll learn how to keep them," she teased. "But very shortly, you're going to have a common and overpowering reaction to what you've just been through. Little brother, you're about to find out about werewolf sex."

His burst of laughter made several people turn to look. "Werewolf sex?" he said, mystified. "Are you joking?" He laughed again.

"Laugh while you can, kid. But I suggest you get your tail uptown, and fast."

She stood up suddenly and waved at the curb. A cab stopped almost instantly for her: things like that happened to Sylvie. She opened the door for him. As Walt slid inside, she murmured, "Hope it doesn't hit you in the cab. That driver looks like he wouldn't appreciate a pass."

Walt laughed again. "You're absolutely insane. I'll call you tomorrow."

The cab shot off, and Walt looked fondly back at Sylvie, who was waving comically from the sidewalk and making movie monster faces. He realized that, though he had always loved Sylvie as his sister, the love between them now was even more profound. No one could have given him the gift exactly as she had given it, and with more unselfish love.

He gave the cabbie Mathilde's address and settled back in the seat. He laughed again. Werewolf sex, he thought, amused.

The position was highly improbable, but equally as enjoyable.

He was sitting up on his knees on the floor, between one set of wide-spread female legs wrapped tightly around his hips, moving rhythmically in and out of that sweet, moist, impossibly tight opening. All the while, facedown and supporting herself on her well-developed forearms, straddling the first woman between her elbows, Matty had Walt's head caught between her thighs. He drank long and deeply, his tongue catching every tart drop of juice. He and one woman formed a right angle; Matty was the heavenly hypotenuse.

If I'd known triangles could be like this, Walt decided, I'd have paid more attention in geometry class.

The women seemed to take it less seriously than Walt

did. Every once in a while their eyes would meet and they'd both be overtaken with giggles like a pair of naughty debs. Which was astonishing, considering that one of them was a professional.

A couple of times he caught sight of the three of them in the bedroom's floor-to-ceiling mirrored wall, and he was simply flabbergasted. If he didn't go insane with lust, he was thinking—when he was able to think at all—or pull a goddamn muscle, he was going to be the happiest man on earth.

How they'd gotten to this position, he didn't remember, but he was aware of Matty's superb muscular development and control, and her insatiable desire to show it off. This position, not listed in any version of the *Kama Sutra*, was her idea, and he was going to be forever grateful to her for it.

He *did* remember what had come before this moment. It was almost just as Sylvie had said: it didn't hit him in the cab, but damn near. He was so jumpy by the time the cab pulled up at Matty's building that he just stuffed some bills into the cab's payment slot and rushed out. He had a key to Matty's front door, so he didn't even bother to knock. He located her in a split second; with his sharp senses, he smelled her, unmistakably.

She was in the tub, soaking in hot water and bubbles, when Walt burst into the bathroom. She looked up, started to smile, and was cut off completely when Walt reached down and scooped her up, dripping and soapy, out of the water. When she had caught her breath, she managed to breathe his name, once, and to begin to ask what all this was about, but when Walt pinned her to the bed and began to devour her body with his mouth, she decided that she really didn't give a damn *what* had come over him, so long as it didn't go away.

Matty was used to passion. Opera singers are fiery, emotional people: it comes with the territory and with submerging oneself in high drama every night, twice if there was a matinee. Singers are never halfhearted about lovemaking, and can sometimes frighten non-singers with their intensity.

But Matty had never experienced anything like *this*! Walt had always been good at sex, but this went way beyond technique. It went beyond mind, and was all body, all primitive and primal. She had no idea how he managed it, but every orgasm, instead of depleting him, seemed to rejuvenate him. She was vaguely aware that, in other circumstances, she could have felt used, simply a sex toy that Walt was using for his own pleasure. Usually, he talked to her, and tonight—so far—he hadn't said a word. But Matty felt swept along, caught up in whatever tide was carrying Walt, and she found that thinking was the most useless thing she could do right then. She simply turned her mind off, and let her body express itself.

The other woman became involved in all this at about two in the morning.

Walt and Matty had finally reached a stopping point, but they could tell it was just going to be a lull.

"Matty," he said, his voice still vibrating with a strange exuberance, "haven't you ever wanted to do something totally wild, totally unlike you?"

"Wilder than *this*?" she said, confused.

"I mean, we could..." He thought a minute. Then he smiled as if he had thought of something monumental.

Ten minutes later, Matty was on the phone.

"I don't believe we're doing this," she whispered, her hand momentarily over the mouthpiece. She meant it, too. He might have suggested it, but it was Matty, always diving into life from the deep end, who'd picked up the phone.

They had called the most exclusive, expensive call girl

service in New York. Matty'd gotten the number from her
soon-to-be ex-husband, a scandalously rich playboy who
seemed merely amused by her request. Matty and Walt had
them send over five of their finest harlots. They only
wanted one, but Walt wanted to be certain that whoever
they picked was healthy. He wasn't worried about himself;
he was no longer human and human diseases meant nothing
to him. But he didn't want to take a chance with Mathilde.
He could tell who was healthy the same way he could tell
that the man in the park was guilty.

This service certainly knew their business. Each one of
the women was a stunner, looked like anything except a
call girl, and was in perfect health.

He asked them all to sit down and offered them drinks
while he and Matty retired to the other room.

"You're sure you're okay with this, Matty?" he said.

She gave a short laugh. "I can't believe it, but I really
am." She pressed her breasts against his chest and murmured hotly against his neck. "God, Walt, let's just do it,"
she said urgently. "Pick one and let's get on with it."

"You choose," he said gallantly.

"Oh, no, sweetheart," she said seriously. "It's going to
be your birthday present from me." Somehow, she thought,
the Cartier watch she had actually bought him didn't seem
like nearly enough.

Walt chose a refined blonde who looked like Grace
Kelly, the exact opposite from Matty. Mathilde, ever the
gracious hostess, gave each girl a hundred dollars for just
showing up and called taxis for them.

Later, Matty and the whore, whose name was Roxane,
theorized that it would be nice if they each reclined on two
different portions of Walt's anatomy at the same time while
he relaxed on his back, and it would also be nice if they
inserted a small vibrating device of Roxane's, only the

comfortable width of a feminine finger, just inside Walt's anus, where it would drive him absolutely bonkers.

"Does he scream when he comes?" Roxane asked politely.

"He will now," Matty assured her.

Walt decided that he'd died and gone to heaven.

Just before Roxane lowered herself gently over his waiting mouth, Walt gave a brief, secretive smile. He would have laughed, but was sure it would have been misinterpreted.

Werewolf sex, was what he was thinking.

If that night of his nineteenth birthday was the high point of his life, Walt reflected, this trip to New Orleans might well be one of the lows.

Walt had his family's strong love of the sea and of water. The elegant architecture of Rowe's Wharf was quickly receding behind him as the water taxi carried him across Boston Harbor to Logan Airport. The other passengers huddled in the tiny cabin, hungry for warmth, but Walt couldn't resist standing on deck as the boat chugged over the choppy winter water. He liked the sting of the wind against his face; it jolted him out of his problems, made him feel clean and decisive, connected to the element of water that fed his spirit.

This trip was the right thing to do; he had to believe that. He hadn't been home to New Orleans in two years, had avoided all but the most dutiful Christmas, anniversary, and birthday calls to his parents, and even then, he kept it short. It wasn't out of resentment or anger; it was out of self-preservation. There were certain things that he and his parents were never going to be able to talk about. Unfortunately, those things were central to Walt's life. He wasn't asking them to agree with his choices, only to respect his decision, and it was this that they could never do.

The water taxi slowed and pulled into the dock, where a shuttle bus was waiting to take the passengers to Logan. Walt picked up his bags and walked carefully up the swaying dock.

That night of transformation and blood and passion had been four years ago. It had not only changed his life, but it had changed his relationship with the people around him. He got along with human beings, and he certainly wasn't going to give up Mathilde, but he vastly preferred the company of other loups-garous. Because of that, he grew closer to Sylvie and Lucien, and to his Aunt Georgiana. He had known Georgiana was a loup-garou, but this had previously been something unspoken between them, Georgiana knowing that it was Sylvie's place to educate Walt. Now those invisible walls were smashed, and Walt took his place not as a sibling or a nephew, but as a respected member of the New England loups-garous' exclusive company.

After that summer, Walt went back to Boston, but not to Harvard. Sylvie had read him right: he was never sure he belonged there, or in any school. His life had always been proscribed by doing what was expected of him, following the rules, *waiting* somehow for his life to get started. And everyone around him, friends, family, teachers, all had bought into the illusion that your life didn't start until you were out of college and got a job. They all called it "doing something with your life." Walt never thought that doing something with your life had to be put on hold until you passed all the accepted milestones: you could do it at any point you wished. And right now, what he wanted to do with his life was be a loup-garou. To feel and touch the world around him in a new way. To serve justice as its darkest instrument.

Oh, all right, he admitted to himself, maybe he was putting off some things. Maybe he hadn't exactly decided what he wanted to do later. But right now, being a werewolf was all-consuming to him. It was so new, so strange; the emotions and sensations were all marvelous to him and he wanted to enjoy every minute of it while it was still fresh.

And he wanted to have a little fun. Okay, a *lot* of fun.

That was why he moved in with Georgiana in her fabulous house on Louisburg Square. She had the best of both worlds. She lived a luxurious public life—or, as luxurious as you can get in a low-key place like Boston—filled with fashionable people, theater parties, operas, music, trips abroad. Georgiana was a famous patron of the arts. She sat on the boards of museums and musical organizations and gave generously to all of them. Most of her energy and money went to children's charities.

She also lived an extravagant life as a loup-garou, a life that her socially prominent friends never suspected existed—except those few friends who were also werewolves. She moved in a charmed, decadent circle of international werewolves who traveled the world to be with their own kind. She was happy to sweep Walt along with her in an exuberant swirl of fabulous parties, exotic people, and erotic kills.

Georgiana had always loved children, but had never had any. Unlike Walt and Sylvie, who had chosen the loup-garou's life and had it lovingly given to them through the werewolf's kiss, Georgiana had the life forced on her, unawares, because of a family curse. And on her wedding night in 1910, unable to control herself or what was happening to her, her first kill was her young husband.

It had taken years for Georgiana to come to terms with what she was. She was actually at the point of suicide when she was rescued by Lucien's mother, Zizi. Zizi took her under her wing and taught Georgiana to control her powers.

She also taught Georgiana to live again, and to love, but for Geo, some damage could not be repaired, some agonies never comforted. She never remarried or formed another permanent attachment to any of her lovers, although several loups-garous were enchanted with her. And though she desperately wanted children, something inside her was terrified of passing on the family curse, although it had been broken long ago.

Sylvie, Walt, and their sister, Georgiana's namesake, were actually the children of her great-nephew, Andrew Marley. Like Georgiana, Andrew had inherited the family curse; like Georgiana, he had almost been destroyed by it. Andrew never came to terms with what he was, and after many tragedies and much heartbreak, discovered the woman who had cursed his family. She was his last kill, and with her death the curse died. But Georgiana, used to the life and the freedom, had long before elected to continue living as a werewolf. Andrew resumed his human life, married, and had children. Georgiana resumed her dizzying life in Boston and on the Continent. She was happy, but always conscious of the space in her life that should have been filled with children. When Andrew's children were born, Georgiana loved them like her own.

Walt had always been aware of Georgiana's sad history. He was glad that he could ease some of her pain. As it happened, Walt and Georgiana were perfect for each other. He loved his mother, but if he'd had to pick another one, it would have been Geo, no question. She loved his smart mouth, his quick wit, his sense of fun, and his keen attunement to the injustice of the world, which he was now armed to correct.

His budding eroticism, now coming into full bloom with the animal nature of the loup-garou, fascinated her. Georgiana had the same instincts, the same earthy passions: that was why her lovers found it almost impossible to keep away from her when the affair was over. She was always the one to leave. It was always with good grace, too. Walt was amazed when old lovers from fifty or sixty years ago would turn up at the Louisburg Square house, and Geo and the gentleman would uproariously relive old times.

Walt thought it amusing that Georgiana knew everything about his affair with Mathilde Grimaud. She didn't even have to read his mind for the details: he told her. It was a relief for him to have a confidante. Georgiana told him that a human woman, no matter how passionate, couldn't possibly match a female loup-garou. It was simply a question of nature.

"But this singer sounds like she comes close," Georgiana commented one morning when Walt had dragged himself in. Mathilde was singing a week's engagement with the Boston opera. "And where have you been since the curtain went down?"

"I'm pleased to tell you, madame, that I went down, too," Walt said with a formal little bow. "Matty and I have been ruining both the sheets and the reputation of the Ritz Carleton."

Geo raised an eyebrow. "If Matty wasn't so famous, and you weren't so rich, you would both have found yourselves chucked out on Arlington Avenue and on your way to a Motel 6."

That evening Geo and Walt were sitting in her box at the opera. "You should make her a loup-garou," Georgiana suggested. They were listening to Matty sing *Lakmè*.

"I can barely keep up with her as it is," Walt whispered. "If she had our strength, she'd kill me."

"You nasty, lascivious boy!" Geo hissed with mock outrage. "I meant that you could preserve that glorious voice for at least eight more generations of opera lovers." But, after a few minutes reflection: "Of course, she probably *would* fuck you to your grave."

Walt's life with Georgiana had been wonderful. His relationship with his parents, however, was declining at an alarming rate.

His family had only barely tolerated Sylvie's life choice. When they found out that she had given Walt the werewolf's kiss, they were aghast. In their eyes, she couldn't have done worse if she had sold her brother into white slavery in a Chinese opium den.

That his mother and younger sister might not understand was logical to Walt. But for his father, who knew what it meant to run free under the moon, who knew what the werewolf's code of ethics involved, who had actually experienced the transfiguring euphoria of the night—his father's stern disapproval struck Walt as nothing less than hypocrisy. When Walt said that he didn't intend to return to school right away, the ensuing argument had created a breach between them that had still not been bridged.

If not for that gulf of misunderstanding separating him and his father, Walt would have felt that his life was happy, content, and fulfilled. For now.

But even Georgiana was suggesting that Walt return to school.

"I still have my trust fund," Walt said. "It's not like I have to work. Besides, the economy is nasty; people who *need* jobs can't find them. I'm supposed to take a job I don't need and don't want away from someone who both needs and wants it?"

"I'm not talking about your working," Georgiana said, "I'm talking about your becoming educated. I don't want anyone at my dinner parties who can't keep up, mentally. Eventually, you're going to be a social liability."

He laughed. "I've got eight or nine hundred years to

become educated,'' he said. ''And I *am* becoming educated. Just ask Mathilde.''

That conversation had been only two weeks ago, and since then his suspicion that Georgiana was right, in her indirect, joking way, was creeping up on him. Living a dilettante's life was fun, but superficial. And look at his own sister. Sylvie had been meant for better things, but she stopped her life short when she married Lucien and had Claire. She tried to redirect her ambitions into being Superwife and Mom, and it was starting to wear very thin. Not that she realized it. She could see that she wasn't living happily ever after, but not why. Walt was sure that, for the first few years, she had been just as deliriously happy simply living the werewolf's life as Walt was right now. But when did the novelty wear off for her? How soon would it wear off for him?

He had no doubt at all that what he was doing as a loup-garou—serving as the instrument of justice—was beyond question a noble calling, and one that he would never regret.

But was there something else that he should be doing as well?

As he boarded the plane for New Orleans, these questions were no nearer to being resolved for him than they were in the beginning. In Louisiana, he hoped, he could think things over. He could talk with his father and try to reach some compromise. Besides, it was almost Mardi Gras time, a good time for any Orleanian to be home. He'd always loved the giddy mood of the city then, in which all problems of the real world seemed to dissolve. But most of all, in New Orleans, he could see the one person to whom every loup-garou turned when he or she was in real trouble.

Apollonius.

Walt adjusted the pillow behind his head and relaxed in his seat. Apollonius had been taking care of the loups-garous for two thousand years. He could certainly tell Walt how to handle this.

The plane climbed, and Walt slept peacefully for the first time in weeks, wrapped in clouds and sunshine.

5

Apollonius closed his eyes and concentrated on a white candle that existed only in his mind. The flame flickered and cast a circle of glowing comfort in the surrounding darkness.

As he had been taught by the Zen masters, Apollonius began to still the jittering flame. It was an old exercise to quiet the mind: the flame must stand perfectly still and no other thoughts must distract the mind.

Apollonius had been doing this for hundreds of years. He found that it helped him shut off his naturally well developed psychic attunement. He wanted silence, both in his mind and his surroundings. That was why he was doing this in the predawn hours. Even the streets were quiet; the tourists had already worn themselves out and the real inhabitants of the French Quarter weren't up yet.

The candle flame gave one last shiver and held still, and Apollonius relaxed.

But the darkness surrounding the candle had changed, from total blackness to a deep red that seemed to be spreading outward from the flame. It was liquid, moving. Suddenly the flame caught the red stain and the whole vision burst into fire.

Apollonius opened his eyes, puzzled. This had never happened before. The candle meditation had always been as sure and dependable as it was calming. He shook his head to clear it and started over.

The candle appeared, the flame flickered, held still . . . and disappeared into a vision of a city. The flaming red liquid advanced again, this time engulfing streets, flooding houses, washing the steps of skyscrapers. Apollonius put out his hand, as if he could touch what he saw, and at once he smelled blood. A sea of blood and fire.

He opened his eyes again, but the vision persisted, blinding him. He struggled to bring back the candle, knowing that he must regain control.

The candle floated over his consciousness again and he desperately tried to hold it there, but it kept fading. He tried something else: he gave in to the vision of blood and willed it to subside. He saw the flames extinguished, the scarlet tide withdrawn until it was nothing but a faint glow of red. He willed it into oblivion.

For some moments there was only darkness. And out of the darkness rose a mountain of glass, its sheer, slippery sides unassailable as a fortress.

This was no random vision. Someone was sending him this message, someone who knew that only he could receive it.

There was a man on the glass mountain, surrounded by werewolves. Far from the werewolves who served justice, these were mindless monsters who indulged a passion for human flesh and human suffering. They carried horror about them.

Apollonius tried to bring back the dark, to revive the candle, to regain control of his consciousness.

The werewolves on the mountain turned toward him, so that he could see their faces. Their faces!

With his right hand, Apollonius bent one finger of his

left hand back until he heard it snap. The pain shattered his trance.

He found that his breath was coming very fast, his heart racing even faster. He used a controlled breathing method to slow his body and calm it. His broken finger hurt, but it would heal in a few minutes; no injury was permanent for a werewolf unless it had been caused by silver. He stood up, trying to shake off the memory, and wandered aimlessly through the rooms of the house, not really seeing anything or having any objective in mind, simply trying to clear his senses. He knew that talking to someone would help, would put it all into perspective, but it was four in the morning and everyone he knew would be asleep.

Apollonius didn't need sleep. Two thousand years ago, on one of his wanderings in Egypt, he had been led by a dying priest of the goddess Isis to a sacred place in the desert. Every hundred years, the priest told him, Isis caused water to gush out of the sand. It was in this water, not in the Nile, the priest said, that Isis had laid the dead god Osiris and brought about his resurrection. To drink the water, if Isis permitted it, meant immortality.

They spent two days and nights there, taking no food and no drink, letting their throats parch in the hot desert air. They didn't speak and didn't move, even when poisonous insects crawled over their still bodies, concentrating only on purifying their souls through denial of the flesh. They offered their suffering as a sacrifice to Isis.

At midnight of the second night, when the moon hung clear and full in the heart of the sky, they heard at first a trickling, then a gush of water at their feet. With grateful thanks to Isis, Apollonius let the old man, with the privilege of age and learning, drink first.

The priest cupped his hands and drank, his eyes filled with bliss as the water cooled his throat. Apollonius took several drafts of the water, finding it sweet and oddly cold in the desert heat. The old priest looked at Apollonius expectantly and, with the smile still on his lips, he died.

Apollonius, horrified, waited for his own death. He was motionless with terror as the minutes passed. But he didn't die. Instead, he began to feel a renewal of life, nothing as dramatic as he'd expected, but a sense of well-being and peace.

He remembered that the priest had said that immortality would be granted only if Isis willed it.

He never knew why Isis had chosen him and not the priest who had served her, but in the years to come, he knew that she had. As long as he lived, long after the worship of Isis had vanished from Egypt, Apollonius made a shrine to her, no matter where he roamed. He kept one still, a small statue that was now priceless because of its antiquity, which sat in an honored place in the house.

In granting him immortality, Isis had also freed him from the need to eat, drink, or sleep. He could do these things if he chose—and Apollonius often chose all three—but they weren't necessary. He especially enjoyed staying awake, being up and about when all the town was silent.

On this particular morning, however, the silence was a drawback. A little noise and distraction would have pushed this whole nasty scenario aside. He thought of transforming, then going outdoors for a cleansing run through the Quarter, past the Central Business District, down St. Charles and out to the Parish. Just a little morning's jog for a werewolf. But action alone wouldn't do it: he needed conversation.

He thought about waking Zizi. She'd talk to him. She'd probably make love to him, especially if she thought he was troubled. But he wasn't sure he wanted to push this particular nightmare on Zizi, or on anyone, not until he knew more.

What chilled Apollonius was the certainty that what he had seen was not simply a vision. It was the future. He knew the man who had sent it to him. Lycaon. His old enemy. His exact opposite. The same man who had made him a werewolf, knowing full well that Apollonius's immortality would ensure that Lycaon would never be alone in his lycanthropy.

Lycaon's immortality, however, had not been a gift from the gods. It had been their curse.

Lycaon's true power, Apollonius knew, resided not in his lycanthropy or his immortality, but in his empathy. He could see into the hearts of people, could pinpoint their most vulnerable pain, fears, and inadequacies; their most volatile passions; and he could exploit them to his advantage.

Lycaon had been silent a long time. Long enough so that Apollonius had been lulled into a false sense of security. But that silence may have been merely a quiet marshaling of his forces.

It would be typical of Lycaon, Apollonius knew, to attempt to seduce the world's werewolves to his own amoral principles, and for no better reason than the satisfaction of his perverse sense of amusement.

The rooms were getting lighter as Apollonius roamed the house. The world was taking on that peculiarly promising shade of violet that at twilight darkens to night, and at night lightens to morning.

Apollonius sighed. He had seen so many dawns, so many twilights. He tried to summon some enthusiasm for the sight, but his immortality had jaded him to this as well as to so many other things. He wondered if Lycaon, in his long absence, had found a renewed passion for the small things that make up everyday life. Is that what it took? he thought. Would a complete denial of the senses result in a rebirth of them?

He realized that he was being presumptuous. Just because he hadn't seen Lycaon in centuries didn't mean that Lycaon's existence had been suspended or that he'd been hidden away in some cave.

He was intensely curious, and uneasy, about what Lycaon wanted after all this time.

He was sitting at the lacy iron table in the courtyard, reading the morning paper, when Zizi finally came outside. She hadn't dressed; she was wrapped in layers and layers of intricate lace, tied together at the throat with ribbons, her blond hair tumbling over her shoulders. Apollonius thought, not for the first time, how grateful he was to her for having saved his life when he was so determined not to let her do it.

It was in eighteenth-century France that they had met. She was an exuberant sixteen-year-old, newly made a loup-garou, and he was wrapped in the distancing cloak of his immortality. But Marie-Thérèse, as she had been called then, was so much wiser than he had been. She had known all about love, and he had known nothing except his fear of it. Because he was so terrified of losing the people he loved, he solved his problem by simply never letting anyone touch his life. Marie-Thérèse had not only touched him, she had ripped open his carefully woven shroud. But he was determined to be unhappy, and Marie-Thérèse had left France to make a new life in Louisiana. And making a new life was literally what she had done: she was pregnant when she got on the boat. She and her son, Lucien, were the first loups-garous in Louisiana. They created more of their own kind through the *baiser du loup-garou,* the werewolf's kiss, the erotic bite that transforms mind and body.

Apollonius never knew he had a son. Not until over two hundred years later. At that point, Marie-Thérèse figured that he was mature enough to handle it. Not Lucien; Apollonius. She finally persuaded Apollonius to abandon his centuries of wandering, the life that had left him so unsatisfied, and she offered him another chance to learn about love.

He was not such a fool as the first time. He took this chance gratefully and without reservation.

Apollonius had had the belated luxury of being a father for only a few years before Lucien and Sylvie moved away, but they were wonderful years. He envied Marie-Thérèse all that time she'd had with Lucien, his birth, his childhood, all the large and small daily joys and trials of parenthood. He wasn't bitter; he had never given Marie-Thérèse any reason to expect that he'd be able to accept a child into his tightly confined life. He'd had only himself to blame for that.

Still, he and Lucien had had a marvelous time getting to know each other. They were both adults, both able to meet on an equal ground, and there was great respect on each side. Apollonius was grateful to learn that Lucien had absorbed his father's most cherished principles of justice, and had even studied Pythagoras's work on numbers and musical tones. Lucien laughed and said that he could never quite get over the fact that Pythagoras's most famous student was right here, giving him the facts straight from the source.

Now he and Marie-Thérèse had settled into an orderly routine, more or less. They spent most of the year in New Orleans and the unbearable summer months in Rome, in the Palatine Hill house Apollonius had owned for a long time. In the winter, the house was occupied by Apollonius's friend and Sylvie's great-aunt, Georgiana Marley, who filled it with more interesting people and fabulous parties than Apollonius had managed to cram into it in almost twelve hundred years. Plenty of loups-garous who wintered in Italy said that there hadn't been a party giver like Georgiana since maybe Caligula.

"I don't care if we *do* miss the Jazz Festival every year," Zizi once told Achille, who pointed out that she'd miss New Orleans's summer fun if they decided to summer in Rome. "You're joking, right? Fun? I've put up with this miserable humidity for two hundred years—Italy's got to be better."

Because he had learned over the centuries what it was like to be alone, he began each day with a keen awareness that he would never have that particular torture again. And though Marie-Thérèse and Lucien and Sylvie and Achille and all the loups-garous that he loved were not immortal and would eventually die, he had finally allowed himself to be happy now, with them, and knew that what they had taught him would see him through the sorrow when the time came. "It will actually be a comfort," Lucien had once told him, "to know that you'll be here for my children, and their children, and all the generations of loups-garous. You'll have all the memories, Apollonius, all the history. You can teach the kids. It's strange, but it's as if we'll never die, either; not really, not as long as you remember us. What a wonderful adventure that will be!"

Amazing what wisdom the children have for the fathers, Apollonius thought, remembering it.

Zizi came up behind him and put her arms around him, her hair falling forward like a yellow silk curtain over his face. Her perfume wafted around him and he took a long breath of it. "*What* is that scent?" he asked her. "It's absolutely maddening."

"It's a perfume essence," she told him. "Tunisian frankincense. I was going to blend it with some other fragrance, but I decided to try it straight.''

''Well, it's wonderful.''

She pushed her hair back and looked over his shoulder at the paper. ''Anything earthshaking?''

''Not in the paper, but I had an interesting phone call while you were asleep. Lucien called.''

She straightened up and smacked his shoulder lightly. ''And you didn't wake me for *that*?'' She sat down opposite him.

''He didn't talk long. He just wanted to say that he and Sylvie and Claire are coming for a visit next week.'' He grinned. ''Isn't that great?''

Zizi whooped loud enough to wake the house ghosts. ''About time! How long are they staying? Oh, I've got to get the little apartment cleaned . . .'' She stood up as though she were going to do it right then.

He laughed and grabbed her arm, pulling her into his lap. That perfume distracted him again, filling his mind with all sorts of interesting images.

He pulled at one of the ribbons that held her lace peignoir together.

''Well . . . ,'' she said, ''I guess the maid can clean in there . . . later. . .''

A few minutes later, she sighed, ''You know, *chéri*, for a Greek philosopher, you certainly have some French ideas.''

6

Achille had always liked Addis. It was a tiny town, very parochial, and everyone knew everyone else's business. That was not such a bad thing, in Achille's opinion. Everyone knew him, they knew why he was here, and they were kind enough not to talk about what had happened to his wife.

Some, but very few, knew he was a loup-garou. Achille was surprised at first at the casual way this was accepted, but he realized that he had been away from the bayous for way too long. He had forgotten how deep-seated the superstitions were in this part of the country, and how matter-of-factly people took strange happenings. Ghosts in the old houses, Voodoo charms and hexes, the loup-garou; they were part of life here. People were cautious, but not afraid: they knew that the supernatural world had its own rules, as surely as the real world did, and if you obeyed the rules nothing would hurt you. Mothers might threaten bad children with "the loup-garou gonna get you!" or "If you bad, Marie Laveau gonna fly in the window and catch you!" but children and adults alike knew that to avoid fate, one only had to keep to the straight and narrow. The loup-garou, they knew, only got you if you were really bad. Keep your nose clean and the most he'd do is scare you.

Eventually, Achille found that he had acquired a new

reputation, one that surprised him. It started with a timid knock on his back door, so light that he wasn't sure he'd heard it. He opened the door just to reassure himself that it wasn't his imagination.

Two little black kids stood there, looking as if they'd wet their pants if he made any sudden moves. Their eyes were round as Easter eggs as they looked up at him. The girl was about nine or ten, her brother considerably younger, maybe six or seven. He was a terrible judge of kids' ages.

He thought at first they were selling cookies or candy bars for some school fund-raiser, and he instinctively looked around to see where he'd left his wallet. But they just stood there in awed silence.

He was as puzzled as they were, but he smiled to put them at ease.

"Hey. Where ya at?" he said. The universal New Orleans opening line. It didn't work so well here. "Uh . . . y'all want to come on in and have some Barq's root beer or something?"

The boy looked intrigued at this, but the girl shook her head. They didn't look so much scared as interested, and Achille had the feeling that this visit was satisfying some intense childish curiosity. He remembered his own childhood, when knocking on the door of the local bogeyman/hermit was absolutely de rigueur for getting in with the right crowd.

"Okay. You must want something, though. Am I right?"

The little girl found her courage. "My mama says tell you you gotta come."

This didn't clear anything up for Achille.

"Come where? For what?"

"To our house. My mama sent me to bring you to our house. My little sister's real bad sick. She got a bad fever.

Mama's afraid she might . . ." The child choked on her fear. "She's afraid she might die if you don't come."

The child's voice had taken a desperate tone. She was obviously afraid that she wasn't getting through to Achille and she didn't know what to do now that she had delivered her message. Her lower lip trembled as she held tight to her brother's hand.

Achille was terribly confused. "Did you get a doctor? You want me to call one for you?" He knew that some bayou houses didn't have phones, and sometimes the doctor was distant from his far-flung patients.

"Mama says you can make Sissy well. She says to me, 'Child, you go get that Voodoo man, Madame Mae Charteris's husband. He'll know what to do.' "

It all became clear to Achille then. Of course. Everyone in Louisiana had known Mae, and her power as a healer was as famous as her charms and spells. If he had been sick, he sure would have gone to Mae first. She could cure you faster than the doctor and for free. But Mae was gone, and Achille had never felt so helpless.

"I think y'all made a mistake, 'tite chers. I'm no Voodoo man."

But they just kept looking at him. The little girl's face looked even more troubled as she tried to assimilate what he'd just said.

He tried frantically to remember Mae's cures for fever. She'd told him often enough about what herbs were good for what ailments, and sometimes he even knew enough to brew up a few remedies himself, but it was Mae who had the gift. She could heal by laying on of hands alone.

"You ain't comin'?" The little girl looked like she was on the verge of panic now.

Achille ran his hands through his hair. "Shee-it," he said to himself. Then to the kids, he said, "Yeah, I'm comin'.

Just let me grab a few things here. Y'all go out to the driveway and get in my car. You give me directions."

When he had left Mae's house in the Quarter, he had taken most of her things with him. The innumerable jars of herbs and roots and precious resins were all packed away in boxes, fortunately all labeled with the contents. One of Mae's enormous books of formulas for healing brews, all in her own handwriting, was sitting on the bookshelf.

Ordinarily, he wouldn't have touched anything of Mae's. They were like a saint's relics to him, and the sight of them was still painful. He hesitated at the bookshelf. "Damn, Mae. How do you get me into these things, dawlin'?" he said, sighing. He grabbed the book, leafed through it until he found what he was looking for, then made for the warm, dry attic where he'd stored the jars. He ripped open the boxes, stuffed several jars into a canvas overnight bag, laid the book on top of them, and carried everything out to the car where the kids waited.

But before he'd reached the car, he'd made a stop in the kitchen for a six-pack of frosty Barq's root beer. He'd also dumped an entire bowl full of fruit into a paper grocery bag.

If he was gonna be Dr. Achille the Voodoo man, he thought, then he'd start by seeing that those skinny kids got some vitamins.

It was past midnight when he got home, but he was pretty sure the kid would be all right. All he could do now was pray to God, the saints, and throw in a couple of offerings to the Voodoo saints as well. He remembered Mae's special relationship with Erzulie, the gentle goddess of love. Erzulie had seen Mae through lots of hard troubles.

He had breathed a supplication to Erzulie more than once throughout that day and night. He'd also had a heart-to-

heart talk with Saints Marron, Expedite, and Jude, and had
called on Jesus quite often, deliberately or not.

It hadn't looked so good from the very first. The girl,
about eight or so, had been raving with fever, about a hundred and three. Normally, if the fever had been slight,
Achille would have eased the child into a hot bath and kept
her there, then bundled her in layers of clothes and under
lots of blankets. Achille knew that fever was the body's
way of burning off the germs causing disease.

But this kind of fever was its own malady. This was
frighteningly high. He cursed himself for not calling EMS
first thing, before he left home, but he could see that moving the child wasn't going to do a damned thing. Fortunately, the ramshackle bayou house had a good refrigerator
and there was a little grocery down the road that sold ice.
He sent the kids there in shifts, giving them money to buy
bags of ice that he packed around the burning Sissy. He
put her mother to work bathing the child with ice water
and feeding her ice chips to suck, while he brewed the
special teas from the herbs he'd brought.

Sissy was so deranged with fever that her throat was
parched, and at first, Achille considered forcing the tea
down her throat with a plastic turkey baster, all that was at
hand. It might even be a pleasant alternative: some of these
cures were amazingly effective, but they tasted like hell.
Mae used to dump great quantities of honey in them to ease
the taste, and he didn't intend to depart from that little trick.

He started out with infusions of goosegrass, one of the
best things for bringing down a fever. He was amazed at
what he remembered. Living with Mae all that time, listening and watching her spells and cures, helping her tend her
herb gardens, he'd absorbed more than he was aware of.
For fevers, he knew that wild indigo, echinacea, myrrh, or
garlic were good, but that cleavers—called goosegrass—

was better. He'd also brought along vervain, to help the child after her fever broke. Please, God, he thought, that it *would* break, and soon.

Despite the taste, the girl managed to drink his goose-grass tea, and to keep it down. He knew that this was a hopeful sign. He alternated the tea with beef broth, to keep up the child's strength, and as much water as she could keep down for the dehydration. She sure couldn't eat solid food.

He knew immediately what was wrong with her, the minute he'd seen the swollen glands under her jaw and looked down her throat. Her tonsils had become infected. It's stupid, he thought, nobody dies of tonsillitis anymore!

Nobody but kids whose parents couldn't afford to have the tonsils removed, and who couldn't afford regular medical care. Kids got sick all the time, and Achille knew that among the poor, it was always a crapshoot as to whether the kid was sick enough to warrant the expense of a doctor. It wasn't irresponsibility: it was that the parents actually had to choose between medical care for one child and adequate food for the family. They couldn't afford both.

That's why Mae never took money for healing, and why she had such a big clientele. She could cure a lot of things outright, but she also knew when medical intervention was called for. And she was the AMA's worst nightmare, calling in favors and shaming some of the town's most expensive doctors into taking her charity cases.

He sure wished for some of Mae's juice now, he thought more than once as he watched Sissy. He had to give her credit, the kid fought that fever like a champ. She choked down his evil-tasting brews, though he tried to pump enough honey in them to curb the bitterness, and she tried desperately to do everything he told her, even though she wandered in and out of consciousness.

Achille tried to help, saying every prayer he knew, to every god that man had ever invented.

At about ten that night, it looked like Sissy was taking a turn for the worse. She gagged on the tea and spit it up. Achille was terrified that she was going to empty her stomach of the rest of the healing teas, but she didn't.

The mother started to cry, and Achille would have, too, except that he was too desperate. Come on, honey, he thought, you gotta pull out of this. As if she'd heard him, the girl looked at him with weary eyes. She looked so defeated that Achille wanted to scream his frustration.

"Jesus, Jesus, Jesus!" he muttered frantically. "Mae, darlin' . . . help me here. Don't let this little child down. I may be an idiot, but you know what to do, so help me do it for you."

Sissy gave a slight cough and Achille almost jumped out of his chair. In desperation, he grabbed hold of both the child's hands. From out of nowhere, he felt a burst of strength through him. He concentrated on the energy, the life in his own body, feeling it like electricity, the same kind of energy he got when he transformed under the moon. But he wasn't going to use it for that. He willed it out through his arms, through his hands, pumping it into the child.

Come on, darlin', he commanded the child silently, you gonna be all right; you gonna get well. Just feel all this strong stuff flowing through you, burning away all the infection.

He closed his eyes and concentrated on their linked hands, giving it everything he had. There was nothing in the world at that moment but him and that little girl, linked by their hands, like two pairs of copper wires completing a circuit. A picture came to him of Sissy's fever, swirling like dark smoke around her body. He willed the smoke to lighten, to evaporate, to vanish, sailing out the window. He concentrated everything on this picture, trying to make it real.

The energy reached a peak and Achille felt his breath come faster, the little girl echoing the sound. He opened his eyes and couldn't believe it.

He saw Mae, as real as if she'd been there, standing on the other side of the bed. Her tumble of black gypsy curls, her glowing *café au lait* skin set off by her favorite scarlet silk dress—it was Mae, no question.

She smiled at him. "You done real good, white boy," she said, then vanished.

He was so surprised he dropped Sissy's hands.

The girl sighed and sank back on the pillow. Her mother gave a sob.

"Oh, Jesus God!" Achille said in alarm.

But she had fallen asleep. A real sleep, not a fevered state of unconsciousness. Achille stuck the thermometer under her tongue. Ninety-nine. He showed the numbers to the mother, who started to cry. Achille, too tired to cry himself, merely slumped back in his chair. Some odd things popped into his mind. He would have said they were thoughts out of nowhere, except that he was sure that somewhere Mae was still doing her stuff, one last time. He remembered things he'd long forgotten; his old Cajun ancestors who used to rely on the gifted community healers, men and women who knew the old herbs and the old remedies, things that had largely been forgotten in these days where science and medicine have to be slick and packaged to have credibility.

Those old Cajun healers were still around. Not as many as before, but they existed. They carried on the old traditions, kept the old ways. He vaguely remembered being taken to one when he was very young. The herbs were just as bitter as the ones he'd given Sissy, and just as effective.

More and more people were coming back to the old ways these days, only now they dressed it up by calling it "holistic health alternatives" and buying their herbs and tinctures in expensive health food stores. Call it what you want, he thought, it was still the old way of the Cajuns, the Native Americans, the Witches, the Pennsylvania Pow-Wow doctors, the Voodoos . . . all the traditional healers.

Achille smiled thinking about it. A loup-garou healer. Now there was an oxymoron for you.

Sissy's fever returned to normal about midnight. She woke a couple of times and had some more tea and warm broth. She drank a big glass of ice water, then fell back to sleep, exhausted by everything she'd been through.

Achille stayed for another two hours, watching her as her fever subsided, but he knew she'd be all right. Just to be on the safe side, he'd make sure that a doctor was out here first thing tomorrow, and he'd pay for it.

As he left the house, the little boy was still awake, sitting on the front stoop.

"What are you doin' hangin' out here?" Achille said. "Go on in and go to sleep. Your sister's gonna be all right."

The little boy looked at him wisely. "You goin' home now, Voodoo man?"

Achille thought about it. "You know what, *'tite cher'?*" he said. "I think I've already come home. I just didn't recognize it when I saw it."

7

The windows of Gabriel Breaux's shop in the lower Pontalba building always attracted a crowd of tourists. He was the best goldsmith and jeweler in the city, if not in the United States, and his fantasy creations were even featured in museums, usually next to the work of Carl Fabergé.

Fabergé, who had created those unbelievable clockwork Easter eggs for Tsar Nicholas II and his family, would have been respectful, and maybe a little envious, of Gabriel's work. Everyone else was merely delighted.

Besides the usual line of fine jewelry, Gabriel specialized in tiny, working models of Mardi Gras floats. Every fine detail was perfect. The enameled colors on the gold and silver sparkled like liquid jewels. Miniature maskers rotated and waved to the mesmerized crowds outside Breaux's window, some dangling strings of Mardi Gras beads in their infinitesimal gilt hands. They rode atop wonderful floats shaped like dragons or alligators, mechanized creatures who nodded their heads and waved their tails, sparks flying out of their roaring mouths. Some played Mardi Gras tunes from ingeniously hidden music box works. Sometimes, Gabriel made his small floats from imagination, sometimes he copied real floats of the previous Mardi Gras parades, working with Blaine Kern, who made the big ones. Some of the floats were traditional clockwork: they had to be hand-wound with purposefully elaborate keys. Some were powered by watch batteries: you touched one of the little maskers, which was actually a power switch.

He didn't just set them out on black velvet. He turned the entire window into a Mardi Gras afternoon, with a diorama of Canal Street, cheering crowds, trees and grass, and pavement littered with beads and trinkets. A spray of Carnival doubloons arched through the air on invisible plastic filaments. Tiny banners, ribbons, and streamers in green, purple, and gold festooned balconies and lampposts. Some of this was three dimensional: he had built the front of the Boston Club, a scaffolding, and a tiny pavilion holding plaster images of the Queen of Carnival and her court. The ladies were mostly imaginary, except for the Queen. He had modeled her on a real woman: his friend Sylvie Marley, only seventeen when she was Rex's queen. She stood in Gabriel's window now as she stood in front of the Boston Club then, in her white suit, her red hair flaming against her ivory skin, her eyes real chips of turquoise. On the street below her, the Rex float with its animated figures played the Mardi Gras anthem, "If Ever I Cease to Love."

All day, tourists were arrested in their flights between Jackson Square and the French Market, caught as if by invisible hands to stare at the windows with the tiny, magical Mardi Gras parade. Gabriel had gone the real thing one better: in a single glance you could see the kings' floats of Rex, Bacchus, Zulu, Momus, and Comus with Krewe officers mounted on white horses, one after the other, all in one parade.

More often than one would expect, considering the astronomical prices, one of the little floats would be sold and would disappear from the display, to be replaced with another. But not another just like it: Gabriel only made one of each. He often worked on commission, with the piece paid for in advance, but he still reserved the right to display it in his window for two weeks before it was delivered in a special glass display case to its owner.

Those who expected Gabriel Breaux to be old, or at least middle-aged, were surprised when they met him. He was very young, somewhere in his early twenties, a dark-haired young Cajun with intense dark eyes. People marveled that he had attained such control and such artistry while he was still so young. He was certainly a prodigy: talented and imaginative.

However imaginative Gabriel was, it was as nothing compared to the imagination of his lover, Delilah Faust. Delilah was a lovely, innocent-looking blonde with big blue eyes that opened wide when she was thinking up deviltry, which was a lot of the time. Delilah was at least twenty pounds over what was usually considered fashionable weight, which gave her soft, erotic curves that made men want desperately to touch her buttery skin and sink into her.

Which was what Gabriel was trying very hard to do at just that moment.

It wasn't easy. Delilah had a perfect penchant for sex in strange places or under strange circumstances. It had forced her husband, a prominent surgeon, finally to refuse to make love to her anyplace but in bed—or at least, at home and indoors. This was after Delilah's insistence that she couldn't wait, she absolutely *had to have it* in the backseat of the bridal limousine parked at the curb of the country club during her sister's wedding reception. The driver, coming back a little early, had glanced into the backseat, choked discreetly, and walked off.

"That's it, Delilah," poor Dr. Faust said, pulling his pants back up. "The only saving grace here is that the limo is rented and we don't know the driver."

She had stretched luxuriously. "Oh, I don't know," she drawled, "I thought it was kind of exciting."

"It was entirely humiliating," he declared.

Delilah told Gabriel that he was much more adventurous than the doctor. There was no question, though, that she loved her husband to distraction. "The very sight of him makes me wet," she sighed to Gabriel. "Those blue-gray eyes. That body. He's got great hands, you know, all surgeons do. But it gets pretty boring doing it in the same old house all the time." She considered a moment. "I guess it's good we have all those rooms," she concluded.

She often told Gabriel that she loved the physical contrast between him and her husband. Gabriel was dark, with an elegantly elongated body. He reminded her, she said, of Lord Byron. Dr. Faust, on the other hand, looked like a Teutonic prince.

She did it everywhere with Gabriel, whose willingness to go along with this was fueled partly by his fascination with what she'd come up with next. They had sex under the bandstand in City Park, behind the animal cages at the zoo, standing up in the deserted confessional in St. Louis Cathedral (Gabriel hated to admit it, but that was one of his favorites), and in the parking lot of the Canal-Villère supermarket, near the entrance, in Gabriel's convertible. (She at least agreed to have the top up.) And those were just the places for full-scale sex. When it came to hand jobs, she was at her most flamboyantly inventive.

But the place she'd picked this time made Gabriel really uneasy; so uneasy, in fact, that he was having trouble managing the act itself.

They were in an examining room at her husband's office.

"It's a big office," Delilah assured him. "Nobody'll know, and besides, he has locks on the doors, back from when the building was still a private house. It takes these big old skeleton keys. See?" She held up an enormous antique key.

Still, the mechanics were a trifle difficult.

"You have to stand on that little step," Delilah said informatively as she reclined on an examining table, "and I'll just wrap my legs around you, and you can lean forward . . ."

"Jesus, Delilah," Gabriel complained, "do you realize we've never done it in my apartment? Wouldn't that be a welcome change?"

Nevertheless, he had maneuvered himself into position and was just getting into the rhythm of it when they heard the door rattle.

"You *did* lock it?" Gabriel asked her, alarmed.

"I think I did," she said, her eyes opening wide.

They heard a softly spoken swear word and the rattle of keys.

"Oh," Delilah said, remembering, "I guess the staff has keys."

A handsome, glacially blond man was standing in the door, regarding the two of them in mild shock. After a surprised second, he shut the door behind him.

"Hi, honey!" Delilah said with a little wave. "It's only me."

"Yes, dear, I recognize the birthmark," he said, still a little stunned. "Gabriel," Dr. Faust sighed in quiet exasperation, "why do you encourage her like this? It only makes her worse." His voice was slightly tinted by his lilting Viennese accent, incongruous considering how long he had lived in New Orleans.

Gabriel straightened up slowly and shrugged. "I try to be accommodating, Christian."

"You can afford to be," Christian said, going to the

cabinet and picking up the lab slides he'd come in for, "you're not married to her."

He retrieved the slides, then bent briefly to kiss his wife, still reclining on the table. "Delilah, try to show a little restraint. What if it had been a patient or a nurse who'd found you two, instead of me?"

"Don't forget tonight, honey," she said to Christian. "Gabriel's birthday party? We have at least twenty people coming for dinner, so be home early." She gave a little wave as he moved toward the door. "I love you, sweetheart!"

Christian sighed. "You know, only the three of us could possibly understand that statement." He laughed briefly as he left the room. "Good-bye until tonight, Gabriel. Happy birthday. Hope you get everything you want!"

He shut the door, still shaking his head in amusement.

"This is hopeless now," Gabriel said, pulling on his clothes.

Delilah raised herself on her elbows and sighed. "He's such a sweet man," she said dreamily.

To an outsider who may have been looking on, Gabriel's birthday party that night would have seemed like any intimate black-tie New Orleans dinner. Just another Garden District gala. Besides Dr. and Mrs. Faust and Gabriel, there was the governor of Louisiana, Darryl Dozier, newly elected for his second term, and his animal-rights activist wife. He had married Evangeline Leigh during his first term, just after she had sued the state for destroying wetlands nesting areas and won the case. "Damn!" Darryl had said after the honeymoon. "Court wasn't the only place that li'l gal managed to screw the daylights outta the state a' Looziana."

There was the conductor, Lucien Drago, and his wife

Sylvie, just arrived from New York. Their tiny, gorgeous daughter, Claire, darted among the guests like a fairy, in a white lace dress that was only slightly marred by the chocolate icing from an eclair that had dripped onto her skirt. At the moment, Claire was sitting cross-legged on the floor, letting Daisy Buchanan, the Faust's furry red Chow dog, lick the chocolate off the lace while Claire had another pastry. She kept breaking off bites for Daisy, who was in dog ecstasy.

Lucien's parents, Apollonius and Zizi, were there; and Sylvie's younger brother, Walter. There was a tall, exotic black woman who owned New Orleans's most prestigious art gallery, in the company of a famous chef who had made the reputation of a restaurant in the Garden District. There was the CEO of an oil company who had managed to keep his offshore operations feeding money profitably into the state, even after the oil crash. A shadow-haired lady writer moved like a mysterious wraith through the nineteenth-century rooms of the house as if she were one of the original inhabitants. The guest list comprised the eccentric, the powerful, and the famous of New Orleans.

And, except for little Claire, none of them was human.

Long before the actual dinner commenced and people were seated at the long table, Claire had dropped off to sleep in one of the bedrooms. Daisy Buchanan stretched out alongside her, one huge paw draped protectively over Claire's arm.

The Fausts' dining room was cozy and intimate, with a large fireplace at one end and a set of glass-paned French doors at the other, leading to larger rooms. The entire party was softly lit with a combination of low, indirect lighting and candlelight, glinting discreetly off the Baccarat wineglasses, casting prism-colored sparkles around the room when the light caught in the perfect cuts of the crystal.

The governor looked around the table wistfully. "I ain't seen so many loups-garous together since the last full moon at Bayou Goula," he said. "And even then, not all of us were able to make it there. Remember when nobody would miss a full moon on the bayou?"

"Time intercedes," Apollonius said, "life intrudes."

"Look how scattered we are," Christian said. "Lucien and Sylvie in New York, Brenda gone on book tours half the time, Henry in Saudi Arabia arguing with OPEC. Apollonius and Zizi in Rome for half the year. The lovely Georgiana never leaves Boston anymore except to take young Walt here to Europe. And Achille..."

Everyone fell silent thinking of Achille. Sylvie Drago felt tears swelling in her eyes and blinked hard to keep them away.

"He shoulda been here," the governor said sadly, "even if we'd gone out there to Addis and dragged him here."

"He'll be back," Apollonius said positively, "in his own time. And he'll be a better man for it. The strength we gain is in proportion to the troubles we have to overcome."

Delilah, seeing the depressing turn the party was taking, signaled a waiting maid. In a few minutes, an enormous birthday cake, blazing with candles, was wheeled into the room and stationed beside Gabriel.

"Damn, boy!" the governor complained. "All that light makes my eyes hurt!"

"Good heavens, Delilah!" Zizi said. "How many candles did you have them put on that thing?"

"I only put his real age, thirty-five," Delilah said defensively.

"Be glad it wasn't mine," Apollonius advised, "or we'd have had to build a bonfire. It's a good thing he's just a baby."

"Wait a minute . . ." Sylvie said. "Delilah . . . what's on

top of that cake?'' It was hard to see in the glare of all the candles. Sylvie let out a whoop. "Oh, my God!" she laughed. "It's the Wolf Man!"

"No, it isn't!" Delilah said indignantly.

They all looked closer.

"It's in much worse taste than that," Apollonius said, amused. "Congratulations, Delilah, you've outdone yourself."

Lucien's eyes widened. "That's not . . . oh, my *God*!" He burst out laughing.

On top of the cake, perfectly rendered in lifelike colors, were two werewolves, in that halfway state of transformation between human and loup-garou. A full moon shone yellow behind them. They were fucking their brains out.

Delilah looked at the group in smug pride. "I took the bakers a picture from that movie, you know . . . *The Howling*? Remember that scene where—"

"We remember it, Delilah. Good grief," Zizi said.

"Didn't they do a nice job?" Delilah asked with pride. "And look . . . they've got the little pendants of the Krewe of Apollonius on. I had the bakers add that part myself." Indeed, the jewels that all of them wore, a gold howling wolf set against a sterling silver full moon, were rendered in icing on the busy werewolf couple. The little icing female wore hers like Zizi and Sylvie did—mounted on a ring.

"Very ingenious," Gabriel commented dryly.

Christian laughed, and sank back in his chair. "Trust Delilah to liven up a party, one way or another."

Gabriel blew out the candles and Delilah handed him a ribbon-bedecked cake knife. "The piece with the boy loup-garou's for you," Delilah said. "Be careful and don't cut his little thing off."

"Thanks a lot, Delilah. Now I'm not gonna be able to eat my own birthday cake."

Sylvie looked over his shoulder. "I remember at birthday parties when the big deal was to get one of the icing roses. I guess times have changed."

Gabriel hesitated before he cut. "I'm trying to find a non–X-rated piece to save for Claire," he explained.

They lost themselves in laughter, champagne, and birthday cake.

They were having such a good time that, for several moments, no one noticed the maid standing in the dining room doorway. Beside her was a stranger, a tall man with neat, graying hair and a craggy face. He looked tired and terribly uncomfortable.

The maid cleared her throat. No response from the revelers. She decided to be more assertive. *"Miz Faust!"* she commanded loudly.

All conversation stopped and everyone turned. The maid smiled with satisfaction. "This man here come to see Mr. Apollonius," she said, then turned and left with the air of one who has done her job well.

There was no movement among the startled loups garous for a moment, and the man looked more uncomfortable than ever. Then, his eyes lighting with pleasure, Apollonius strode to the man and embraced him.

"Giovanni, my old friend," Apollonius said in perfect Latin. "How wonderful to see you again!"

Giovanni looked relieved. He held Apollonius close for a moment, then backed off to look at him. "Still the same," he said in the same language. "The wonders of immortality, Apollonius. You look exactly as you did on that day when I asked you to teach me the ways of the loup-garou."

Apollonius turned to the crowd of curious werewolves. "This is an old, old friend. The last time I saw him, he was a Hell's Angel going by the name of John Luparo. But when I *first* met him," Apollonius laughed, "he was going by his real name, Cesare Giovanni Orsini. He was a loup-garou, and he was a prince of the church."

"I apologize for crashing the party," John said, "but I have important news. And it isn't good."

Apollonius pulled out a chair at the table for him. "Then you'd better sit and tell us, John. But I think I know what you're going to say."

John told them about his meeting with Lycaon in Boston. "Boston!" Walt said. "My God, perhaps I shouldn't have left Georgiana there alone." Georgiana wasn't exactly alone, but Walt obviously felt that only he could protect her adequately.

"Don't worry," John said, taking a swallow of the pale gold Riesling Delilah had poured for him. "He's not there now. All he wanted was to make his presence known to the New England loups-garous. They're probably the largest East Coast community, you know. But it's pretty certain that his real mission is here in New Orleans."

"I know why," Zizi said grimly. "It's Apollonius he wants to see."

Some of the younger loups-garous still looked blank.

"A few of you might not know about Lycaon," Apollonius said, "because he simply dropped out of sight a few hundred years ago, longer than some of you have been alive. But Lycaon's theories of lycanthropic principles are very different from ours. He doesn't believe in killing for justice, he hasn't dedicated himself to the service of Hecate. At one time, he had a very large following of werewolves who killed as he did: brutally and for the blood pleasure of it. They seemed to die out when he disappeared around the seventeenth century."

"Like most of us," John said, "Lycaon would take on various identities, and in each one of them he was in a position to cause as much destruction as possible. Sometimes he and his werewolves would go on rampages throughout the countrysides, even through the cities, leaving carnage behind them that defied description. Several times, he was thought to be the devil." John paused a moment. "I'm not sure he isn't."

Some of the loups-garous shivered, hearing this.

Delilah put her hand gently on Apollonius's arm, as if she were afraid. "But he couldn't be more powerful than you, Apollonius," she said in a slightly quavering voice. "You're immortal, the oldest of all the werewolves."

Apollonius shook his head. "Lycaon was born the same year, the same month as I was, and he gained his immortality at about the same time, but in a very different way. No, his bond to me is an emotional one: I was the first werewolf he ever made, the first human to receive the werewolf's kiss. I refused to join him in his philosophy of slaughter for slaughter's sake, and he's never forgiven me. And on the other hand, he admires me for it: he finds it so beyond his understanding that a loup-garou would refuse to kill for anything but justice that it exerts a sort of mystical fascination over him. So immortality has nothing to do with it. It's principle that's at issue.

"The real contest here is the oldest story in the world. Which is stronger? Good or evil? The balance of power has been swinging back and forth between us for centuries, and I suppose Lycaon wants the issue settled."

The loups-garous were very quiet, considering the awful implications that this information might carry.

"I'm still confused, John," Gabriel said, "but maybe what you've told us may make some sense out of this." He fished briefly in his pocket and pulled out a square of paper. He smoothed it out on the table between them, so Apollonius could get a good look at it.

It was a sketch of a piece of jewelry, rendered in colored pencil. A gold wolf's fang, from which dripped a single scarlet pear shape.

"This was commissioned by a customer I'd never seen before," Gabriel said. "That dangling drop is supposed to be blood: it's a pear-shaped ruby."

The others, curious, had gathered around to look at the sketch.

"That ruby's going to cost somebody a small fortune," Evangeline said. "I mean, if you've drawn it to scale, it's going to be at least five carats."

"Who's your customer for this, Gabriel?" Apollonius asked. He could feel the hair prickle on his neck.

"Well, that's the weird part. This strange man came into the shop. Not that there was anything out of line about him . . . in fact, he was one of the most charismatic men I've ever met. Chestnut-colored hair, some silver streaks, but dramatically placed, you know? Strong cheekbones, straight nose, very full lips. Handsome man. He carried himself like royalty, had the most unshakable self-confidence and a hypnotic presence. It's hard to describe. But what really spooked me was that he was a loup-garou. I knew immediately *what* he was, of course, but I had no idea *who* he was." Gabriel broke off for a moment to gather his thoughts. "For some reason, he scared the shit out of me. I couldn't tell you why, either. He gave me a crude, penciled picture of what he wanted, described the materials he wanted me to use, and while he watched and made comments on it, I made this sketch. I'm to make a pair of them; they're pendants to hang from gold chains, like the Krewe's."

"You're going to get a *pair* of rubies like that?" Christian asked.

"It's not going to be easy to find them. I told him that, but he said that time wasn't a problem." Gabriel shrugged. "As if I didn't know that."

"Why does he need two?" Apollonius asked.

"I guess one for him and one for the woman," Gabriel said. "There was this woman with him, another loup-garou. What a beauty! But cold, you know? Absolutely pitiless. I got the impression that she was older than any of us, though it was hard to tell how old she really was. They were a good pair, I tell you. The funny thing was, I could see she was beautiful, but I couldn't tell you what her eyes or hair looked like. She was wearing big sunglasses and one of those silky turban-type hats that hid her hair. She had a triple string of pearls any jeweler would kill for, and they were *old*! You can't match pearls like that these days. And the clasp was set with a half-carat rose-cut diamond. We don't do rose-cut anymore, and round-cut is different.

"The whole scene just spooked me; I couldn't get those two out of my mind for hours. So now, from what John's said, I guess the man was Lycaon. The woman's a mystery, though."

Apollonius looked up from the sketch, his eyes fixed on the distance, seeing things not in this time or place, thinking, remembering. He knew this was going happen, had always known it. Lycaon's silence had lulled him into a sense of security; now he was jolted out of it and he felt that he had been stupidly careless.

He should have known that Lycaon couldn't have simply confronted him. That wasn't Lycaon's way. His way was subterfuge, games, intrigues, puzzles. And so the challenge was thrown and the game begun.

Suddenly, Apollonius felt the weight of his centuries of

existence, the exhaustion of his years. To be dragged into this fight again, this argument that had no possible resolution, was more than he could bear. And he knew he had to bear it, for himself and for them all. There was no one else.

Zizi moved behind Apollonius, her hands on his shoulders. He could feel her strength moving into him, renewing his energy. He and Zizi could do that for each other, every time.

"What does this mean, Apollonius?" Zizi asked. "Why is he here? And why now?"

Apollonius looked again at the sketch. "He's here to reclaim what he feels is rightly his: all of you. All the werewolves who have worked so hard to become disciplined, who have struggled to do what is right and just. He wants to distort you and use you, to convert you to his way of thinking, to make of you mindless killers."

"Well, he can't do that," Lucien said positively. "We follow your principles of justice, Apollonius. All of us were born into them, we know no other way. We *want* no other way."

"If he thinks his manipulative little tricks will work on us, he's wrong," Walt said.

The other loups-garous murmured their agreement.

Apollonius looked at him curiously. "Is he? I wonder. Walt, why are you home at just this time? Why are Lucien and Sylvie here?"

Walt looked baffled. "Well, I had the time . . . and it's Mardi Gras . . ."

"You're all here because you've reached some crisis in your lives. You're confused and unhappy with things as they are. And it isn't only the three of you. Darryl, you're in political hot water. You know that the legislature and a powerful lobby are going to fight you on that environmental protection bill and they're trying to slander your wife to do it. They're saying that Evangeline's leading you by the balls on this issue."

He turned his glance to the oil-company CEO. "And, Henry, you're in the middle of this fight, too. You agree with Darryl and your stockholders want to crucify you for it. Brenda . . ." He turned to the writer. "Your last six books have done so well, you'd think you had no troubles. But you're sick of doing the same thing. You want to break new ground, but your fans won't accept it and you're frightened. Your publishers think you're about to kill the golden goose and you're afraid they're right, that you have more technique than talent."

Brenda dropped her face into her hands.

"And Achille, in the worst pain of all of us, and resisting the hardest. You're all at difficult points," Apollonius told them gently. "Your mental strength is weakest, your self-esteem shattered. It's no accident that you're all in New Orleans now, that some of you came from far away to be here. It was the werewolf's bond that pulled you here. All of you—all of *us*— without being aware of it, sent out the same signals: come home. We're in trouble. We have to be together now, or we might never be together again."

The werewolves silently moved closer and, still without a word, clasped each other's hands around the table. Darryl impulsively brought his wife's hand to his lips and she looked at him gratefully.

"He isn't going to give up without a fight," Apollonius said. "He's going to use your troubles to drive wedges between you. And you might not even be aware he's doing it."

"Let him try it," Lucien said tightly. "He might be immortal but he's never had a fight like this."

"Your way of lycanthropy is the only way we know,"

Sylvie said. "As far as we're concerned, there is no other life for a loup-garou."

Only Zizi said nothing. Zizi, who remembered another way, who had begun so long ago with werewolves who followed Lycaon's principles—or lack of them—and who had witnessed for herself the destruction and damnation that could come of it. And who knew how easy it could be to slip back into heedless, orgiastic killing. She sometimes thought about what would have become of her if she hadn't met Apollonius so early in her life as a loup-garou, when he taught her about justice and the dignity of death. It made her shiver.

She looked at the other loups-garous, so indignant, so sure of their powers and their commitments to justice, united now in their rejection of Lycaon's way of life. You don't know, she was thinking, you can't possibly know how easy it is to rouse the secret part of your natures, the lust hidden even from yourselves. You have no idea how close to the surface it lies, and how terribly fragile is the veneer of respectability. And once it cracks, there's no turning back.

Lycaon knew it. He felt their weaknesses from worlds away. Time meant even less to him than it meant to any of them, except Apollonius. As the two immortal loups-garous, they could wait indefinitely for what they wanted.

But for Lycaon, the time had come. And what he wanted was certainly within his grasp.

For the first time since she had become a loup-garou, Zizi was terrified of the future, because she knew the stories of the past.

PART TWO

†

The Adversary

8

In the Papal Court of Honorius V, Avignon, France, ca. 1340

"Wolves have become the masters of the Church."
—*Alvaro Pelago*

Odile was determined not to let her lover see that she was frightened, but she knew that he would sense it. She and Honorius were too much alike for pretense, which was precisely why they were together.

She had been more than his mistress. She had been his protégée, then his passion, and there was more between them than simple lust. Honorius said many times, sometimes with amusement and sometimes with wonder, that Odile was his female self.

Now their mutual agreement had brought Odile to this room, in which they had hidden themselves time and again to do what they could not resist, and for the first time, she was apprehensive. The opulence of the delicately painted frieze of nymphs and satyrs on the walls, the tapestried bed with the hangings pulled back, the imported silver mirrors, the yellow light from the wavering candles, and the warm fire didn't move her as they had on previous occasions. Then her very passage through the heavy oak door pro-

voked a deep, erotic response, so that she was ready for
Honorius the moment he touched her.

Now she was not so sure. Waiting for his arrival, she
was both terrified and excited, and she thanked the gods
for the generations of good breeding that allowed none of
this to show.

Standing in the middle of the room, bewildered and shivering, was a young girl, not yet twenty. Odile had chosen
her according to Honorius's preferences, which corre-
sponded so naturally with her own. She had paid a handsome sum to the loathsome woman who kept the girl, but
she was perfect, and what did it matter to Odile that she
had to pay a fortune for her? The girl was a virgin. Odile
must have had to deal with a dozen such harridans and a
hundred whores before she found the right one. The hu-
miliation was a fresh-cut wound every time. And Honorius
knew it.

She was exactly as he had requested she be; not naked,
but nearly, wearing only a silk shift. It was one of Odile's,
given to her by Honorius and still bearing the scent of his
body as it covered her on one of the many occasions when
they couldn't wait to get undressed.

The girl was bewildered, but trying to be professional.
Her keeper had obviously told her the usual rules. Well,
thought Odile, the usual rules will certainly not apply tonight. The girl still wore the air of the country. Odile felt
an odd compassion for her; she only hoped for the girl's
sake that Honorius's preferences that night would be gentle
ones.

"Come over here, girl," Odile told her. When she stood
before her, Odile impulsively let loose the girl's hair, a pale
gold cloud falling over her shoulders. Something in her
eyes stirred Odile and she felt . . . she wasn't sure what.
Pity? Envy? Lust? She stroked the girl's hair, then her

shoulders, very softly. She had no idea why. The girl inclined her head and looked into Odile's eyes. Her innocence aroused in Odile a lust and a longing; her virginity stirred a sympathetic memory.

Odile could tell that the girl was thoroughly intimidated. By her dress, her jewels, the diamond buckles on her slippers, and the power of Odile's ancient name and title. The girl has no idea, thought Odile, of how little they mean.

"You're very beautiful," she told the girl.

She looked at Odile with artless innocence. "So are you, madame," she said with no guile. But the girl, though a virgin, was wise in the ways of perversion, more from observation than from experience. "Am I here for you?" she asked Odile.

Odile's hand, caressing that gold cloud, stopped. Her voice faltered. "No," she told the girl. "Yes . . . oh . . . I don't know."

They stood there for a moment, both in confusion.

There was a knock on the door. The girl didn't move, but Odile's reaction was violently unsettling. She steadied herself on the edge of a little gilded chair, sat down in it, got up, walked agitatedly around it, then pulled the chair over to an alcove and sat down in it again, hidden in the shadows.

The knock sounded again.

"Oh, go, girl! For Jesus' sake!" Odile hissed, with a wave of her hand. "Open the door!"

The advantage to Odile's seat was that she could see perfectly clearly everything in the room, while she herself was concealed. For instance, she could see the shock on the girl's face when Honorius entered. Not because of who he was, though she had been informed, but because she clearly never expected him to look like that. People of her class saw him from afar, in processions, on balconies and terraces, from the extreme back of great cathedrals. Odile was sure she expected some old, balding cleric elevated to great rank through wisdom and age, and was not remotely prepared for a man with Honorius's charisma and grace of movement.

Odile saw that he looked especially compelling. He was in pale blue silk, the soft color bringing out the marvelous planes of his face, the luster of his eyes. A fine white wool cloak was thrown over his shoulders and fastened with a marvelously wrought gold pin set with an enormous sapphire. It was all Odile could do not to rise and throw herself at his feet, pleading with him not to do this. It was a game they'd planned together, even looked eagerly to, and now she wasn't at all sure she still wanted to play.

But she stayed in the chair, twisting her rings and trying to keep her hands still.

Honorius went immediately to the fire to warm his hands. The whore looked toward Odile in confusion and Odile waved surreptitiously to her, gesturing for her to get on with it.

But the girl, overwhelmed, dropped to her knees. "Holy Father . . . ," she said in awe, pressing her lips to his ring.

Honorius, amused, raised an eyebrow and winked at Odile, then looked down at the girl. He made the sign of the cross over her bowed head.

Monstrous, thought Odile disloyally.

"And what is your name, child?" Honorius asked. His voice was warm and light.

"Louise," she replied, her voice unsure, her accent rural.

He stopped momentarily and raised an eyebrow. "Louise," he said. "Well. A name for a lady." He cast a sidelong glance at where he knew Odile was concealed, his only acknowledgment that she was there. "Or for a jaded comtesse, isn't that right, Louise?"

Odile, more properly Odile Louise Catherine de Valois, Comtesse de Coudreuil, stiffened in her chair. She could have slapped him, but she didn't move.

Louise took his cloak and folded it with reverence, as if it were his holy vestment. He sat on the bed and she removed his boots. She began to unfasten his tunic, but he caught her hand.

He touched her hair, in exactly the same way Odile did, and his hands moved to her shoulders. Unloosing a slight ribbon, he let her shift fall open, exposing her delicate breasts. The nipples were like pale pink sugar, topping mounds of smooth white cake. With one hand he gathered her hair and pulled it back, tilting her head, the arch of her chin and throat forming a pure and enticing line.

He tasted her throat, his lips moving lower over her skin, slowly, letting the salty sweetness of her linger on his tongue.

What fascinated Odile at that moment was that the girl didn't know what to do with her hands. She made a tentative motion, as if she would hold him, but still in awe of who he was, her hands found only the air. She finally held them at her sides, the fingers splayed and stiff with nervousness.

But Honorius, as Odile knew, was very good at what he did. His lips moved lower, lower, teasing Louise's nerve endings and exciting her out of her nervousness by giving her other things to think about. He pushed the shift down around her hips, then took one of her perfect nipples in his mouth. He had a special fondness for this, and tended to take his time.

Louise's hands relaxed, then moved almost of their own accord, one around his back, one tangled in his hair.

Odile dug her nails into the tapestry of the chair and leaned forward, her throat suddenly parched.

Honorius knelt and pulled the garment off Louise, slowly revealing the soft hair that hid her virginity. She looked down at herself as though she had just discovered her own body, still nervous, but losing her fear as rapidly as her passion awoke.

His hand parted her thighs, reaching back between them to cup her buttocks and tilt her closer. It was the same thing he and Odile had done a hundred times in this room, and she realized that she never knew before the complete, stirring picture of his body as they made love. She also realized, with a growing excitement, that she wanted to see him in a new way. She wanted to know what he looked like making love; not just his face, but his whole body, his nuances, his expressions, the way he moved in entirety. She could not do that while she was engaged in it with him.

Honorius glanced at her. She caught a glimpse of herself in one of the mirrors. It was simply astounding. She looked interested, but completely composed, exactly the way she knew she must look sitting at court listening to an especially fine singer. Seeing her face, her bearing, no one would dream that she was actually watching the man she loved—and loved so completely that the thought of being without him produced an empty terror—taking his perverse pleasure with a whore that she had paid for. Her perfectly calm reflection only heightened her excitement.

Honorius smiled slightly and turned his complete attention back to the girl, his hand moving between her thighs, tickling her with his fingers, teasing her. He turned her body slightly so that Odile had an unobstructed view. She saw the light catch the beginning wetness on his fingertips. Odile knew the effects of his movements so well that it was as if his hands touched her, too, mastering her body as he always did with such skill. It was something Odile insisted that he never rush.

But it was all new to the girl, these sensations, and with the impatience of the young, she was ready all too quickly.

And when she was, he knew it. He stood and pushed her back on the bed, parting her legs, bending and raising her knees. She struck Odile as oddly passive. Odile watched and wondered. Was that passivity something he wanted, had *always* wanted, in her? Something she'd not given him? Was that why all this was necessary? Odile was a headstrong, demanding lover, she knew. Honorius said, even after she became his mistress, that she was a challenge to him. Had it lost its charm?

The girl gasped a little when she saw Honorius's erection. Well she might, Odile thought with wry amusement. His eyes never leaving her body, he ran his hand over himself with a light, easy stroke, as if to confirm his hardness. It was a little habit of his that Odile always found irresistible.

He reached out and ran his hands over Louise's legs, up her thighs, again between her legs. She moaned and squirmed under his hands.

It was evident to Odile, but not to Louise, what he was going to do, so Louise was caught off guard when he grasped her hips and pulled her to the very edge of the high bed, where he stood very straight. He took his cock in one hand and teased it against her, each long stroke making her lift her hips to meet it. Her eyes opened wide, then closed in pleasure. She moaned again, more sustained this time, and her breath came in little, sharp catches.

Like his fingers, his cock began to take on that same glistening wetness. "Wrap your legs around me, girl," he told her, his voice harsh.

Odile became lost in the sight on the bed. She admired the wonderful lines of his body in the candlelight, the way his hips moved, the strength in his arms and shoulders. It

was because of this peculiar grace of motion that she had
known, the first time she saw him, that they would be lovers. He had been walking in the palace gardens with his
defiant stride more at home on the battlefield than before
the altar. She had been, of course, in the company of her
husband, but when she knelt to kiss the papal ring and she
looked surreptitiously into Honorius's eyes as she rose, she
had never wanted a man so quickly and with such intensity.

That had never changed.

The urgency washed over Odile and she found it very
hard to sit there. She wanted to scream, to rip off her own
clothes, to touch herself in all the places that he knew how
to arouse. It seemed to Odile that the whore's body and her
own were the same body, connected by the bonds of his
passion.

She watched his hand stroke Louise's body, his finger-
nails trailing over her skin. Odile found this tiny detail
erotic in the extreme, and her physical reactions were violent out of all proportion to it. She felt her own moisture,
that sweet liquid that he loved to take on his tongue, begin
to flow as it never had before. The scent rose to her nostrils,
intoxicatingly. She had the almost overwhelming urge to
run her own fingers first there, then over her own lips.

She watched Honorius take his first stab against the girl,
gently, and Louise stiffened. He leaned over and kissed her
breast and murmured something that Odile couldn't hear,
and the girl relaxed. The second thrust was more decisive;
the third broke the seal and the girl gave a little scream.
Her legs locked tighter around his hips and her hands
clutched at the embroidered coverlet. She was obviously in
pain, but just as obviously in heat; Odile could have told
her that the pain would pass, but the heat would stay with
her always.

His strokes were gentle at first, then longer, harder, as

he drove into her body. Odile watched him move and marveled again at how beautiful he·was, how graceful. She wanted him so badly she felt she could suffocate from it. The longing stuck in her throat, in her chest between her breasts. Every stroke he took, every touch on the whore's skin, she could feel on her own body, and when he finally shuddered inside the whore and she screamed her pleasure with it, Odile felt her own back arch, her own breasts burst into flame, her body aching with the familiar fullness of him.

He looked frankly at Odile and saw the first crack in her demeanor: the bright crystal of her soundless tears.

He withdrew, slowly and gently, and left the lightest film of blood, the faintest trickle of it on the coverlet. He leaned over the girl and smiled, and touched her cheek, and told her she was a good girl, the sweetest, and that he must be going.

She seemed disoriented and confused, not from what he had done but that he wasn't going to do it again.

He cleaned himself off with water and towels that had been left by the bed, and instructed the girl to bring him his clothes.

She dressed him, moving as if hypnotized.

Honorius moved to Odile's chair, pulled her to her feet, and kissed her with more passion than he ever had, murmuring against her throat that he had never loved her more.

And then he was gone.

Odile sank back into the chair and sighed. How had this happened, she thought. How did she get to this point in her life, when did she decide to participate so willingly in her own seduction by Honorius, a seduction not only of the body but of the soul? She saw that she had sacrificed her own conscience on the altar of Honorius's perversity, but she would find it unthinkable to go back.

By degrees, she was becoming what Honorius wanted her to be.

Louise still looked dazed.

Odile walked over to her and stroked her hair again, softly. She gave Louise a small bag containing more gold than the girl would ever have seen in her lifetime.

"Here," Odile said, not unkindly, "use one piece to buy yourself back from that hag who owns you. Take the rest and leave Avignon. Go to Paris, go to Naples, to Rome or Venice. You have enough there to set yourself up as a great courtesan and have a good, secure life. But, my dear"— Odile kissed her gently and with regret—"don't ever let me set eyes on you again."

Odile didn't see Honorius again until after supper, after all the guests had left and the household had grown quiet. She wandered, unable to sleep, into one of the many palace chapels. She sat on a velvet chair and wondered what she was doing there: she had long ago dispensed with the need for religion.

"And?" Honorius's voice came from behind her, gently. "Did you kill her after I left? Did your jealousy get the best of you?"

She didn't answer.

"You needn't be ashamed of that," he told her. "Not to kill when you feel the urge for blood is to deny your nature. A loup-garou needs no conscience, Odile, haven't I taught you that? And haven't you been my most avid student?"

Her cool demeanor broke and her anguish was beyond anything she had ever felt. It terrified her; she was in danger of being out of control, and she had never permitted that. "Tell me again that what I do is right!"

"It's neither right nor wrong," he said, stroking her cheek. "It simply is. Never resist the kill, Odile. Never resist anything if it gives you pleasure. And creatures like us, my love, demand more refined forms of pleasure than human beings.''

But Odile was not consoled. "What have I become, Lycaon?'' she said, so distraught that she used his real name for the first time in months. "Why have you done this to me?'' She was not referring to her lycanthropy, which had little to do with her anguish, and he knew it.

He held her close. "Because,'' he said, laughing gently, "you never once tried to stop me.''

He looked at her more closely. "Do you love me, Odile?'' he asked. His voice was gentle, but there was a mocking tone underneath the satin of it.

She couldn't meet his eyes.

"Your husband and children, your reputation, your position in a great family, perhaps even your soul . . . all those are lost to you for my sake. And do you hate me, Odile?''

She stared at her lap, her eyes stinging, her face drained.

"Perhaps if you're in such pain, I should put you out of your misery. Is that what you want? Would that be proper penance for your sins?'' He tilted her face up to him so that he could see her tears. "But how would I live without your beauty?''

She sank to her knees, clinging to him as he stroked her hair, hating herself more than she loved him.

And so the days passed in Avignon. The mornings and afternoons filled themselves with the business of the church, conducted by Pope Honorius with skill, but with an amused detachment, almost a contempt, invisible to all but Odile.

The nights were for sumptuous entertainments, lavish meals, indulgences in sensuality by the French cardinals and their succulent mistresses, over which the pontiff presided with the same detached attitude he brought to the Holy Offices. And for Honorius and Odile, unknown to the others, some nights were for the pleasures of the chase and the kill.

They killed brutally across the placid countryside until they were satiated. Sometimes they disposed of the bodies, sometimes not. Blame would never fall on them; the odor of scandal and murder would never waft from the papal palace.

But the blame did fall somewhere. In superstitious France at that time, the cry of "loup-garou" often rang out when bodies were found mutilated. There were hunting parties, there were the accused, there were quick trials. And there were executions. Always the executions. Hanging. Burning at the stake. Dismemberment.

For a while, the killings stopped. Or seemed to stop— there were no more telltale bodies. And then, when the people began to breathe easy again, when they had forgotten about the killings and were not so careful of danger, it would all begin again.

Over it all, Honorius presided. The courts were convened in his name and the name of the king. The guilty parties were excommunicated in the churches and executed.

For Honorius, these were all distracting little sidelights in an extremely long life, a life that could all too quickly become boring.

Then, swiftly and inexorably, the Black Death cast its shroud over Europe. It swept into tiny hamlets and great cities, catching up the powerful and the powerless in the final dance of death. The grave diggers couldn't keep up with the bodies; the priests couldn't say Mass fast enough. Death moved as regularly as the tides. The healthy child baptized that morning would be dead by Evensong. Entire families were wiped out in a week.

Where the horror of death is commonplace, a few more bodies caused not even a comment. The whole world, it seemed, was dying and lying unburied in the gutters, on overburdened carts or in great stacks of corpses at the edge of the cemeteries.

Except at Avignon.

Within the self-contained papal city, there were fresh vegetables and healthy meats, sparkling wines from old cellars. The air was perfumed by rich spices. The people within the palace walls were fat and healthy, their faces glowing like their jewels.

There was very little death at Avignon, few tears for lost children or lovers; the mass for the dead, constantly chanted on the altars of Europe, was rarely said at Avignon, most often for the old, who had died in peace.

Cesare Giovanni, Cardinal Orsini, often thought how ironic it was that he was here, nestled in safety. He had come to Avignon against his will and had been trapped by the epidemic. To attempt the return to his father's family in Rome, where he had been living since the papal court had moved to France, would be to sign his own death warrant.

Orsini loved his God, but he had no wish to meet him earlier than planned.

He stretched luxuriously in bed as the first light of the sun caught his face. He knew he had to get up and dress, but not too quickly: they said Matins a little late in this parish. At the bedside was a tray covered with a white cloth, embroidered—like all the linen in this household—with the gold crossed keys of the pontiff. The cloth covered his breakfast, left there only moments before by a silent monk.

He sat up and lifted the cloth on the tray. The aroma alone made him salivate. There was poached, firm-skinned

fish, floating in a pale lemon-spice sauce. Bread thick with
fresh butter. Glazed fruits. A flagon of new milk sat beside
a gold cup. Giovanni inhaled the spicy scent of the fish.
Ah, yes: it was Friday, a day of sacrifice. In the rarefied
atmosphere of Honorius's court, this was meager fare.

Giovanni got up, crossed the room to the little prie-dieu,
and proceeded to say his Divine Office, trying to keep his
mind off the meal on the table.

This whole tenor of life in the papal palace distressed
him. And what distressed him the most was how used to it
he had become in such a short time. True, the life of a
highly placed cardinal, in or out of the court, was not exactly one of poverty and self-sacrifice. Made a cardinal at
only seventeen, a political move by his father's influential
family, he had served under two popes and was no stranger
to luxury. One had to keep up appearances, and it was
thought that for a prince of the church to live like a peasant
was disrespectful to his office. One should serve his God
in an atmosphere of pomp and richness, and if he couldn't
afford it, he shouldn't have bothered to seek the highest
rank in the church in the first place. Cardinals, like all powerful churchmen, were expected also to maintain armies, to
be placed at the disposal of the pope when fighting enemies
of God and the church.

What a pity that most of the cardinals and popes for the
past few centuries had considered the enemies of God to
be each other. Some of the most mighty ecclesiastical armies, Giovanni knew, were there to protect the individual
bishop or cardinal from his fellow priests, who had been
known to murder each other for their lands, their money,
or simply to get them out of the way on their road to Rome
and the Holy See.

Things had come to cross points in 1296. Peter Murrone,
the holy monk, had been flushed from his hermit's lair,

taken unawares, and been put on the Throne of Peter as Celestine V, a puppet for the powerful and warring families of Europe. Ignorant of politics, he had tried to be a real spiritual leader and guide the church back to peace. But he had been destroyed by those who were not so innocent. He abdicated, wanting only to go back to his mountainside hermitage, but was imprisoned at the Vatican. The heartbroken monk was found in his cell, suffocated with a red velvet cushion, the preferred death for papal prisoners. His successor, Boniface VIII, proceeded to destroy most of Europe through torture, massacre, wholesale excommunications, and a reign of terror more suited to Attila or the Visigoths than the supreme pontiff. For real or imagined slights, he ordered the entire town of Palestrina destroyed. The buildings were razed, and the whole population, right down to the babies and animals, was murdered. It took nine more years before Boniface was found dead in the Vatican, his brains smashed out.

Small wonder that his successor, Benedict XI, had decided to leave Rome. The power of the church had long been split between the French cardinals and the Italians, and Benedict, a Frenchman, declared that he'd had enough of the barbaric place. Besides, terrible things had happened—and recently—to churchmen who stayed in Rome. There were poisonings, strangulations, the ever-present red velvet cushion, and worse. Much worse. No fool, Benedict fled the unhealthy climate of Rome for Perugia. Unfortunately, it wasn't far enough. Like the Emperor Tiberius centuries before him, he succumbed to poisoned figs.

In the meantime, civil wars were breaking out between the Gaetani, Orsini, and Colonna families of Italy, supporters of Charles of Naples, and the factions of King Ferdinand of Sicily. Added to this unholy brew were various other pro-French and pro-Italian groups. To control the church was to control all Europe.

Clement V was elected in 1305 and refused to go to Rome at all. He accepted the papal crown in France and settled in Avignon. King Philip of France extended his protection, delighted to have the church under his control at last.

Avignon was healthier than Rome in more ways than one. It was paradise on earth, an unspoiled Eden. The Rhone and Durance rivers fed fertile valleys, vineyards, and orchards. Cool springs flowed from the snowy peaks of the hills. The people of Avignon were cosmopolitan, the city was sophisticated, the houses and buildings beautifully proportioned and lavishly decorated by local artisans.

And the church would rather that the pope stayed in Rome? That decaying, degenerate city filled with murderers and thieves? Why, even then cattle were grazing in St. Peter's, the floors covered with dung and filth. *Ah, mais non,* said Clement when various churchmen broached the subject of his return to Rome; *addio* and *buona fortuna* to the Italians. And be sure to send his regards to the warring families. Rome, indeed. They could keep it.

Giovanni Orsini, with an Italian father and a French mother, both of powerful families, was dispatched from the Vatican to plead with the new pope, Honorius.

Honorius was an unknown quantity: in the midst of the chaos following Clement's death, he emerged from the smoke and darkness of political intrigue to sweep the votes of the conclave. It was as if the cardinals were bewitched: for the first time, they managed to agree on a candidate in less than six months and with no bloodshed, though afterward, there were strange stories from some of them who said that they had no clear memory of the conclave. It was said of Honorius that he had been a parish priest; that, like Celestine, he had been a monk; that he was the bastard son of the most powerful of the Gaetani, pushed into the church in lieu of an inheritance. The truth was that no one, when pressed, could swear for certain where he'd come from. But he was flawlessly educated; he could read, write, and speak sixteen languages, including Greek and Latin—classical Latin, not just church Latin—and even Aramaic seamlessly. He seemed very much at home with the machinations of the intrigues of papal politics, and was one of the most charismatic figures to sit on the Throne of Peter in a hundred years.

The most shocking story about him, repeated only in the most private of whispers, concerned his reply to the traditional four questions put to any priest who would presume to be consecrated a bishop. The four questions were: Have you sodomized a boy? Have you fornicated with a nun? Have you sodomized a four-legged animal? Have you committed adultery? Honorius replied with a resounding "No, my lord. I have done none of it." But one of the appalled Byzantine ambassadors caught Honorius's reply, muttered under his breath, "But thanks for the suggestion."

Giovanni Orsini was no master of politics, despite his family's devious reputation. In fact, he was thought of as a little simple, which was fine with him. He was bookish. He was a great admirer of the ascetic Pope Celestine, which was safe enough now that the monk was dead. Like Celestine, he seemed too concerned with spiritual matters and not enough with the realities of power and how it flowed through the arteries of the church. Only Giovanni was aware that he had survived this murderous milieu as long as he had by keeping himself in the background, by making himself useful in small ways, and by disguising the real breadth of his intelligence.

But for matters such as this, appealing to the pope to return the papal court to Rome, he was perfect. With his mixed parentage, he seemed on the surface to have no axes to grind. The Italian cardinals thought him brainless; the French cardinals thought him harmless.

But Orsini was actually that most dangerous of men: a religious idealist. He had no love either for the French *or* the Italians; his love was for Christ and the church, both of which he was convinced were being neglected in the pursuit of temporal power. He firmly believed that the pope should return to Rome and reverse the decay that had set in since its abandonment by the papal court, not because he favored the Italians, but because Rome was the rock upon which Peter had built his church. It was where the bones of the Holy Martyrs lay, the goal of thousands of pilgrims whose lives would be changed by one glance, one blessing by the Holy Father. Orsini's thinking was that simple, that clear, guided only by God, not politics.

It was thought that the young cardinal, now only in his twenties and no more wiser in the ways of the world than at seventeen, would be the perfect Vatican emissary to Avignon. He might not even die for it: this pope was not given much to political execution, and even if he had been, Orsini was little threat. Besides, he belonged to two great families. The wily Honorius would never take the risk of incurring the wrath of both factions by killing an insignificant pup like Orsini.

Giovanni knew all this, but he had come to Avignon just the same. He was delivering the plea that he had been charged to deliver, but for very different reasons of his own.

As Giovanni finished his prayers, then savored his breakfast, there was a discreet tap at his door. In this palace, Giovanni thought with amusement, it was safer to be discreet; one never knew who or how many you could find behind a bedchamber door.

He motioned to his servant, who was arranging his vestments, to open the door. A pair of priests—French, by the look of them—entered respectfully.

"Eminence," one said, bowing, "His Holiness has asked me to convey the message that he will see you this afternoon."

"Very well," Giovanni replied, in Greek, just to make them struggle with it. "And does the Holy Father know about my mission here?"

The two priests exchanged glances. Evidently, one of them knew classical languages better than the other, since he took up the reply. "It is not my business to know that, Eminence."

A good attitude, Giovanni thought. You'll live longer that way.

He dismissed the two priests with his blessing, and went back to his breakfast.

The splendor of the Palace of the Popes impressed even Giovanni, who was used to such things. The evening before, he had dined with the court in the vast banquet hall, remarking to Cardinal Ranieri that if the food started toward them at one end of the hall's 156-foot length, it would be stone cold by the time it reached them. The service was gold plate, and the food was as fine as the dishes.

It was entirely possible to lose oneself in the confusing maze of great halls and intimate salons, chapels large and small, the private apartments of cardinals and bishops, the even more discreet apartments of select ladies, offices where the business of the church was conducted, and lengthy galleries down which one could roam for hours, looking for a specific room. All was done in the latest Gothic style, massively strong, but with a sense inside of light and soaring space. Over the years, the palace had become a storehouse for great art, for decoration, for every aspect of luxurious living. The gardens were an aesthetic delight, fragrant with both cultured roses and with the abundant wildflowers that ran rampant over the fields of Avignon.

Still, there was no mistaking that it was in every sense a fortress. The Avignon popes were taking no chances, considering the past violence against the office. The palace's walls were fifteen feet thick. The architecture was rich with iron gates, battlements, and towers from which the palace's defense could be waged, if necessary.

Honorius's private audiences took place in a reception room much smaller than the great hall used for more public functions. As Giovanni was led to his audience by one of the French priests, he was given to understand that the meeting would have to take place in the Holy Father's private office, since the reception room was in the process of being painted.

Painted? Giovanni was curious. Well, the priest explained, the pope was rather fond of the art of the fresco; it was one of the few things Italian that he admired. He had had the papal bedchamber adorned with a pastoral scene that was, for the priest's taste, classical, but rather a bit too pagan in theme, with half-dressed women cavorting in the woods. Possibly a more suitable subject might be the Holy Martyrs.

From what he had heard of this pope, Giovanni thought, suppressing a smile, the man had no inclination to contemplate a host of suffering saints undergoing grotesque and bloody tortures every time he looked up from his bed.

He had heard, of course, of the lovely Odile de Valois, who, it was said, had posed for one of the nubile nymphs gracing Honorius's walls.

The priest stopped at a pair of carved doors of dark, rich wood, set with polished brass. He knocked, just once, and the doors were opened by a black-robed secretary, an efficient monk, who took over for the priest.

"Giovanni, Cardinal Orsini," the secretary announced in a ringing, authoritative voice.

Giovanni advanced toward the pope, who moved slightly forward to meet him. Honorius had been seated at a long, delicately carved table inundated with books, papers, seals, wax, pens, and inkwells. Honorius held out his hand, and Giovanni kissed the papal ring.

Honorius was much younger than Giovanni had expected. He seemed to be only in his thirties, with dark eyes and long, curling chestnut hair. His grace of movement was exaggerated by the flow of his robes, the sweep of his embroidered sleeves. Giovanni had the distinct impression, however, that no matter how graceful the pope looked, he also looked entirely capable of breaking a man's neck with his sinewy hands and long fingers.

Honorius could be charming, but Giovanni sensed a terrible danger beneath the civilized exterior. This was one pope, Giovanni thought, who was more dangerous to his enemies than they could ever be to him. Honorius might wield political power, but he looked as if he'd be just as happy annihilating any opposition with a swift broadsword stroke.

"I'm overjoyed to meet you at last, Holy Father," Giovanni said.

"Your stay in Italy has been our loss in Avignon," Honorius said. He gestured to a pair of comfortable chairs, arranged opposite each other. "Sit," he said. "I'd rather talk business while making myself comfortable." He gestured to the secretary, who brought a tray bearing alabaster goblets so finely hollowed and polished that they were almost transparent. The secretary poured wine into each goblet and set the tray on a small table.

"French wine, superb." Honorius took a mouthful and let it mellow on his tongue. "Savor it while you can, Orsini; you won't find its like back in Rome."

It *was* excellent, Giovanni thought, but he wasn't here to enjoy the vintages.

"Give me your message, Eminence," Honorius said pleasantly. "Tell me how much better off I'd be in the Vatican, among those deserted and dreary hallways, roaming those miles of depressing catacombs, tearing my hair shirt and moaning *'Mea culpa, mea maxima culpa'* every hour on the hour."

Giovanni couldn't suppress a short laugh.

"I know exactly why you're here, and who put you up to this," Honorius said, "and the answer is still no. However, since I'm sure you have a mightily convincing and impassioned speech planned, you may deliver it and have the satisfaction of having fulfilled your duty." He leaned back in his chair, crossed his legs, took another sip of wine, and said, "Proceed."

"I couldn't possibly, Holy Father," Giovanni said. "Especially after seeing Avignon. I have to ask myself if, in your place, I could leave this Eden for the harsher realities of Rome and the world."

"But you, being a true priest and unafraid of those realities, could make the sacrifice, is that it?"

Giovanni said nothing. Honorius had laid an ingenious trap for him: could he dare imply that he was a better priest than the pope?

"Rome is the seat of the church," Giovanni said simply. "Saint Peter was martyred there, his bones lie there. The very heart and foundation of our faith is in the Vatican."

"But," Honorius said archly, "isn't the seat of the church wherever the pope is? If I travel out of Rome on a pilgrimage, does that mean that I leave the power of the church behind?''

''A pope holds his office because he is the bishop of Rome, not the other way around. Doesn't it seem incongruous that the bishop of Rome is not *in* Rome?''

''Your arguments are spiritual, not secular. Very wily of the people whose emissary you are, not to put words into your mouth, and to let you advance your own arguments. And your arguments, Orsini, obviously come from the heart.'' Honorius leaned closer to Giovanni. ''Let me enlighten you. The real reason that the Italians want the papal court back in the Vatican is because that, as long as I'm in Avignon, the power of the church is controlled by the French king. Or so the Italians believe. And the power of the church has always, without exception, been controlled by the Italians. Back in the Vatican, my French cardinals, who now outnumber the Italians, will suddenly start to disappear, through tragic accidents and mysterious illnesses. And they will *not*, you can be certain, be replaced by other Frenchmen.''

Giovanni was aghast at the man's brutal frankness. ''You believe that your life will be in danger in Rome?'' he whispered. ''Nothing like that will happen again! The men who killed Celestine and Benedict were animals. We've come farther than that, surely.''

For some reason, this perilous question seemed only to amuse Honorius. ''The animals were performing at the bequest of their trainers, Orsini. Your generous attitude regarding the ascendancy of man's nobility over his violent nature is refreshing, if misplaced. But no,'' he said with a brief laugh, ''I have no qualms whatsoever about dying, in Rome or anywhere else.''

Honorius looked toward his secretary and made a small

gesture of dismissal. The man disappeared through a side door.

"Let's be plain with each other, Giovanni," the pope said. "You *do* consider yourself a more religious man than I am, more dedicated to our holy mother the church, more given to self-sacrifice, more concerned with the spiritual than the temporal. You look around you at Avignon and you see a sensuality unbecoming to the austere life of an ideal pope."

"Holy Father!" Giovanni protested, abashed, "I never even *implied*..."

"And, of course, you're right." Honorius didn't sound particularly upset at this. "You have no idea, naturally, but I've been following your career closely. I know that you have always been above politics. That's a difficult thing to do in the church as it is now, and especially for a man in your family. I know that you have deeper religious values than most of the cardinals and bishops around you, and that you'd probably be just as happy as a parish priest or a monk."

It just struck Giovanni that since the secretary left, Honorius had been addressing him in Greek, and that he had been answering in the same language without thinking about it.

As if Honorius could read his mind, he smiled. Was this some sort of test?

"I also know that you play the simpleton, and that there is very little about you that is simple, except for the innocence of your faith. That, my friend, is strong and uncomplicated. Your very simplicity makes you a complex man, Orsini, but a man of true principle and moral strength. The men around you, possessing none of those traits themselves, are unable to see you for what you are. Instead, they judge you by their own warped measures, and cannot understand that the temporal power and wealth that is of prime importance to *them* is of little or no value to *you*. So you hide your intellect and your convictions, biding your time until the day when both of them will bloom in a world where they will have true value."

Giovanni was stunned at how thoroughly right Honorius was. He was also frightened beyond reason.

"The men of our time, Orsini, use their gifts of intelligence as weapons to destroy, not tools to build. It cannot continue indefinitely, but it will continue long after you are dead. So you might as well let your own light shine now. Become joined to the battle. Beat them at their own games."

Orsini was surprised at the depth of his own bitterness. All the rage that he had felt for so long, at seeing the church raped, at seeing the faithful treated like no more than fodder to keep the gold and the land flowing into the church coffers, at having to deal with priests who sold absolutions and indulgences to the highest bidders and who did nothing for the salvation of the people entrusted to their care, thinking only of their own advancement . . . all this seemed to rise from nowhere. It was the sour gall that poisoned the sweetest region of his soul, and he had been living with it for longer than he thought possible. It was a boil beneath the skin, and now Honorius had lanced it. "Become so greedy that I would sell the sacraments to a dying man? Abandon the teachings of Christ for the acquisition of power? And what would I do with that power, Holy Father? Would it make me a better man, a better priest? Would it ease the suffering of the poor or console the grieving? Would it teach men how to live in Christ?"

"Why, of course it would! With enough power, you can do anything. Reform the church, if you would. Bend it to your will."

"To the will of *God,* Holy Father!" Orsini said bitterly. "As men rise up the ladder, they forget to look down. They kick loose the rungs that supported them. Look at history; how many powerful men of the church have used that power to help the faithful? Only Christ, only Peter, only the holy apostles remembered where they came from, and they died for it at the hands of the powerful. No, the poor and suffering of this world are not to be succored by the church, they are to be ignored!"

Giovanni realized that he was saying far, far too much, but it was quite beyond him to stop. Let it out, let the poison pour forth, and if it killed him, better to die with the truth on his lips than prolong the lies.

"Look into your own eyes, Honorius," he said. "You must have started as a simple priest, you must have felt that God called you. Is *this*"—he swept his arm around, encompassing the sumptuous room—"... is this what you envisioned as doing God's work? What have you gained? And what have you thrown away?" He moved forward, unable to stay still. "At night, just before dawn, when the entire city is asleep, do you sometimes lie awake thinking about who you were and who you've become? Do you question yourself without mercy, and does your heart break for it? Do you ever admit to yourself what you can admit only to God: that you may have been *wrong*?"

Honorius was very still. When his anguish passed, Orsini realized that the silence, blank and questioning, was filled with peril. Too exhausted to care, he sank back into his chair, his head in his hands.

"Those questions," Honorius said softly, "are not my questions. Not any longer. In the beginning, perhaps, so very long ago, longer than you can even suspect. But I know they're yours. I know that you ask them of yourself every morning since you became a cardinal and you realized that sometimes power is useless, is—ironically—powerless in itself.

"Your devotion, I admit, fascinates me," Honorius continued. "I've only met one other man like you, a long time ago, in Ephesus. He was a man of principle also, and he came to grief for it. I seem to have a particular attraction for people of high moral value."

Although you seem to have none of your own, Orsini thought.

"Oh, but I do have principles," Honorius said, as if in admonition.

Orsini looked up, shocked. Had he said it aloud?

"You ask if I was a parish priest. Sadly, no. You may not know that one only has to be a baptized male, technically, to be pope. One does not have to rise through the ranks, and there are many, many shortcuts on the road to the Holy See. One merely has to survive the election and the politics. If I had been a priest, well"—he shrugged—"things might have been different. But perhaps not. We are what we are, Orsini, and it is sometimes the will of the gods that we stay the same, fundamentally, throughout our lives."

"I can't believe that," Orsini said, horrified at the heresy. "Otherwise, why follow the teachings of Christ, if one cannot make a better life?"

Honorius waved his hand carelessly. "We follow the teachings of Christ, or the teachings of Buddha, or listen to the Delphic Oracle, or celebrate the Dionysian Mysteries or dedicate ourselves to the study of the Torah because we must have rules to follow. We cannot accept that there may be only ourselves to answer to, that we are responsible for the choices we make. The burden of that self-government is too heavy to carry. And so we let the church make the rules, and we follow, clinging with a tenacity that outstrips

all reason, assured that if we only do what we are told, and
confess and repent and try again if we fail—as we surely
will—that we will not suffer."

"No," the horrified Orsini whispered. "Christ wanted to
elevate men to saints! And by his death he gave us the
means to do it."

"Do you really believe that?" the pontiff asked curiously. "No, Jesus merely wanted everyone to conform to
what he thought was right. He thought that following his
way would make a better world, so you can't say that his
motives weren't pure. But who is to say that what *you* think
is right is not just as valid as his opinion? I actually feel a
great sympathy for Jesus," Honorius said, reflecting. "He
was trying to end political corruption in his church and put
faith back in the hands of the people. He believed in what
he was doing so much that he willingly died for it. And
here we are, thirteen hundred years later, still in the same
condition." He seemed to stop and consider this for a moment. "A pity, really.

"At any rate," he continued briskly, "the apostles were
religious fanatics. And astounding magicians: they discovered the secret of turning men into sheep. A really imaginative system, that," Honorius said with admiration. "You
invent a heaven and a hell. You promise people that if they
follow your rules absolutely, they will see this paradise—
but only when they die. And if they don't keep to the rules,
they will burn in hell. Ingenious. There doesn't have to
actually *be* a heaven or hell, you don't have to prove they
exist, just as long as the people believe and are afraid. Then
you set up the concept of sin, and invent a complicated set
of rules for avoiding it. Sin, of course, consists of anything
that you don't approve of, or that will not advance your
own cause. If the people have already been following a
religion other than yours, make sure that the tenets of that

religion are the most heinous sins of all. For example, if that religion says that pleasure is a sacrament, then pleasure of any sort must be a sin. If they have a pantheon of much-loved gods, tell the people that those gods are devils and demons. That's how we dealt with Paganism and we were quite successful.

"Jesus never said any of this, you understand. He was more concerned with kindness. We have only the word of the fanatical apostles, the earliest accounts written a full generation after Jesus died. What he really said is lost."

Orsini was growing more appalled by the minute, his eyes wild with the beginnings of terror. You are the Antichrist, he was thinking, and God help us all, you wield the power of the church to fuel your insanity!

Honorius laughed, his eyes dark. "Oh, no! Not me! The Antichrist was Apollonius of Tyana. Even the remaining apostles of his day said it. He could perform the same miracles as Jesus. He could raise the dead, he could speak with spirits. He wandered the earth seeking truth, and was obsessed with justice. And it is said that he overcame death itself."

Horror burst over Orsini. He knew—was certain!—that he had not spoken. And Honorius knew his thoughts! He would have run, but was fascinated by fear.

"But back to the church," Honorius said. "You must wonder why and how I attained this most holy office. Well, the 'how' cannot concern you. But the 'why' may interest you. I've lived a very long life, my good cardinal, longer than you can imagine. And through it all, my views of human nature have always been confirmed: that man is fundamentally evil."

"But, Saint Paul said...," Orsini began.

"Saint Paul!" Honorius chortled. "Now, *there* was the perfect religious fanatic. Believe me, Orsini, there's no one as sanctimonious as a reformed whore. And such an honorable view of women! Mark me, it will be centuries, if ever, before women will open their mouths to disagree with men again. There must not be even the slightest chance that they will reestablish the ancient matriarchies that we so carefully crushed. Because Paul despised and distrusted them, he gave men the perfect excuses to blame them for our own weaknesses. *Men* don't sin, Paul whined, *women* tempt them into it. Paul set a useful pattern: create a scapegoat. And we've used it well. Pagans, Jews, Moors, Turks, heretics . . . give the people someone to hate, someone to *blame* and they'll unite behind you. And you can control them. Any atrocity will be permissible in the name of God. I tell you, Orsini, you must never underestimate the power of religion to make people do what they would ordinarily find repugnant. Just convince them that the enemy is threatening their way of life and they'll never question you.''

Honorius, seemingly unheeding of Orsini's numbed shock, rose, moved toward a large table, and refilled his goblet from a silver jug. He savored the wine with obvious delight.

''And the scapegoat serves another purpose. Misdirection. You don't want people examining the workings of the church too closely. Just look at what we've done to the faithful. Guilt. Fear. Awe. While they starve, we cover our churches in gold and ourselves in ermine. We demand their money, their lands; we tell them what to eat and when to stop eating; how to raise their children . . . we even tell them when they can make love and with whom, and they've never put up any argument. They're too terrified of hell, too convinced that they are insignificant and that God talks only to us. If they start to examine it all too closely, we conjure another holy war as a distraction. In short order, they're waving swords and raising armies, screaming things like "We must save the birthplace of Jesus from the infidel!" or some such nonsense. We've distracted them once more.

"Why, Orsini, if the people ever realized how they've been controlled and cheated, they'd tear the churches to rubble. And you and me right along with them." He took another sip from his goblet. "We've convinced them that God wants great basilicas, and rich ornamentation, and the sacrifice of their lives. Save us all if they ever realize they can talk to God just as well, or maybe better, than we can."

Honorius relaxed, drank the rest of his wine, and seemed to disregard Orsini, who was now weeping as violently as a child over a dead father.

Finally, Honorius spoke again. "You cry because you want to believe that I'm a madman. Because my truth has just destroyed your life. Because you can see that there are very few churchmen who are any more honorable than I am; they simply don't see the truth as I do.

"Look at me, Giovanni: *I am the church*. The parish priests, the bishops . . . they have no power. It is the papal court, the wealthy cardinals from ancient families like yours, the governments, the corrupt, controlling fortunes behind us all . . . *that* is the church! And it will never change. Not as long as the people let us get away with it. The church has concerned itself with temporal power because there is no such thing as spiritual power. Spiritual power is individual, it comes from inside a man, it cannot be governed. It is a connection between man and God that needs no intermediary. There are many who say now, have said in the past, and will say in the future, that they can interpret the word of God, and people will believe them. But they will believe only because they have been trained to stop listening on their own. The word of God is available

to any who want to hear, at any time. and without the aid
of the church.''

Orsini lifted his head, his eyes ravaged. "And you, Honorius. Do you hear the word of God? Do you even bother
to listen?''

And then Honorius made a statement that Orsini did not
understand at all, that made no sense.

"When I was young, many centuries ago," he said, "I
challenged the gods. I had stopped listening then. And now
they have given me no choice but to listen, to do what they
have assigned me. To play the role they have written for
me.''

Orsini was struck by the strange phrase, "the gods." As
if the man were some Pagan idolater.

"Have you ever heard of the Hermetic Laws, Orsini?
Perhaps you wouldn't have, or if you have you've been
taught that they are heresy. They were put forth by a great
man, a great philosopher-king and priest, perhaps a god
himself. Hermes Trismegistus. The Hermetic Law of Po-
larity states that everything contains its opposite, that for
something to exist, its opposite must also exist. To state an
example in Christian terms: because God exists, Satan, his
opposite, exists. If there were no Satan, there would be no
God. Everything, every man, every being and spirit, contains both good and evil. Therefore, nothing is black or
white, but is both. All truths are half-truths. What we become depends on what part of ourselves we choose to ac-
knowledge. If we choose evil, then we are evil.

"So it is with me, good Cardinal. I exist because my
opposite exists. If either one of us dies, we would both die.
If either one of us changes and is no longer the exact op-
posite of the other, then both of us would cease to exist.
And like God created Satan, I created my own adversary. I
And even though I have not seen him for many ages, I

know he lives, still. Because I live."

Honorius seemed to be in a trance. His face was placid, yet a shadow of pain crossed his eyes for only a second.

"You asked if I wanted you to become like your fellow cardinals: corrupt, greedy," Honorius said. He turned his hypnotic eyes on Orsini. "No, I don't ask you to become like them. I ask you to become like me."

Honorius looked up. Orsini became aware of a woman in the room. She must have slipped in so quietly that he didn't hear her, or perhaps the numbness of his fear deadened his senses. In other circumstances he would have acknowledged her beauty, her hair black as polished onyx with strings of gold beads braided into it, her skin pale as pearls, a jewel as rare as any other that Honorius possessed.

"I grow lonely here, Orsini, deprived of the companionship of another male of my own species. And you are so like my adversary, that opposite created so long ago and whom I no longer see. You have his principles, his sense of honor, his intelligence. You're worthy of me, perhaps the only man in this century who could be my equal. Shall I do it? Shall I make you my equal?"

Orsini, in terror and never taking his eyes off Honorius, rose from his chair, so violently that it tumbled on its side. But he *should* have been looking at Odile. She came from behind, clasping him in arms strong as a man's, stronger. He tried to struggle free, but she pinned his arms behind him, holding him with one hand. With the other, she reached in front of him and with a single stroke of her nails, seemingly grown into claws, ripped his vestments away from his chest. He felt a dizzy panic overcome him, as if he might faint, but he fought to stay conscious. All he could see was Honorius's eyes.

He had an eerie hallucination, he was sure it was from a hysteria induced by his own terror and Honorius's unsettling gaze. Honorius seemed to be changing, mutating into something monstrous. With a swiftness too fast for Orsini to see, Honorius was upon him, his gaping mouth fastened over Orsini's heart.

The pain stunned him, but only for a minute. He felt himself sucked into a vortex in which his mind was swept away as well as his body. He had no real understanding of what was happening to him, but he knew that he was being changed forever, and that his old life was being drained away from him as surely as his consciousness waned.

With the last of his strength, he staggered back against Odile, supported by her arms and body. He opened his eyes to see Honorius, monstrous, unthinkable, but deviously beautiful. Truly, the wolf in the clothes of the lamb. The lamb of God, Orsini thought hysterically, and who will protect us now from our predators?

9

In a town not far from Avignon, ravaged by the Black Death, a distraught woman stood at the door of her house, very close by the side of the road. It wasn't her poverty that made her noticeable, though her clothes and her broken demeanor certainly marked her as one of the poor, but it was her pathetic desperation. She begged of everyone who passed, "Please, please . . . I cannot leave my children to die alone. Please bring the priest . . . tell the priest to come! I cannot go myself and leave them. What if they die without the sacraments, with no hope of Heaven! The youngest hasn't even been baptized."

But very few people passed, and those who did either ignored her or were frightened. If her children were dying, there was every chance that she, too, was infected. No one wanted to draw too close.

But she stood there, without pride, with only the love and anguish for her children keeping her begging by the road. Every so often, a tiny cry or a moan would come from inside the house, and she would dart inside to wipe a small, sweat-soaked forehead or administer a cool draft of water to a fever-dry throat, or simply to hold one of her children until its fear subsided into febrile dreams. One of the children was so far gone with the disease that he couldn't be touched; if he was moved, whole sections of his skin would slough off.

At last, she saw the parish priest coming down the road on his mare. He had just left the prosperous home of a merchant and his belly was full of roast kid and good wine.

At the sight of him, the woman sobbed with relief. "Thank you, Father, oh, thank God that he has sent you."

The priest saw the woman. He hesitated. The distinctive smell of the Black Death was rolling out of the open door. Pulling an embroidered handkerchief from his pocket, the priest covered his nose and spurred the horse to a gallop, away from any possible contagion.

The woman stood stunned at her door. When she realized what had happened, she felt the full weight of hopelessness overcome her. She sat heavily in the doorway. Her sobs were so deep and her eyes so blinded that she almost didn't hear the sound of horse's hooves. They stopped at her door. In relief and gratitude, she looked up, expecting to see the returning priest. God hadn't deserted her and her children!

But it wasn't the priest. It was a young man, covered completely in a light brown wool cloak, such as a monk would wear.

He got down from his horse and approached the woman. She looked up.

"Have you asked for a priest?" the man said. "I heard it in the village."

"Yes, yes . . . are you a priest?" she said, her hope rising.

He helped her to her feet. "Yes. Where are your children?"

She led him inside, where her children lay in fever. The man opened a small bag and brought out the priest's tools: a small jar of chrism, the priest's stole, a number of consecrated Hosts, and a stoppered silver jar of holy water. He spread a clean white cloth on the table and laid these things reverently on it. He took off his cloak.

The woman gasped to see the splendid scarlet vestments of a prince of the church.

He closed his eyes, murmured a prayer, kissed the stole, and draped it over his shoulders. His magnificent cardinal's ring winking in the dim light, he proceeded to baptize the baby and to give extreme unction to each dying child.

The mother felt her desperation lighten. She would grieve the rest of her life, but at least her babies would die with the sacraments.

The cardinal finished with the children and turned to her. "Would you like to make your confession?" he asked.

He heard her confession and gave her absolution and penance.

"Thank you, Eminence, thank you," she said. She suddenly found that she was so tired, as if all her efforts had drained her. It was hard to get the words out. She passed one hand over her eyes. "When the priest wouldn't stop, I was so afraid."

He looked at her, his face darkening. "What do you mean, he wouldn't stop? Did the parish priest come here?"

"He rode by, but he wouldn't come in."

"Did he know your children were dying?"

"Yes, Eminence. I said so."

An absolute fury passed over the cardinal's face and he turned his head away. The woman heard him mutter softly and harshly, "Sacrilege!"

After a moment, he reached into his purse and brought out four gold coins.

"Three of these are for your children, that they may have a proper burial. The fourth is for your grief, and is a poor apology for your callous mistreatment at the hands of the clergy. The church asks your forgiveness."

She had never heard of such a thing! Before she could even recover from her surprise to reply, the cardinal had packed up his things and mounted his horse. Still speechless, she followed him outside.

He looked down at her, and the bleakness in his eyes struck a sorrow in her that she couldn't understand. "Pray for me, my child, that I may always do what is right and be forgiven my sins," he said, and then he was gone.

There was a weak wail from inside the house and she hurried inside, a blessing and a prayer for the nameless cardinal already on her lips.

Giovanni was furious. Here was a perfect example of what the love of earthly things led to. A woman of simple faith who placed her trust in the church, and the church had failed her. *God* had not failed her; *Christ* had not failed her. But the very people to whom St. Peter had entrusted the Bride of Christ had betrayed her. Was there no end to this? Had the corruption from above seeped through the entire body of the church? When a simple parish priest cannot find the charity to baptize a dying child, trusting that God would protect him? Giovanni thought about visiting the priest's bishop: a visit from a cardinal would surely carry some weight.

And then he remembered that the bishop of this part of the country was another scheming political pawn. And the parish priest was from a family close to the king. The bishop would listen respectfully to the cardinal. He would cluck his tongue, he would feign indignation at the priest. He might even mention it to the man—over a good dinner, Giovanni was certain.

But nothing would be done.

The more Giovanni thought about it, the more hopeless it seemed, and the angrier he grew. How could he fight the

entire church? For the first time he understood the anger
that Christ must have felt, standing in the Temple confront-
ing the money changers, the last straw in a haystack of
frustration. Jesus had tried truth and soft words and no one
had listened; clearly, it had been time for violent action. It
seemed to Giovanni that a vast army of immorality lum-
bered unstoppably toward him, ready to engulf him. If he
vanquished one, a hundred stood to take up the charge. It
was an impossible task for one man.

True, Giovanni's rise in the church had been partially
due to just the system he abhorred. He was well aware that
his being placed as a cardinal was not because of his faith
or the outstanding performance of his offices. It was ironic
that he had always wanted to be a priest, it was a boyhood
ambition; his family's chessboard moves had only put him
where he had wanted to be in the first place. He despised
Honorius but had to admit that he was right: Giovanni
might just as well have been happier as a parish priest, well
out of the intrigues of Rome and Avignon.

Giovanni was not really aware of how far he had ridden,
or in what direction. He was simply galloping his horse to
clear his anger. He reined the horse in, dismounted, and led
the animal to a quiet stream to rest and drink.

He hadn't realized how late it was getting, and was taken
quite by surprise at the sudden pain that seemed to rip
through his midsection. He looked in the sky and saw the
faint shadow of the full moon, just beginning to make herself known.

He managed to tie his horse to a nearby tree. Then, staggering a few yards away, in hopes that he wouldn't terrify
the animal, he gave himself over to his transmutation.

It wasn't totally unfamiliar: he had changed before, the
night that Honorius had raped him. On that first night he
had refused to run with Honorius and Odile when they

changed, had refused to kill. Honorius had explained to him that he might be able to refuse that night, but on the full moon, he would have no choice. A loup-garou must feed on that night.

And the night had come.

As he writhed on the ground, changing rapidly, he found that the pain was secondary to his real thoughts. Tonight his mind was occupied with rage at the parish priest. What the man had done was an unforgivable sin, and there was no one to punish him for it. No one who would even be interested.

No one but Giovanni.

The transformation was over. He stood up straight, and for the first time was grateful for his strength, his heightened senses, his supernatural speed. He thought again of irony. In bestowing on Giovanni his blasphemous gift, hoping to break him and win him to evil, Honorius had in reality given Giovanni the strength to do what must be done to restore God's justice to the world.

He found that, despite the frustration he had felt earlier, he was not helpless against evil at all.

He took in a deep, renewing breath of night air and looked up at the stars. Following an instinct that recognized no politics, no dirty deals, no bastard alchemy that transmuted the prayers of the faithful into gold, Cardinal Orsini, no longer himself but an instrument of pure justice, set out toward the town, to instruct a negligent priest on the finer points of doing penance.

An hour before dawn, Giovanni ran in righteous joy under the moon, the priest's blood drying on his pelt, clotting in his claws. He found a stream and plunged in, enjoying the cold water as it washed over him and carried the blood away.

He regained the place where he had begun the night, his clothes hidden in the branches of a tree. He lifted his face to the moon and, for the last time that evening, drank in her silvery light, feeling his power melt into her own, a kind of quicksilver energy running from his body to the moon and back again, gaining in strength with each exchange.

Giovanni thought about what he'd done to the priest. He remembered that, just before taking action that night, he had been nervous and unsure. Suppose he was doing wrong, suppose the priest had been a good man and his behavior toward the poor woman had been one slip of bad judgment in what had been a pious life? For that, he didn't deserve to pay such a high price. Perhaps there was some rational explanation for what was, on the surface, a despicable act.

But he hadn't been wrong about the priest. Like Honorius, Giovanni now could read men's thoughts and see their souls. The priest was everything he despised; he was a microcosm of all that had corrupted the church. Greedy, power mad, licentious, smug in the complacency of his position. From the pulpit, he preached humility, self-sacrifice, chastity, and charity for his flock while believing none of it for himself.

It had been a pleasure to kill him. The look on the man's face, especially when the loup-garou reminded him of his neglect of the woman and her dying children, was to Giovanni's greatest satisfaction.

"We reap the rewards for the good we do," he had growled at the terrified priest, pinning him to the wall of his richly gilded church, "and we pay the price for the bad. Think of me as merely the tax collector."

The priest, like most country Frenchmen, was no stranger to the tales of the loups-garous, but he had obviously never expected to see one, glaring fire into his eyes and breathing the breath of destruction into his face.

The priest started to babble some excuse.

"Save your lies," the loup-garou told him. "Make your explanations before the judgment of God, to which I am about to consign you."

He snapped the man's neck and it was over. Giovanni believed in a merciful death: why prolong it, when dispensing justice was all that was really important? He fed on the priest's heart, as a werewolf must do to live, then took the body with him to be disposed of deep in the woods.

This, his first kill, exalted Giovanni. He was surprised. The guilt and the horror of murder that he had expected to feel had not come. Instead, he felt a vindication for his existence as if, for the first time, he was doing what he had been born to do. He realized that his elevation to cardinal had not been the best thing for him: it had caught him up much too soon, at too young an age, and had thrown him too deeply into the politics that he despised. For years he had felt like a man buried under a snowdrift: he wanted and tried to dig himself out, but he had no idea where to start digging or in what direction. And the snow kept falling. His frustration at what he saw happening to his beloved church had left him angry and impotent: he was only one man. What could he do?

For the first time in years, he felt that he had done what was right and just. He was the Angel of Destruction sent to wield a sword of righteousness.

He completed his transformation back into his human form and was just pulling on the last of his clothes, straightening and pulling sleeves and fastening buckles, when he noticed something streak by him, so fast it was blurred.

Seemingly out of nowhere, Odile stood before him. She

had obviously completed her own kill and was still in loup-garou form. In one massive paw she carried a bundle of clothes. She dropped these on the ground and began her change. When it was over, she stared frankly at Giovanni.

He tried not to look at her. Her beautiful nude body was much too distracting. He was astounded to see that she was shaved, all over. The smoothness of her human body con-strasted shockingly with the sight of her as a fur-coated loup-garou. He was also quite mystified that her tender nether parts were rouged the same color as her lips. A vir-gin himself, he had no way of knowing that this was a fashionable cosmetic affectation of upper-class ladies. The sight was so strange and so suddenly erotic that it riveted his attention.

Shaking himself out of his fascination, he picked up her cloak and held it out to her.

"Cover yourself, lady," he told her with exquisite sar-casm. "I would hate for your keeper to accuse me of having violated your chastity. Where is he, by the way?"

"Home," she said, making the magnificent papal palace sound like a warm little cottage. "He's with the emissaries from Rome. There is trouble there: a man who has set him-self up to rule the city."

"Cola di Rienzo," Giovanni said, with a negligent wave of his hand. "He thinks he's been called on by the Holy Spirit to restore the glory of the Roman republic. He won't last long. The Papal States are in too much of an uproar from the warring families. Di Rienzo is simply another passing demagogue. Honorius will have more to worry about from Visconti of Bologna and Emperor Louis of Ba-varia. Provided, of course, that Honorius is interested at all in the church. But of course, this isn't spiritual business; it's temporal power. So it may get all his attention."

"I know what you think of him. But you mustn't judge

him harshly. He may be cynical, but he is still doing good. Every day he has flour distributed to the poor so that they may have bread. He has built up the papal hospitals and opened new cemeteries for the plague victims and hired grave diggers and carters that the dead may be decently buried.''

Her tone was odd. It sounded like a speech that she had memorized, not something she really felt.

''Has it ever occurred to you that he does this so that his baser actions won't be suspect?''

''The people love him!''

''I'm sure the families of the people he's killed would fall on their knees to him in gratitude if they only knew.''

She wrapped the cloak around her and sat gracefully on the grass, still looking at Giovanni. She seemed completely at ease, but there was something very sad about this woman. Giovanni had thought so from the first time he saw her. She had been sitting in one of the palace gardens, all alone, and he saw her drop the public face she used at the court. She'd looked like a trapped animal.

''So you've had your first kill,'' she said pointedly. ''What was it like? How did you feel? Are you still so much more virtuous than he is?''

''I feel quite well, lady,'' he said coldly. ''Are you surprised? Did you and your keeper mean for me to suffer? Is that why he did this to me?''

She shook her head. ''You don't understand, Giovanni.''

''Oh, then educate me. Please.''

She looked up at his face, his tall form towering over her. ''I can't talk to you unless you sit with me.''

He sat opposite her, studying her face. He relaxed back against a tree and observed her beauty. She didn't look like a monster. No one, seeing her graceful form and gentle face, would suspect that she was anything more than another sheltered, cultured lady.

"Why are you here alone? Did your keeper let you out?"

"Stop saying that! He isn't my keeper."

"Your tender and ardent lover then, madame. A shameful union, to be sure."

She turned her face away. "That may be. But the shame is mine, Eminence, because I cannot leave him."

"He *is* spellbinding, I'll say that for him."

"I'm not spellbound. I've let him shape me like this. I've allowed him to influence my thoughts and my life because I'm terrified of losing him. I cannot live without him." The simplicity and honesty in her voice moved Orsini.

"You love him that much?" Giovanni asked. She gave no reply.

"Then that is your misfortune, lady," he said more gently, "because someday he will leave you. Without a word. He is a man without responsibility to anything or anyone. His interest is caught periodically by events and circumstances and even people. He plays at them awhile, then discards them. I've seen men like him before. You and I, lady, will have long lives, but we don't share his immortality. We are nothing but passing moments to him. To love him is to allow him to further ruin you until you are beyond hope. I would advise you to find a more stable partner; better yet, take holy orders and repent of your sins."

She burst into laughter at the absurdity of this last suggestion.

"I can hardly do that, Eminence. I am going to have a child and, when I inform him, I doubt that Honorius would want his child born anywhere but in the palace, close to him."

Suddenly, as if he could see her life laid out in a brightly colored map, Giovanni had the truth of her future before him.

"Listen to me," he said, leaning closer to her, "Honorius cannot afford that scandal. No man in his position can, no matter how powerful he is. It will be inconvenient for him—*you* will become inconvenient. A man like him loves a woman only so long as she is beautiful, enticing, and no trouble. You, lady, are about to become a heavy burden of trouble. He will send you away to have your child, and he will no longer be in love with you.

"Go back to your family, madame, or to the husband you deserted for Honorius," he advised her. "Throw yourself on their mercies and forgiveness. Let them care for you and your child. Very shortly, no more place will be made for you at the papal palace."

She jerked her hand back from him in anger. "He will love this child!"

He shook his head. "It will, like everything else, simply amuse him for a while."

The pain in her face was unbearable to him. She suddenly looked a half-score years older and frightened. Because of that, he lied to her.

"But then, lady," he shrugged, "I'm no prophet. And my dislike of the man colors my judgment. I could be wrong about all of it."

He patted her hand. "Now tell me what you have to tell me. You didn't come here and we didn't meet by accident."

She still looked frightened, but it was a different kind of fright. Even after his transformation, Giovanni found that his psychic powers were not completely faded. Odile was torn between apprehension and duty. Some remnant of honor in her, some fragment of principles that must have once been part of her upbringing had not been entirely crushed.

She was struggling now to find that remnant. It was what had brought her here, looking for him.

"It's because you seem so . . . helpless," she said, "so vulnerable in the generosity of your nature. Honorius says that people are evil, that any charity or kindness is only a facade erected to get them what they want. But in you, I think, there is real kindness. Honorius made you as he is because he knows that. He is much taken with the idea of opposites; sometimes, it seems to me that the idea doesn't intrigue him so much as frighten him."

What Honorius had said came back to Giovanni. "His adversary."

"Yes," Odile said, grateful to be understood. "The adversary still exists. He is the opposite of Honorius in every way: kindness against brutality; good against evil; a belief in nobility of man instead of degradation. And he kills only for justice. Justice, when he was human, was his highest ideal, and now, in his lycanthropy, he has developed an entire philosophy for the behavior of werewolves. He preaches control over the bestial side of our nature, so that we can turn our curse to a gift."

"And do you believe this adversary, Odile?"

The terrible pain crossed her face again. "It doesn't matter whether I do or don't. I chose my road, and I chose to walk it with Honorius. But it is a road, I think, that you are unable to travel. It would destroy you, to live like we live and kill like we kill."

The priest in him, the ultimate believer in salvation for any sinner, rose irresistibly to the surface. The desire to ease the pain of this young woman, seduced into a life that was now ruining her, filled Giovanni with compassion.

"I'm not sure that you are able to travel it, either, Odile.

You can leave it if you wish."

She hesitated, then shook her head. "The truth is that I've become too used to the pleasures he's taught me. I never knew those preferences were there, but he saw them, he knew. Something inside me that *wanted* to yield to his ways. And how could I go backward? You asked me if I loved him? How could I love him? I think, most of the time, that I hate him. Yet I can't leave."

"Think of your child, Odile."

The fright flickered again in her eyes, then was blotted out by the elaborate fantasy she had built around herself and her lover: Honorius would love her, would take care of her, would treasure their child. When it was born, he would change his ways and their happiness would be idyllic.

Giovanni grieved to see the age-old lie that women persist in telling themselves about abusive lovers, including the self-deceptive fantasy that it was partly her fault. He could see that she was immobile.

Still . . . "If you're too ashamed to go to your family, surely mine would take you in. My mother is a most charitable Christian woman."

But Odile's own web held her trapped.

"You should find the adversary," she said, dismissing the subject of herself. "He can teach you so many things. I don't know where he is, he is a wanderer. It was said of him that he was a great magician, a thaumaturge, performing miracles. Apollonius of Tyana, he was called."

Of course Giovanni had heard of him. Apollonius had been the first great Antichrist, promoted as such by the enemies of early Christianity. His miracles were exactly the same as those brought about by Jesus, or so they said.

"I don't fully understand this," Giovanni said. "What has Apollonius to do with Honorius?"

"His name isn't Honorius. It's Lycaon. In ancient times, he lived in Arcadia. Arcadia was like Eden, a paradise. A temperate climate, gentle people, a beautiful country of hills and valleys abundant with fruit and grain, of fast-running streams live with fishes. And over all this, Lycaon was king.

"But Lycaon's flaw was in his character. He was selfish and vain in those days. He felt that his intelligence and his birth placed him far above other men, not seeing that real peace comes from the love of friends and family. That simple satisfaction was beyond him. He accepted no equals and scorned those who he felt were not as accomplished as himself. Lycaon was a man to whom the comradeship and enjoyment of the race meant nothing and victory meant everything. Being better than the rest obsessed him, drove him to the ultimate folly.

"He became fixed on the idea that Jupiter was his rival. He would permit no one of his household to sacrifice to the god; instead, he desecrated Jupiter's temples and had them rededicated to himself. He broke apart Jupiter's statues and replaced them with his own.

"Eventually, he conceived the idea to murder Jupiter in order to assume the god's place on Olympus. It was madness, but the methods by which he might accomplish this raged incessantly in Lycaon's soul. It drove everything else out of his mind.

"Jupiter, of course, was furious. The people of Arcadia, devoted to the god, had sacrificed to him in secret and kept his Mysteries, even with the threat of death over them if they had been discovered. They prayed to be delivered of their blasphemous king. Their devotion to Jupiter saved the country, I believe, else he would have destroyed it.

"Instead, Jupiter took his vengeance on Lycaon alone. He condemned Lycaon to live as half-man, half-beast. His life, unspeakably changed, was to be his sentence, that he may contemplate his true nature and repent of it.

"Unlike all the werewolves to come, who age one year to a human's ten, Lycaon was created immortal. He didn't see that his curse was also his potential salvation: that in the centuries he would live that he might learn from his affliction and repent of his audacity.

"But he *hasn't* repented!" she said hopelessly. "And, Giovanni . . . I've waited so long for that repentance to come to him! If anything, he has grown worse. His transformations merely gave him another weapon with which to vent his anger in murder and debauchery."

Giovanni listened to this tale with growing unease. "But, Odile," he said, "you say that the god Jupiter cursed him. Surely there is no god except the one true God. This story can't be true."

Odile shrugged. "Jupiter, Jehovah, Allah, Ishtar, Isis . . . all gods are one, Giovanni. Lycaon is right about the nature of gods: you must push aside the veil of your chosen faith and look clearly at the truth. Any religion is merely the way one chooses to *interpret* the gods; it isn't the gods themselves. They will continue with or without us."

"And what happened with Apollonius of Tyana?"

"Here was a man who had always been considered extraordinary. A great philosopher. A renowned magician of whom there were many wonderful tales. He was the most promising student of Pythagoras, and saw the world in terms of the greatest good. Lycaon, as you have seen, regards it in terms of the greatest evil.

"Lycaon believes that justice is irrelevant. Apollonius held that man has an obligation to his fellow man. Lycaon venerates selfishness as the ultimate goal of all actions. Now that you know Lycaon's theory of opposites, you can see the hold Apollonius had over Lycaon's imagination.

"Lycaon had heard of Apollonius, of course. So he plotted to meet him. Lycaon traveled to Ephesus, where he started an epidemic of killing, knowing that the tales of how horrible the murders were would reach Apollonius. The Ephesians, never having had anything this terrible happen to them before, referred to the rash of murders as a 'plague' and sent for Apollonius. Among his miracles was supposedly the ability to lift plagues.

"So Apollonius came to Ephesus, where he met Lycaon. And Lycaon did to him what he did to you: he made him a werewolf."

Giovanni was fascinated by this story. "And made him immortal, like himself, so that he'd always have an adversary."

"No," Odile said. "Apollonius was already immortal. This was irresistible to Lycaon because it meant that an adversary would always exist: he'd never have to worry about finding another one. The adversary doesn't have to be immortal, there doesn't even have to be a single adversary—there could be many, but there must always be at least one. There must always be one werewolf who upholds the principles of justice, who has never killed for any other reason, who believes that the loup-garou is the servant of the gods.

"In the centuries that have followed, Apollonius has gained many followers among werewolves. You must know this about him: Apollonius, even when human, was a priest of the goddess Hecate, who governs all things hidden and secret, patroness of the magical arts. Because she reveals secrets, she also metes out justice. Apollonius has always taught that our abilities to know men's minds, our human reasoning and conscience, and our swift power to kill obligates us to kill only in the name of justice. The werewolves who follow him dedicate themselves to Hecate.

Apollonius himself, it is said, has never killed for any other reason. And that small distinction is the true secret of the adversary.

"You think that Lycaon is evil, but there's a deeper taproot to Lycaon's beliefs. Like Apollonius, Lycaon was a priest, but his goddess was Eris, the goddess of discord. It was Eris who led him into the disastrous attempt to murder Jupiter. And still, he worships Eris. Lycaon creates chaos whenever he can: it is part of his belief, it is what gives him power. When people are forced to live in a state of chaos, when things are constantly going wrong, the anger and frustration generated in the situation are tremendous sources of energy. Lycaon is able to drink that energy like a vampire drinks blood. It strengthens him."

Giovanni was beginning to see. "And that is why there is such discord now in the church."

"And why Lycaon is so powerful. Yes." She paused and caught her breath.

Giovanni was intrigued. This singular young woman, thought of as merely an ornament for a licentious pope, had a mind of her own.

"Like religion," Odile mused, "a werewolf's belief in himself is a matter of choice. Lycaon's followers believe that a werewolf is fundamentally a savage beast with the advantage of human cunning. Apollonius's followers believe that a werewolf is a rational human being with the advantage of an animal's power."

She looked slyly at Giovanni. "Which is true, Eminence? Or are both positions true? One must eventually choose, and you, I feel sure, must choose Apollonius's way. For myself"—her shoulders sagged as she turned away—"I no longer have a choice."

*   *   *

Giovanni left Avignon to search for Apollonius of Tyana. He found him, studying the mysticism of the East. He told Apollonius who he was and how he came to be a werewolf, and Apollonius took Giovanni under his wing and taught him about justice and honor. Eventually, young Cardinal Orsini returned to the Vatican, determined to save the church from her keepers.

Orsini never saw Odile de Valois again. But to his sorrow, he heard her story.

It was exactly as he had told her. When Honorius learned of her pregnancy, he sent her to a convent to have the child, he replaced her with another mistress, and it was as though she had never resided at Avignon. Throughout her pregnancy, she never doubted that Honorius would return to her, that his sending her away was merely for her own health and safety, and it was only this pitiful thought, from which she could not be deterred, that sustained her.

And Honorius did return to her when his daughter was six months old. Even the sisters said that they had never seen such a beautiful child: Annette Louise Catherine de Valois had not only her mother's honorable family name, but her mother's dark, silky hair and white velvety skin. Honorius, looking at the little girl, was delighted with her.

So delighted that he took Catherine away from her mother, to raise as his daughter, *only* his. Odile was never to see her again or influence her. Catherine would, he told the shattered Odile, be himself in female form.

Very soon after that, Giovanni learned, Odile had died a suicide. Her method had mystified everyone but himself and Honorius. She had stolen an elaborate rosary from the mother superior and had swallowed it, choking to death before anyone could pull the thing out of her throat.

The rosary was retrieved finally by the sisters who prepared Odile for her ignominious burial in unhallowed ground. They felt uneasy about it, but the rosary was very valuable. Its crucifix was encrusted with precious stones, all set in the purest silver.

Shortly after claiming his daughter, Honorius abdicated the papal throne on one day and disappeared the next, taking his child. It threw both Avignon and Rome into chaos.

But then, the church had survived worse things, and would survive worse still, and the loss of one pope more or less was not a fatal blow. There was another raucous conclave, another powerful puppet elected to the Throne of Peter, and the church, still wound in its own cocoon of treachery and intrigue, carried on.

PART THREE

†

The Golden Apples
of Discord

10

Present-day Louisiana

"Damn, *chérie*," Achille complained to the lady lying next to him, "I think you done broke it, dawlin.' Just look at that.

He reached down and held up his unresponsive member, which amused itself by flopping to one side. He flipped it irreverently back and forth a few times.

"Oh, yeah," he said positively, "it's done for."

The lady, whose silky black hair and velvety white skin had been the hallmark of beauties in her family for generations, looked dispassionately at the offending appendage. "I'm not fooled by appearances," she said.

But Achille wasn't so sure. He dropped the thing, laid his head back on the pillow, and sighed. "Don't be too sure," he advised. "I'm not as young as I used to be."

She gave him a very sour look: she was older than Achille. "Don't be insulting." She spoke fluent English, but with a lovely French lilt, like Zizi's. And like Zizi, she had originally come from France. He knew that much about her, but not much else, and that was fine with him.

He ran a hand through her long hair and over her face, only slightly etched with lines. "How much older than me are you again? It just knocks me out when you say it."

She laughed. "Five hundred and thirty-three, more or less."

He peeped under the sheet. "Ooo-*wee!* You held together real good, girl."

"The loup-garou's gift, *mon ange,*" she said, getting out of bed and wrapping Achille's old terry-cloth robe around her. She opened the curtains and looked out at the mid-morning light. The sun streamed in brilliant ribbons through the old trees, and the gray stone birdbath was full of late risers taking the waters, chirping and chattering at each other.

"It's absolutely beautiful outside," she said. "I'm getting coffee. Want some?"

"Nuh uh, dawlin'. It might age me, and then I couldn't keep up with you. Then that husband of yours might come after me and my tail'd be draggin'."

"I told you," she said patiently, "he's not my husband. You know how these things work. As far as looks, some of us age slower and some age faster. He's one of the real slow ones. Now we look too close in age for anyone to guess we're really father and daughter. So we tell everyone we're a married couple. It's less explaining to do."

"Even worse," Achille said with mock alarm. "One thing I don't need is somebody's daddy in here, horse-whippin' me for seducin' his five-hundred-year-old baby girl. You must be a slow ager, too, dawlin'. You should look fifty, nearly sixty and you look about late thirties. You got good genes from your daddy, whoever he is."

"How old are you, again?" She looked at him curiously. He was a young loup-garou, to be sure, born into the life at age eighteen, he had told her.

He had genuinely forgotten. "Human years? Um . . . maybe mid-fifties, damn near it. Who counts?"

"Not me," she said, leaning over and pulling the sheet away from his hard body. "I don't measure in years. I measure in performance." She turned toward the kitchen, leaving a trail of musky perfume behind her.

He looked down at himself again. *"Damn!"* he said to his still-sleeping parts.

He was grateful for Catherine. She would never take Mae's place and both of them knew it, but neither one of them was looking for love. Achille was looking for an anesthetic for his pain; she was looking for sex and a few little adventures. But Cat was charming and could make him laugh again. She was also sexually voracious, even for a loup-garou, and could keep his body so busy that his mind didn't have a prayer of keeping up.

It interested him that she was a loup-garou, and a stranger to the insular little Louisiana loup-garou community. It had been so long that Achille had made love to another of his own kind that he had forgotten how all-encompassing it could be, how primitive.

With Mae, he had had love and all the attendant emotions. Those parts of his heart and mind were still too painful to touch. With Cat, he was getting raw, brainless sex with no attachments. He could have gotten the same thing with one of the Louisiana loups-garous, but they had all known Mae and loved her. It would have been as difficult for them as for him.

He had met her totally by accident. He had been running on the bayou, transformed at the full moon, and there she was, darting among the moss-dripping cypress trees. He had been so shocked to find a strange werewolf out there that it had stopped him cold. But there was something about her, something alluring that called to him. It wasn't love, he knew, but whatever it was, it would do for now.

Without a word being spoken, he loped to her side and

they took off together. He was gratified to see that she
preferred to run as he did, flat out, creating his own small
hurricane of rushing wind around his body, turning the
sights of the countryside into blurred shapes passing by.

It was in the kill, however, that the difference between
them became glaringly obvious. Here was a werewolf that
killed not for justice but for the sheer blood pleasure of it.
Even those werewolves who don't kill in the service of
Hecate, the ones who kill because they have to in order to
live, who toy with their prey, extracting the scent of fear
that was so intoxicating, and giving the prey a sportsman-
like chance to escape, even those werewolves make the
actual moment of death fast and painless.

Catherine did none of that. She didn't toy with her victims, she tortured them. Her kills were violent, and indis-
criminate. Because she didn't bother seeking out those who
deserved killing, she pounced on the first human who met
her requirements. And her requirements changed on whim:
a husky dockworker one night, a scrawny, studious type
the next, a woman the night after. She killed more than
once a night. Achille knew that this wasn't so unusual, even
among werewolves who kill for justice, though Achille
himself only took one life a night. But there was something
driven and brutal about Cat, and her manner of killing disturbed him for days afterward. He quit running and killing
with her, and settled for just fucking her, which was plenty
for both of them.

It was plain that, wherever she came from, she either
hadn't heard of Apollonius of Tyana—which was almost
impossible—or she didn't care. He would have said that
she was one of Lycaon's werewolves, but no one had heard
anything of him since he disappeared around the sixteenth
or seventeenth century. The few werewolves who bothered
to keep up with their history—and there were fewer each

decade who even knew Lycaon's name—thought that his immortality was just a myth and that old age or a silver bullet had gotten him. If he had really existed at all.

Still, Catherine was very old. So old that she had probably heard of Lycaon. Achille wondered if she had known him and if she had taken his principles as her own, perhaps not knowing anything about Apollonius.

He thought about introducing her to Apollonius or at least teaching her the ways of justice, but Achille had started to question his right to do any moral judging these days.

Besides, Cat wasn't going to be the love of his life. She wasn't even sure she was going to stay in Louisiana. They weren't going to spend the next couple of hundred years together—hell, he was never sure whether Cat would still be around the next morning. She was her daddy's problem, whoever he was, and not Achille's.

He pulled on a pair of pants and joined Cat in the kitchen, lured by the irresistible smell of coffee and chicory. She was studying his newly built rows of shelves, lined with jars of herbs. He had stuck little notes on some of the jars, reminders to himself.

" 'Make ointment for old man Landry'?'' she asked, reading a note.

"Oh, yeah," he said uneasily. He was still not completely comfortable in his new role as Voodoo doctor, but his cures worked and people had started coming to him. "That's plantain. Landry's got hemorrhoids. That stuff's good for poison ivy, too: you jus' crush the leaf and rub it on. Usually grows where poison ivy grows. Funny about that, sometimes the cure grows right beside the problem."

"You like playing doctor?" she purred sexily.

For some reason, this annoyed him. He wasn't "playing doctor," he was providing a service, making himself useful.

He didn't feel like explaining himself to Cat.

"Oh, *chéri*," she cooed, "now I've hurt your feelings. But I have to ask myself why a cop who worked his way up to captain of the homicide division is back here in the sticks, making cough drops and hemorrhoid cures. That's a pretty big life change. I know you weren't worried about getting shot, not unless crooks are using silver bullets these days."

"Things just got . . . *complicated* . . . in New Orleans." He hoped that would hold off further conversation.

"And your wife getting killed had nothing to do with it?"

He stared at her, a quick surge of rage rising in him. He had been very careful to shield his thoughts on this subject. He wasn't quite sure why, but he didn't want to discuss this with her. "How did you know about that?"

"I'm sorry, *bébé*, but everyone in New Orleans knows. It's still in the news and on everybody's mind. It was a terrible, terrible thing."

Achille couldn't think of anything that he wanted to say. Perhaps his unresponsiveness would force her to change the subject.

"Forgive me, but I wonder," she said, "why that preacher's still running loose. I understand the legalities, that he's out on bail, but why he's still alive is a mystery. Anyone who killed someone I loved would suffer the most painful death I could give."

"Perhaps you're just more ruthless than I am," he said.

"I don't think so. I think that you're even more ferocious than me. But you hold it in, you push your most primitive instincts back. Now, why is that, Achille? Why deny what you are? You bury yourself back here in this little town, you get involved in healing—all very well and good, but what is it that you're trying to prove? Are you ashamed of your werewolf nature? Are you ashamed of what we do?"

"Ashamed!" he exploded in surprise. "I'm doing some good here with my herbs and teas and ointments, for myself as well as for other people. And as for lycanthropy, I use it for the highest purpose, to kill for justice. What have I got to be ashamed of? Or is it you who should be ashamed?"

"Me?" She was genuinely baffled.

Achille knew he shouldn't even be bringing this up, that she wasn't his business, the way she killed wasn't his business, nothing about her was his business aside from the enthusiastic fucks she'd been giving him. He was no reformer; he'd had enough of teaching werewolves the principles of justice. Apollonius was no longer wandering the world, he was here in New Orleans, settled with Zizi. If justice was to be taught, let Apollonius do it. But he couldn't seem to stop himself in this particular argument.

"Look at the way you kill, Catherine. For no reason. And they're the most brutal deaths I've ever seen; they're almost sadistic. Are you proud of that?"

"I'm neither proud nor ashamed," she said reasonably. "Killing's just a fact of life, Achille."

"It's more than that. Or . . . it *should* be more."

"You're taking a very basic act and dressing it up in an elaborate philosophy," she said. "Why is that necessary? Look at the situation it's gotten you into. You have the power to avenge an awful crime, a crime against someone you loved . . . a crime against *you*, if you'd admit it. And you want to do it. It just eats away at you, all the time. It drove you out of your job, out of your home, out of the city, away from your friends, because what you *want* to do and what it's *morally acceptable* to do—at least, among your kind of loup-garou—are at odds. You've been taught that killing that man would be as great a crime as what he did. But that's not true. You're beginning to suspect as much. And that scares you."

She leaned very close to him and looked into his grief-stricken eyes. "I think you're ready for a new way of living your life, Achille. And very soon, you'll be ready to admit it. You can't hold out that much longer."

"You'll never understand justice, Cat."

"You're right. I never will," she said simply.

But what frightened Achille the most was that he was beginning to believe that he didn't understand it, either.

11

The woman in Christian Faust's examining room wasn't like the rest of his patients. When he opened the door, he found her seated in a chair, fully clothed, as composed as if she were sitting in a restaurant waiting for a gentleman. She was holding her hand in front of her, fingers elegantly outstretched, examining her perfect nails. Dangling from a gold chain around her throat was a gold wolf's fang, dripping a single ruby.

Maybe he didn't know her name, but he immediately knew who she was.

Flustered, he retreated into routine: he checked the clipboard in his hand, looking for the name on her chart. There was no chart.

She smiled, and it was as if a wave of steam had rolled over Christian. The woman's seductive power was almost tangible. Inadvertently, he took a step backward, when what he really wanted was to move forward with all possible speed. He had a quick memory of Delilah and Gabriel coupled together on that very same examining table, only the figures dissolved into himself and this woman.

He shook his head slightly. He wasn't sure why she was here, but he was positive that this mind fucking was part of her game. Best to play it professionally until he knew what was going on.

"What seems to be the problem?" he asked by rote.

She laughed. "Oh no, I have no problem . . . I'm here to help *you*!" Her voice was low, full of sexual intimidation.

"I'm not aware that I need any help at all, miss," he said politely but firmly.

"Oh, but you *do*," she cooed. "You know, Dr. Faust," she said, "you're incredibly handsome. You're just the yummiest man I've ever seen." Her voice was like melting ice cream. "If I were your wife, I wouldn't let you out of my sight for a *minute*."

She shifted back in the chair, and Christian could see that her cocoa silk blouse had the top three buttons undone, far enough so that he could see the curve of her breast, outlined in scalloped peach lace. It was more erotic than if she'd been naked, and he couldn't take his eyes off it.

"Look, lady," Christian said firmly, "I know you're up to something here, and it isn't going to work. You may as well leave, and tell your friend Lycaon that the Louisiana loups-garous won't be seduced." He grinned wryly. "In *any* sense of the word."

"You think I'm not telling the truth?" she said, her eyes wide and appealing. "I'm just intrigued, that's all. I would think that you'd be more than enough man for any woman," she continued to purr. "Why would your wife want that silly boy when she's got you?"

How did she know about that? Christian thought. "Gabriel's my friend." His voice wasn't working right, he noticed.

"I'm sure he is," she said. "You've shared everything with him, haven't you? Before Apollonius came to Louisiana fifteen years ago, you both lived with Zizi. You shared her life, her bed. The three of you were inseparable. You loved Zizi, didn't you? And you know what? I bet she loved you. Or she might have. But Gabriel was always there. Always taking half of what should have been yours alone.''

"Delilah loves me. Both of us love Gabriel, and he loves us. No outsider could understand what the three of us share. And *you*,'' he said, looking pointedly at her necklace, "should know all about the werewolves' bond between lovers. It isn't restricted to the traditional pair of one man and one woman.''

She stood up and moved closer to him. Her breasts swayed with her stalking walk, as if they were free inside her blouse. It seemed to Christian that he was looking at her through one of those trick lenses: the spots of light in her long black hair seemed distorted into stars. He was mesmerized by the sight and scents of her, and the sound of her voice.

"But one man and one woman can generate a lot of heat,'' she murmured. She moved very close to him, unbearably close. Christian knew that if she came just one inch closer, he couldn't control himself. He had no idea why she had this effect, but he was just on the edge of not concerning himself with reason.

"Gabriel has fooled you, Christian. And now he wants your wife. You love Delilah, the same way you loved Zizi, and yet here Gabriel is again. He and Delilah are making a fool out of you, when she should really be on her knees, thankful she has a man as beautiful as you.'' She hesitated only a moment. "I'd go on my knees for you. Right now, as a matter of fact. Would you like that?''

She reached out and lightly touched his fly. Christian drew in a sharp breath.

It's true, he thought in a split second of illumination, Gabriel had always been there, claiming half of his life. Gabriel had transgressed all the boundaries of friendship. Christian felt an unaccustomed anger; it didn't enter his mind at all that he had never felt the slightest resentment of Gabriel before, that he never before doubted Delilah's love for him and that he understood that her feelings for Gabriel didn't conflict with what she felt for Christian. He forgot that, while it might have been unconventional, the arrangement had always worked perfectly well for the three of them. It didn't occur to him to question where this sudden surge of anger came from. It blinded all logic.

Catherine ran her fingers between his legs, cupping the weight of his testicles, moving her face a little closer to his, her other hand in his hair. "Gabriel doesn't have a life of his own," she whispered, "he's always stolen yours. Perhaps it's time to repay the favor? To repay both your faithless friend and your silly wife?"

Walt had never been to Bayou Goula, not as a human and not as a werewolf. But he had always heard the stories, and the longing for the sacred ground of the Louisiana loup-garou ran as strong in his blood as it did in the older werewolves'.

"The old bayou can tell you stories," Achille had once told him. "All you have to do is go out there and listen, and the souls of all the loups-garous and all the old Indian shape-shifters and shamans will speak to you. They're still there, still waiting."

And so he went out to the bayou alone. Not to think, but to listen.

He did as he had learned, and had done so often. He undressed, folded his clothes neatly in a pile, and stood, naked, preparing for the moon to claim him.

Humans speak of the cold light of the moon and the warmth of the sun. But to the loup-garou the moon is anything but cold. On the nights that he transformed, Walt could feel her light running swiftly into him, igniting his blood, stirring his senses to a tingling awareness. He thought of the kundalini, the Hindus' female serpent of wisdom, who lies coiled and sleeping at the base of the spine. He could always feel her awake at his call and rise toward the light of the moon, opening the hidden power in his body and brain, setting free his true soul.

But tonight, something was missing; some magical element necessary to the alchemy was not there. Transformation, he began to understand, was not what he was there for.

A man appeared at the edge of the clearing. Walt thought it strange that, even with his supernaturally astute vision, he couldn't see him clearly. It was as if the man were wrapped in shadows that he carried with him, moving across the grass toward Walt.

Walt couldn't stop staring. When he came closer, Walt could see that he was a stranger, and yet there was something familiar about him; his dark eyes, his curling chestnut hair, the superbly confident bearing all called to mind someone that Walt remembered but could not place.

"Do I know you?" Walt asked.

The man smiled. "If you know Apollonius, you know me. But the important thing is that I know you, Walt. I know your confusion and your pain."

For some odd reason, Walt believed him.

"I'm an old friend of the Louisiana loups-garous," the man said, "and I'm sorry to hear that you and your father have parted ways over your choice of life." He shook his head sadly.

"You *know* about all that?" Walt said. Then he knew this must be Lycaon.

"I can understand the bewilderment of your sister and mother," the man said. "It's to be expected. They're human. But Andrew . . . ah, there's a different story. What hypocrisy!''

Walt felt stung by this attack on his father. Then again, something inside him felt a righteous satisfaction.

"My father is a bishop, a man of God," Walt explained. "He simply can't understand my choosing the loup-garou's life."

"But he was once a loup-garou himself," the man stated simply.

"It wasn't his choice. He was under a curse. You're a loup-garou, you know the difference between one who chooses our life and one who is cursed. The cursed loup-garou suffers; he doesn't understand the principles of justice and he can't reconcile himself to the kill. For my father, it was a nightmare of guilt. He never knew a moment's peace until he broke the curse."

"And yet, two of his children consciously *chose* the life he'd rejected," the man mused. "I wonder . . . is it that he mourns for what he gave up? The freedom, the strength, the power? Once you have it in your blood, it haunts you. Does it haunt him? Does he wake in the night when the full moon lights the shadows, and does the loss tear at him? And when he thinks of you, Walt, is it jealousy he feels? Is he being tormented because his son has the freedom and the sensuality that he himself will never know again?"

Walt had never even considered the possibility before. Was his father really jealous of Walt's freedom, his release from the normal aging process, his enhanced senses and sexuality? It began to make a sad but logical sense. What had bothered Walt the most was his father's seeming refusal to understand why Walt wanted the loup-garou's life. He remembered the first argument they had had over it; Walt had said that, of all people, Andrew should understand what it felt like, how addictive it was, how being a loup-garou finally brought clarity and purpose to Walt's life. This statement had only served to enrage his father.

"Is it worth it?" Andrew had stormed at him. "Do you have no qualms about committing murder in order to enhance your own life?"

Walt, cut to the quick, tried to explain about justice.

"Oh, don't tell me about *that*," Andrew had said. "I've heard it before. And it still doesn't erase the fact that you're killing. Only God can take a life!"

"Well, maybe God wants me to do it for him!"

Andrew slapped him across the face.

It didn't hurt Walt so much as it shocked him: his father had never so much as spanked any of his children.

Andrew's face had softened and his eyes grew bleak with sorrow. "I'm so sorry, Walt. It's just that I wanted so much more for you than this." The sad desperation in his father's voice at the time had hurt Walt more than the slap.

That was the last time they had spoken.

Walt was mystified by his father's anger. The only reason he could see for it was that his father's religious scruples forbade him from admitting that the ethics of killing in the name of justice justified the act itself. When he thought about it later—and he thought about it more often than he'd wished—Walt was outraged that his father dared to impose his own moral standards on him.

But now, he could see things from a different angle. *Of course* his father was jealous. How could someone have the loup-garou's life and give it up without the slightest backward look of regret? No one could. Not even the bishop of New Orleans.

This explained everything for Walt and, having had it explained, it infuriated him. This split with Andrew had been tearing him apart, forcing him to make a choice between his life and his family. It had made Sylvie miserable, had alienated both of them from their mother and sister. *And for what?* For his father's jealousy and impotence over his own foolishness in throwing away his freedom? Walt had loved his father and had never wanted to make him unhappy, but now he saw that Andrew was using that love to make Walt suffer. The knowledge of Andrew's feelings had stained what should have been the happiest part of Walt's life, and now it would seem that he was manipulating Walt's feelings in the most subtle and nefarious of ways, and had done so deliberately, from the beginning.

And Walt had come home in good faith, willing to throw himself at his father's feet and beg forgiveness! Forgiveness for *what?* For not being such a fool as his father had been? For being man enough to accept the power of the loup-garou when his father could not? He was damned if he'd do that now—let his father instead come to *him.* Walt was the wronged party here.

The more Walt thought about it, the more enraged he became; so much so that he never noticed that the stranger had slipped away, his work accomplished.

And Walt never heard, over the crashing waterfall of his fury, the whispers of the ghosts of Bayou Goula, telling him that his thoughts were not his own, and that he was in the gravest danger.

12

Lucien and Sylvie were staying in their old apartment, part of the small complex of buildings that made up Zizi's shop and house. The apartment, a former slave quarters, had once been made over into guest rooms, then into a single apartment when Lucien and Sylvie married. Sylvie had been staying with Zizi as a houseguest, in one of the airy, antique rooms, when she first met Lucien.

And here he had first made love to her.

- The poignancy of sleeping there now, after so much had intervened, was not lost on them. Their lives at that time had been turbulent, but their love was very simple and all-encompassing, with the optimism that colors love when it first begins. They were certain then that the world would not conquer them—and they were right, it hadn't. Their troubles now, they knew, came from somewhere within, where they were so much harder to vanquish. The world is never as hard on us as we are on ourselves, Sylvie thought.

Claire had been sent to Sylvie's parents for a few days, giving Lucien and Sylvie time to themselves and her parents time to spoil Claire the way they'd never spoiled their own children.

The apartment was separated from the main part of the house by a courtyard, that venerable trademark of an antique French Quarter house. The Royal Street courtyard was one of the Quarter's most beautiful—and most private. Its central fountain splashed, its flowers bloomed and released their sweet early-spring scents, its evening lanterns lit up the trees with pastel lights for only those people who lived in or were invited to Zizi's house.

Sylvie and Lucien sat in the courtyard now, having coffee. Sylvie sipped the rich, slightly bitter chicory-flavored coffee and sighed with relief. Whenever she tasted that particular flavor, inhaled that particular scent, she knew she was home. Sylvie had always felt that nothing bad could ever really happen to her in New Orleans, that even things that looked grim on the surface would work out for the best. It was an optimism that she had somehow lost when she left Louisiana, and it had disappointed her that she was not able to carry that optimism with her. But it was something, she supposed, having to do with the atmosphere in New Orleans and her own special attunement to the rhythms of the city.

It was undefinable, something a tourist never discovers. But sometimes the city reaches out to claim its own. Very often, a tourist will come to New Orleans and find that he has great difficulty getting back on the plane to leave. When he gets home, he finds that the place where he lives has undergone some mystical change: the air is no longer as sweet, the streets not as familiar, the sights and sounds no longer as beautiful as he'd thought. His job, his house, his friends, his favorite places . . . all this now has a slightly used feel, an overlay of dissatisfaction. His thoughts keep turning to old houses with secret courtyards; a free and easy way of living; an insular, small-town sense of community in which everyone spoke a kind of shorthand and shared a way of life that disappeared at the city line. There were things that an Orleanian *just knew*, arcane wisdom that became common knowledge when you lived there, but which

a tourist could never understand. And the unusual thing
about it was that when a tourist finally gave in to his obsession and moved to New Orleans to stay, he found that
he was immediately given the key to that knowledge. He
was welcomed into the club, his ticket for admission being
merely his love for the city, the love that somehow bound
the disparate groups of people living there—no matter what
their backgrounds, ethnic makeup, or other distinguishing
characteristics—into one group: Orleanians. Once you were
there permanently, you were part of the city. And it was
easy to tell when that transmutation took place: it was when
the thought of leaving and never coming back caused a
mild sort of panic. Vacations might be all right, but *really*
leave New Orleans? Unthinkable. It was one of the few
cities in the world where you didn't have to be born there
to be a native. In a very short time, the city made you one.
Even your language and speech patterns would change.
You'd be speaking of going "out in da parish" and asking
"Hey, where y'at?" and demanding of drivers who cut you
off, "You learn to drive at Schwegmann's or what?"
You'd be giving king cake parties and sucking the heads
of crawfish over by the lake or ordering "a po' boy,
dressed" and making groceries. You and your friends
would be bitching about the humidity and the traffic dis-
ruption caused by parades and planning to go on the truck
float at Mardi Gras or dressing up for your Krewe's ball.
You'd look forward to the annual appearance of the Wild
Indians and you'd know a dirty version of "Iko Iko." And
no matter how well you knew the Nine Muses, you'd never
pronounce their names the same way you had before.
You'd sometimes wander through "the Quarters"—where
you probably lived when you first moved to the city—and
shake your head over the stupid remarks made by tourists,
but be secretly pleased that they found your town so irre-

sistible. And you'd look at them and wonder, which one? Which one can't get on the plane? Who'll be sitting in this spot next year or next month, watching the tourists and thinking the same thoughts?

You can move to places like New England, even as a child, and live there fifty years, but you'll always be an out-of-stater. You can move to New Orleans and in a week you'll be one of the initiated. And to have been born there was to have river water running in your veins.

Sylvie closed her eyes and felt the rich wine of the city air wash over her. It wasn't that it was clean, pure air—it wasn't—but that it simply carried on its wings that certain tang of New Orleans, a blend of the scents of pralines and beignets and spicy food, of stale cigarette-choked air from the closed Bourbon Street bars, of fresh blooms from Jackson Square and the Garden District, of old houses, of all the breezes that ever blew between the river and the lake.

"Lucien," she asked, "do you really like New York?"

"Does it make a difference?" he said. "We're stuck there."

New York was also the kind of place you couldn't leave. But, unlike New Orleans, most of the people who lived there hated it. Or at least complained as if they did.

"Well, I wish we could get *unstuck*."

"It's odd that we're in it so little and despise it so much," he said. "Funny about New York, everyone says the same thing: 'I'd leave if it wasn't for my career.' I think I'm in the same rut."

She knew the realities. It was just that in New Orleans the longing to come home and stay here was getting overpowering.

"Is that it, Sylvie?" Lucien asked. "You want to move back home? Would it make a difference for you?"

She thought about it and sighed. "No. Maybe not.

Maybe I'd just be moving my dissatisfaction to a different location. But . . . I don't know. It just seemed that when I lived here I *was* someone, I *did* things. I had some kind of future waiting for me."

"Sylvie," he said patiently, "you were twenty-one when we left here. At twenty-one you have a future waiting for you no matter where you live. Would things have been different if we'd stayed?"

"I don't know!" she said with a slight desperation.

"And you're doing things in New York. You're busy all the time."

She made a wry face. "I'm a *hostess,* Lucien. My life is one party after another, and just because it's for charity or for the advancement of your career doesn't make it any more meaningful."

He was stung by this. "I've never asked you to do anything for my career," he said quietly. He felt that they were about to tread on dangerous ground, and the slightest misstep would plunge them into an argument in which would be said things that couldn't be retracted. "And the parties you organize for charity raise a lot of money."

"Almost as much money as we spend on the damn parties and dresses and hairdressers in the first place," she said with some bitterness.

"If you feel you're not doing anything worthwhile, get a job. Go back to school."

"And stay home while you travel half the time? I'd never see you!"

"Sylvie, what do you want me to say? Are you asking me to stop working? Are you asking me to cut down on my schedule? I can't do that right now—not while I'm hot. I'm cementing a reputation that will follow me all my life or, at least, for the next fifty or sixty years. Eventually I'll be *forced* to give up performing because it'll be too evident that I'm not aging. I'll have to stop until this generation dies off and another is grown up who doesn't remember me. I'll have to pass myself off as my own son or nephew or something. I want to enjoy every moment of this time while I can. But not if I'm going to lose you, and possibly Claire, in the process. Please don't force me to make that choice. I'd never ask it of you.''

"But you *have* asked it of me, never in so many words, but you just assumed I'd follow you wherever you led." She knew as she said it that this wasn't precisely true. If there had been a problem before, she had never said anything to Lucien. He would have listened, the way he was listening now, and would have made concessions for her. But for her to ask for those concessions now, when he was at a point in his life where they would be a great sacrifice, was unfair. She had let him proceed, and he had gone ahead and built his career, trusting that there was no problem on her part.

"I'd never tear you and Claire apart," she said quietly.

This simple statement struck real terror into Lucien. "Does that mean that you're actually thinking about leaving me?" he said slowly. He didn't want to hear her answer, not if there was the slightest chance that she'd say yes.

"No," she said. But it didn't reassure him. He knew that Sylvie didn't know her own mind right then, and she didn't know if she was lying to herself or not.

On impulse, he grabbed her hand and pressed it to his lips, cradled it against his cheek. He thought that if he could only hold her physically, then he wouldn't lose her emotionally. It was absolutely unthinkable. He had thought it was impossible. He and Sylvie had the werewolf's bond, that unbreakable connection that transcends mere human love. If they were off to themselves somewhere, if they didn't have to live human lives at all, this issue of dissatisfaction would never have arisen for either of them. They would live only to run, to kill, to enjoy each other. It had been done by werewolves before them. His own mother, temporarily separated from Apollonius around 1720, had lived like that, or almost like that. She had abandoned civilization to live openly as a loup-garou among Louisiana's Bayougoula tribe, who honored and understood the shamans and shape-shifters. She had served as the tribe's arm of justice, staving off as well as she could the rape of the tribe by the Europeans. When she gave birth to Lucien, the two of them remained with the Bayougoula; Zizi gave him the werewolf's kiss when he was eight, and they had lived as werewolves, sometimes not bothering to change into human shape for days. But, concerned about Lucien's development and longing for her own people, she had returned to New Orleans and had created a community of loups-garous that became the forerunners of today's community. Some of the original members were still among them.

Lucien wondered if he and Sylvie—and Claire—would not have been better off living that simpler life. Maybe that was what Achille was doing out there in Addis. Maybe he'd found the real answers.

Claire. Now there was another thing. Claire was a child of the moon, there was no doubt about it. Often he and Sylvie had found her outside, especially when they were in the country, just staring at the moon or dancing in its light. It had started when she was only three or four. When they were in the city, they'd find her at the window in the morning, sound asleep, curled up on the floor where last night's moonlight had rested.

This delighted Lucien, and he'd thought it would delight Sylvie, too. But though Sylvie professed not to be worried about it, she didn't seem altogether comfortable with it.

Lucien was very confused, but he supposed that it was Sylvie's background, her current estrangement from her family over her transformation of Walt, that was giving her trouble.

Now, he thought it went deeper than that.

Perhaps Sylvie was just now beginning to understand her father's objections to her life, now that she had a daughter. There was no question but that Sylvie considered the loup-garou's life the only way to live, but did she have the right to choose it for Claire? Lucien had reassured Sylvie that Claire would choose the life for herself when she was ready—and she might never choose it at all. But this in itself troubled Sylvie. She never said it, but Lucien knew that Sylvie was afraid that she and Lucien might be exercising undue influence over Claire, without meaning to. Claire was unaware that her parents were loups-garous, or that such a thing even existed, but the child had the loup-garou's eerie psychic powers even when she was a baby. She knew things that children usually didn't know, and was unusually aware of the people and circumstances around her.

Sylvie had responded to this by trying to be Super-Mother, trying to give Claire a life right out of a TV sitcom or old Andy Hardy movies. Claire had a nanny, but she was really more of a baby-sitter when Sylvie and Lucien were out. It was Sylvie that baked Claire's cookies, picked her up at school, read to her at night, took her to other kids' houses to play, took her shopping—all those things that mothers without Sylvie's kind of money did for their kids, but that mothers in Sylvie's social circle had the nanny do. When Sylvie and Lucien traveled together, they almost invariably took Claire, even if it meant hauling her out of school. Sylvie got Claire's lessons from her teachers and made sure she stayed current.

All of this, combined with the full-time demands of simply being Lucien's wife and a semi-pro hostess, was almost more than Sylvie could bear. More and more, she had come to regard everything except Claire and Lucien as superfluous. It didn't seem as if she were on a merry-go-round; it seemed more as if she were the operator of it, and every time she tried to slow down or stop the machine, the people on the horses screamed at her for a faster, longer ride.

"We're here in New Orleans to get *away* from our lives for a while," Lucien told her, "so let's do it. We're away from the pressure and the madhouse: let's see what happens and what we think after we've readjusted. You know, Sylvie," he said thoughtfully, "we keep thinking that New York is where our real lives are and that New Orleans is just a pleasant lull. But maybe what we have back there is illusion and only what is here, in this town, in this house, this courtyard . . . maybe only this is important." He thought again of Achille.

The thought seemed to lull Lucien, but it just confused Sylvie more. She had never thought of New York as real.

She looked at her husband, with whom she had been through so much, and felt the familiar longing for him that had never changed. She wanted so much to put everything right, but she wasn't sure how.

"Lucien, I don't know what's happening," she said. "Really, I wasn't unhappy before. All this discontent just sort of *happened*. One day it wasn't there and the next day it was overwhelming. Do you think this could have anything to do with what John Luparo was telling us? About Lycaon?"

He looked interested. "I don't know. I think there has to be a seed there, though, for him to make anything grow. Although, I'd much rather all our problems were his doing: anything from outside we can fight together, Sylvie. We always have, haven't we?"

He held her hand, then leaned over to kiss her. It was true, Sylvie thought. Lucien and I have been through more than any human couple, even more than loup-garou couples. We fell in love under a bad star and we rode it all out and stayed together.

It mystified her as to what had happened between them, and she wanted to cry.

Apollonius and Zizi emerged from the house, Apollonius smiling and Zizi her usual vague morning self.

Zizi sank down into one of the chairs. Lucien poured her some coffee, without asking if she wanted it. She wanted it, all right. She took two or three grateful gulps, closed her eyes, then looked at Lucien.

"Thank you, *cher bébé*," she said, "I think I may live after all."

"How late were you up, Zizi? Were you running last night?" Sylvie asked.

Zizi just rolled her eyes.

Apollonius, on the other hand, who never needed sleep, was full of energy. "I'll be in the kitchen," he announced. "I feel like eggs Benedict this morning."

Zizi put her head in her hands. "How absolutely disgusting. Don't make me gag, Apollonius," she moaned.

He laughed, kissed the top of her head, and disappeared.

Zizi looked up at Lucien and Sylvie. "The man's an animal," she said informatively.

"That's very enlightening, Mother," Lucien said, raising an eyebrow. "One can only hope it runs in the genes. I'd like to think it bodes well for my own future."

"No argument from me," Sylvie said, sipping her coffee.

"You know that wonderful wine I'd kept for so long? Well, our run last night was so successful—oh, Lucien, it was magnificent! You know that killer who's been carjacking people out on the River Road? He's not going to be doing it again.''

Lucien sighed and waited. Sometimes Zizi tended to get sidetracked.

"Anyway, it just felt so good that when we got home we decided, why keep it around? and we drank it. You know how I feel the day after I drink a lot of wine.''

"Wait a minute. . ." Lucien said. "Good God, Zizi. You don't mean the two-hundred-year-old Bordeaux? You had two bottles of it . . . you didn't . . ."

"We drank both bottles. I feel awful.''

"And well you should," he said indignantly. "You wouldn't even let me open that when I graduated from the conservatory."

"And I was right!" she said defensively. "Look how sick it makes you!"

She moaned and rested her head in one slim hand supported on the table. Her gold hair slipped over one shoulder. Lucien was always startled at how beautiful his mother was, and grateful that the werewolf's slow aging had preserved, and even enhanced, her perfection.

Lucien marveled at the devotion between his mother and father. They had been separated for so long, but since they got back together fifteen years ago they had made up for what they had lost. Odd, he was thinking, that he and Sylvie should be having problems when his parents were like a pair of hot teenagers.

Apollonius appeared a few minutes later with three servings of eggs Benedict.

"And for you, my little hungover darling," he said, "I have a surprise." He set a covered dish in front of her.

"Smells wonderful," she said, lifting the lid. "Oh! French toast!" She gave Apollonius a noisy kiss. "You sweet thing. Just what I needed."

"Two thousand years old you are, Apollonius," Sylvie said, "and as much as you've learned about philosophy and the world, here you are futzing around in the kitchen." Sylvie loved her father-in-law, but she had never quite lost her awe of him.

He savored his first bite of eggs, then smiled. "After two thousand years," he said good-naturedly, "I've earned the right to enjoy the little things."

The maid interrupted, carrying a small envelope. "A messenger service just left this for you, ma'am."

"So early?" Zizi said. "How strange. Something for the store, I expect." She opened the envelope and a small, ivory calling card fell out.

Apollonius smiled. "Really, Marie-Thérèse, you should tell your lovers that a card without the flowers is awfully bad form." But the smile faded as soon as he saw Zizi's reaction.

She had turned stark white, her eyes horrified. Her hand went to her throat as she stared at the card.

"Mother?" Lucien said. "Are you all right?"

She handed the card to Apollonius.

"Good God," he said, frowning at the name.

Sylvie looked over his shoulder at the card. " 'Annette Louise Catherine de Valois,' " she read, noting the little gold coronet above the name and the title after. " 'Marquise de Guibert.' "

"Fancy friends you have, Mother," Lucien said. "I take it she's not your favorite person in the world, however."

Zizi found her voice, but it was shaky. "I knew Catherine in France, before I came to Louisiana . . . your father knew her even earlier than that. Catherine . . ." Zizi's voice faltered. "Catherine made me a loup-garou."

Lucien patted his mother's shaking hand. "Was it that bad an experience?"

"Not the experience. That was the werewolf's kiss . . . it was . . . sublime. But afterward . . . well, Catherine is not our kind of werewolf, Lucien."

"And this Catherine is a follower of Lycaon's?" Sylvie said. "Well, we don't do that kind of thing in New Orleans. She'll have to either change or leave."

"She'll never change," Zizi said bleakly.

"Sylvie," Apollonius explained, "I tried to teach Catherine long ago. And for a while she seemed to espouse the theories of killing for justice. But it just wasn't in her; she couldn't do it. She's not just a follower of Lycaon's: Catherine is his daughter."

"Odd that she wouldn't come see me," Zizi said. "You'd think she'd want to."

"She's always been a little afraid of you," Apollonius said. "You were so much stronger than she was, so much a better person. I think that in the face of your disapproval, her composure would crumple."

"Then perhaps I ought to seek her out."

Lucien felt a vague alarm. "Don't do it, Mother. These people are dangerous."

But Zizi's thoughts were lost in another time.

Apollonius looked at Lucien and Sylvie. "Lycaon's way is chaos; discord for the pure sake of it. He must have it. He cannot appeal to Hecate to give him the power that she gives those of us who are dedicated to her service—he's cut himself off from that. Instead, he feeds on the energy of others to give himself power. And the Louisiana loups-garous are extremely powerful, because we're so close. We've created a group mind: we all think the same way and hold to the same principles, and that's very potent. In creating confusion and dissension, he destroys our unity. And it is that very unity that protects us from the likes of him. Without it, he can drain our power from us to increase his own."

"Just look at what's been happening lately," Zizi pointed out, pulling herself back to the problems at hand. "Did you know that Christian and Gabriel had a real, honest-to-goodness fight? And over Delilah, can you imagine? Those three have always been close, ever since she met them. She could have married either of them; that's how close they were. The world might not have understood it, but the loups-garous did: the three of them love each other, and convention is not always our way. The werewolves' bond binds them.

"And now this?" Zizi said angrily. "Christian actually threw Delilah out of the house. She tried to reason with him but he wouldn't listen; he had all her things carted over to Gabriel's; she's living there now, and both of them are heartbroken. Wherever Lycaon is, it's a victory for him, although a small one."

"Destroying three lives is small?" Sylvie said.

"Oh, yes," Apollonius told her, "for him it is. This is merely a taste for him. He has bigger things in mind. John's coming here last week was really no surprise, though I'm very sad to have my expectations confirmed."

"And what about Achille?" Lucien asked.

"Achille is a very strong piece on our chessboard," Apollonius said. "If Lycaon captures him, our defense could well be weakened. Achille has always been a leader for Louisiana's loups-garous; as he goes, so do they."

"But you're here, Apollonius," Sylvie said, "and even though Achille is strong, your teachings are the basis for the way we live. I should think that it's *you* Lycaon would want to defeat."

Apollonius regarded her sadly. "He does, but he can't. I'm his adversary; he needs me to exist as he does. It's through all of you, those whom I love, that he will be able to hurt me and weaken me. If he can turn you to brutality, he will have won."

"Isn't there some way to kill him?" Sylvie asked.

"He and Apollonius are adversaries," Zizi said quietly, "and Lycaon is immortal. The only way he could die is if his adversary dies. Yes, we can kill him. If we truly want to be rid of Lycaon, we have to sacrifice Apollonius."

She looked up at Apollonius, and the anguish in her eyes brought the horror of truth home to Sylvie and Lucien.

13

The little boy was playing in the yard, sailing boats made of leaves in a large puddle. He caught sight of Achille's car, carefully maneuvering its way around the water-filled potholes. The boy's face brightened and he got up from his puddle to run to the front door, proud to be the first one to announce the news.

"Hey, Mama!" he yelled. "Voodoo man comin'!"

The boy's mother appeared on the front porch, trailed by two little girls. The older one was wiping her hands on an apron, the other, much younger, simply hung behind her mother and sister.

Achille got out of the car and made his way toward the house. The little boy ran to him and jumped into Achille's arms.

"Hey, Achille! Where y'at?" the boy greeted him.

Achille faked a stagger. "Ooo-wee, *'tite cher,* you getting heavy! What you been doing, eh? Lifting weights? Lemme feel them muscles."

"Achille, come on in," the mother said, smiling. "I just made some gumbo."

"Damn, that sounds good, Clarice," Achille said, putting the boy down, "but I can't stay. I gotta go see Titi Dumard, her kids both got the measles. Hey, Tisha, you sure lookin' pretty, dawlin'," he said to the older girl. She gave him a bashful, but proud smile. Tisha was ten, that age where girls start to know they're pretty.

"I just came to check on Sissy, here," he said. He stooped down and felt the glands under the younger girl's jaw. "Okay, lemme look down that throat, little sister," he said. She opened her mouth obediently. "Ooo-*wee!* Looks like the Grand Canyon in there, girl! You got room to hold a party down there! Tell you what, that old doc done a nice job on them tonsils."

He let go and Sissy giggled and hid behind her sister.

"Tisha," her mother said, "go wrap up some of that gumbo so's Achille can take it home. Achille, I sure appreciate you comin' around for the kids, and those tonics you been givin' them."

"Yeah, they look good," Achille said. "Makes my day just lookin' at them."

"I wish I could pay you somethin'."

He frowned, "Shoot, Clarice . . . I wouldn't take it. Mae always said that healers aren't supposed to take money for it, you know that. Of course," he said, considering, "nobody said we have to turn away that good gumbo."

He took the towel-wrapped pot from the girl and smiled.

"You need anything else, Clarice, you know where I am."

She nodded. "Anything we can do for *you,* Achille, well . . ."

He smiled, kissed each of the kids' heads, and stepped back around the muddy potholes to the car.

He headed toward Titi Dumard's house, thinking about his life. Technically, he was still a cop, still Captain Broussard of the Homicide Division of the NOPD. Every time he considered returning to work, however, the very thought made him weary. In his work he saw every nasty little corner of people's souls, and how close to the surface the violence is, always. All day he had to deal with people who were miserably unhappy: there was no good news in his line of work. And even what passed for good news wasn't all that good. The best that could happen might be that you'd get to tell the family of a murder victim that you'd nailed the killer; even then, the cold satisfaction you gave them wasn't exactly healthy.

Yeah, he believed in justice. And the justice he tried to bring about in his police work was important. But he served justice much better as a loup-garou, and the conviction rate was 100 percent. There was a real satisfaction there.

So did he want to finally leave the police department? He wasn't sure. Police work had been his life, and he had to admit that he still had a love for it. But what he was doing back here on the bayou was important, too, and he could see that he was falling in love with this, with being Achille the Voodoo man, the healer, the man everyone was glad to see. It was a welcome change. And he was getting better and better at it; the power that he had been able to summon that first time, the power to heal, hadn't been a fluke, it had been an initiation. He could call it up now whenever he needed it. He had no idea where it came from—although he suspected it was Mae's spirit somehow passed into him—but there was no sign it was going away.

He was still thinking about all this after he finished with Titi Dumard's two kids and was heading home.

It was early evening when he pulled into his graveled driveway, and he was surprised to see the living room lamps glowing yellow through the window glass. He hadn't left them on.

He carefully pushed open the door.

"Achille?" a voice called. Catherine.

He dropped his bag on the table and headed toward the living room. Cat stood up to meet him. He was suddenly so glad to see her: her presence would distract him from all this thinking about the future.

He swept her up close, tangling his hand in her hair and crushing her against his body. The tip of his tongue lightly teased the tender flesh of the inside of her lower lip. She pressed against him, lifting her knee so that her thigh pressed against his sudden erection. She moaned as his lips moved over her face, down her throat.

"Achille . . . no . . . wait. . ."

He pulled back slightly.

"I have something to show you," she said breathlessly. "A surprise."

He resumed his voracious exploration of her body. "I got something to show you, too, darlin'," he murmured against her nipple, "but I doubt you'll be surprised."

"No, not here. At Bayou Goula."

This stopped him short. "Bayou Goula?" Only the Louisiana loups-garous knew about their sacred ground, and he sure hadn't mentioned it to her. For all his attraction to her sexually, Catherine was not Achille's kind of werewolf, not the kind that gathered on Bayou Goula. Taking her out there, he felt in a strange way, would be almost sacrilege.

"Come with me," she said.

"You want to change? Now?"

"No. We're not going to run, we're going to drive there just like real people. Believe me, Achille, you'll be very glad when you see what's out there."

Completely perplexed, and a little wary, Achille followed her out to the car.

They parked as close as they could to the bayou, but still had to walk a ways to the sacred ground. The moon was almost full, so there was enough light so that Achille could see even without his loup-garou's sharpened vision. And what he saw was almost enough to make his knees weak.

Bound, gagged, blindfolded, and sitting against a tree was the Reverend Ely.

"Oh, no . . . no. . ." Achille said in horror. He turned to run away, but Catherine stopped him.

"Come on, Achille. Don't be such a hypocrite. Could anyone have hurt you as much as this man did? Could there be anyone who deserves as much to die? Well, here he is. Why wait?"

Achille couldn't look at Ely: when he did, the anger rose in him fresh and pure in its intensity. He had never hated anyone more, had never wanted to taste blood as passionately.

"Yes, Achille," came an unfamiliar voice out of the darkness. "Why wait?"

Achille spun around. Facing him was an elegant man, tall and composed. He smiled easily at Achille as if this ghoulish situation never existed, as if they were old friends meeting in the spring sunshine in Jackson Square. Achille had never seen this man before, but there was something familiar about him.

Achille, not understanding why he would do such a thing, reached out slowly and touched the man's face. The psychic information came at once, and Achille was a werewolf who knew history.

"Lycaon," he said in dismayed wonder. "Oh, my God . . ." He looked at Catherine and instantly made the connection between father and daughter.

"Now, let's be honest with each other," Lycaon said pleasantly. "I know your arguments against killing this"—he waved his hand to indicate Ely, whimpering in the darkness—"this human garbage. But one thing stands as absolute truth: the man is a cold-blooded murderer. And if, as you believe, the loup-garou exists to mete out justice, then you'll be performing a sacred act. The man has certainly escaped human justice.''

"Not yet, he hasn't,'' Achille said with a real effort. Ely's terror was acting on him like an intoxicant, inflaming him to rip the man apart. He wondered if Catherine and Lycaon felt it as strongly. He could barely resist it: he could feel the resistance of Ely's skin against his teeth as the fangs sank in, deeply, piercing the sheer covering of skin, tearing tough muscle, hitting against bone, then breaking through. He could feel the warm liquid of blood filling his mouth, flowing down his chin, his throat.

He imagined smearing it triumphantly over his own body.

Achille tried to tear his mind away from these images, but they would only pass by for a few seconds, then re-emerge as sharply defined as before. "He still has to stand trial,'' Achille said tightly, the words struggling from his throat, "and he'll be convicted.''

"You sound awfully sure of that,'' Lycaon said. "But you know, Achille . . . he has an excellent lawyer, one of the best that blood money can buy. And that's very good indeed. Several rich murderers are free today because of Russell Berkman. If Ely's acquitted, you can be sure that the same money that hired his lawyer will keep him in safety—far away from you. And probably in luxury as well. He'll be famous, you know. He'll be a celebrity murderer and there'll be book deals, movie deals, TV movies. His 'ministry,' as he calls it, will probably spread. He'll have it all, just like he wants it. And, Achille''—Lycaon moved close to Achille and looked right into his face, enunciating each word so that they would be burned into his brain forever—"your wife's murderer doesn't even feel any remorse for it.''

"If he's acquitted, he'll never be able to run far enough,'' Achille said, trying desperately to believe it.

Lycaon laughed. "You're awfully good at lying to yourself, my friend. In any case, it isn't justice you want. It's
revenge. Why not take it, Achille? What's really stopping
you? Principles? Good God, man: *he* had principles and
look what they allowed him to do with a clear conscience!"

A wave of violent hate so powerful that it blinded him
washed over Achille. It was as if he could see nothing but
Ely screaming as Mae had screamed, falling as she had
fallen, being brutally murdered as she had been. And he
could see himself, in a brilliantly clear vision, exulting over
the death.

Exactly as Ely had exulted.

The thought turned him to ice.

Was he no better than Ely, then? Was this what he
wanted, to be like him? To kill and use the excuse that he
had been ordained to do it?

Achille realized that the answer to that question could
very well destroy him. He had to run, this minute, without
thinking about it, to get away. He might be able to resist
now, but he knew he wouldn't be able to a second time.

He strode quickly to Ely and jerked him to his feet. He
untied his hands but left the blindfold and the gag in place.

"Listen to me, and I mean listen very carefully, because
you could be dead in three seconds. You're free to leave
here, but if I hear one word from anyone about what passed
here tonight, you're a dead man. And it'll be the worst
death you can imagine. It'll be long and slow and agonizing
and you'll be praying to that monstrous God you've invented to take you—provided I haven't ripped your tongue
out by the roots and you can still make a sound besides
screaming. Don't think Jesus is gonna save your ass, because you gave up his mercy when you killed my wife.
Only I will be able to release you and I never will. Don't
make the mistake of thinking that you can have a private

conversation with anyone about this, because I'll know it.
I'll know your thoughts, your dreams, your dirty little whispers in the dark. Not that anyone would believe you. But
I'll come for you, you can be sure of that. And nothing
you've ever conceived of in your worst nightmares will be
anything as bad as what I'll do to you. You have no idea
of how slowly and painfully a man can die, but you'll find
out. Do you think you've got all that?''

Ely nodded his head. Achille was pleased to note that
that man was so scared he could barely stand.

Achille turned and walked away, without looking at
Catherine or Lycaon. But he heard Lycaon's soft laughter
behind him.

As if Lycaon knew that Achille would be back.

14

Joe Ed Landry had seen a lot of dead bodies, in various stages of decomposition and with the evidences of brutality, but this was pretty damn gruesome. Thirty years with the police department and nothing like this had ever come up. This was the kind of thing you'd see in California or Miami, where the drug dealers are little more than animals, or in those little midwestern tank towns where the people get so bored they go nuts. But not in New Orleans.

This was also the quietest crime scene he'd ever seen. No wiseass remarks from the troops, no bitching and moaning, just shocked silence. After the first few whispers, there seemed to be nothing to say. Everyone was going about his or her own business and talk was kept to the bare necessities, and then in low tones. Few of the officers and forensics people would accord this particular victim much sympathy. Some of them would even say that he had gotten exactly what he deserved.

But the sight of it wasn't something you'd forget so easily.

According to what forensics could ascertain at the scene, the Reverend Eric Ely had had his skin flayed off, slowly and in stages. It would seem to the forensics people that he had still been alive when this was done. His heart had been ripped out and was missing. Certain other parts of his body were also not accounted for. His right hand, for instance—the hand that he had used to kill Mae Charteris—was gone.

And when it was over, Ely had been propped up and nailed to a tree by his wrists, his arms stretched over his head, where he hung at that very moment, his dead eyes looking skewered at Joe Ed Landry.

Ely stood against the tree as the police cameras flashed, posing for his death portraits as conscientiously as he had posed for the press during his arraignment and indictment.

Lt. John Sullivan moved closer to Joe Ed and regarded the body. "Funny about the face," Sullivan said.

"Yeah," Landry said, "they left it untouched so that there'd be no question about the ID."

"God," Sullivan said, shuddering. After a moment, he said, "You want me to tell Achille, or do you want to do it? He's going to have to know."

Landry never wanted to do anything less in his life. "Yeah. I'll go out and see him. I don't want him to get no phone call or nothin'."

Landry took one more look at Ely and shook his head. He started to move away.

"Joe Ed," Sullivan said, his voice even lower. He seemed to have a little trouble talking. "While . . . well, as long as you're out there . . ." He swallowed, then spoke more clearly. "Find out where he was last night."

"Aw, for chrissake, John!" Joe Ed's indignant explosion cut through the muffled voices, and several officers turned to look.

"I want to *protect* him, Joe Ed," Sullivan said, "and don't tell me that Achille wasn't the first person you thought of when you saw this scumbag dead. Just remember: you won't be the only person thinking that."

"Achille woulda just shot him. He wouldn't of done *this*!"

Sullivan shook his head. "I don't know. If it had been my wife he killed like that, I think I might have."

Sullivan took another look at the corpse. "While you talk to him, you might tell him to expect a call from the chief. No way the department's gonna let him sit *this* one out. No more fishing and dangling his feet in the warm water of the bayou while he downs a coupla cold Dixies. He's going to have to get his ass back to work."

The loups-garous, stunned with the news about Ely, had gathered again, this time in Zizi's living room. Lucien, Sylvie, Apollonius, Walt, John Luparo, Darryl, Evangeline and a few others were there.

When they'd heard the news about Ely's death, so obviously a loup-garou killing, they became uneasy; some were even terrified. They all felt a cold wind blow through them. If Lycaon could get to Achille and influence him to the point where he'd abandon his principles, then any of them—except Apollonius—was vulnerable.

Achille, sadly, was not there. Apollonius had not only sent out a psychic call for him, but had also taken the more mundane route of using the phone.

Christian was also missing, but Delilah and Gabriel were there. The others were shocked to see the change in Delilah: her charming carelessness and vibrant, innocent sexuality were gone, buried under a dusty film of sorrow. It was as if Delilah's candle, which had always burned so brightly and cast such warmth, had been extinguished. She huddled close to Gabriel, who himself looked very weary.

Apollonius watched Zizi carry a cup of soothing tea to Delilah. Delilah took it and looked up, gratefully, the tears that were always so close to the surface these days giving her eyes the only shine they had. Zizi patted Delilah's hand and whispered something soothing to both Delilah and Gabriel. Gabriel nodded; Delilah just stared at her teacup. Zizi kissed both of them, then settled down next to Delilah, her arm around her.

"I can't believe Achille did this," Lucien said.

"There's no evidence that he did," Apollonius told him.

"I just don't understand why he's not here," Darryl said. "I sure feel sorry for him and I can see why he's holed up in Addis, but this is important. I was hopin' it would kind of snap him out of his troubles."

"It could have been Lycaon or Catherine who killed Ely, couldn't it?" Sylvie asked. "I mean, from what Apollonius and John told us about Lycaon, his objective is to create discord and confusion. That's how he gets his power. And this is certainly creating chaos. Wouldn't it be his style to kill Ely like this, knowing that it would drive us crazy wondering if it had been Achille?"

"You're starting to catch on," Apollonius told Sylvie. "That's exactly his style. He prefers to play games rather than confront me because the uneasiness he's generating among all of you fuels him. The longer he feeds on it, the stronger he becomes. You must understand that Lycaon is sadistic and selfish: he enjoys knowing that you're all suffering in one way or another. Delilah, Christian, Gabriel; Walt estranged from his father; Sylvie and Lucien dealing with problems that have no real root; Achille . . . well, who knows what's happening with Achille? Achille is keeping his thoughts and his actions to himself."

"But some of these problems started before we came to New Orleans," Lucien said.

"Yes. Lycaon has a very long reach, and it isn't confined to New Orleans. John first caught sight of him in Boston, so I called Georgiana. She says that the New England werewolves are having the same kind of problems we're having. He doesn't have to be present to cause trouble."

"He's managed to cut us off from what gives us our strength: our love for each other," Zizi said. "We've always shared our power among ourselves, keeping each other strong and happy. And it is precisely this unity that Lycaon cannot bear."

"So we must stand together now," Apollonius said positively. "No matter what happens."

"And what *is* going to happen, Apollonius?" John Luparo asked quietly.

It seemed that everyone wanted to hear this answer.

"I'm going to find Lycaon, whether he wants to be found or not. He and Catherine have been teasing us—Zizi and me—with tantalizing glimpses of themselves, trying to provoke us into anger and fear."

"Why the two of you?" Sylvie said.

"Because we know them," Zizi replied, "and we know them well. We know their weaknesses and their faults. All of you think of them as ancient werewolves with uncanny power, and they're counting on the fact that your awe of them will weaken you. But Apollonius and I . . ." She shrugged. "Familiarity breeds contempt."

"Finding them is going to be difficult if we rely on our usual psychic powers," Apollonius said. "So we're going to try something that's very old to me, and very new to you. But I must ask you to keep an open mind. If you'll all just join me in the shop?"

Luna had been cleared of the exotic, expensive merchandise except that in the display cases and shelves along the rose-silk walls. The Oriental carpets had been taken up and the wood floor exposed. In the center of the floor was painted a large circle, thirteen feet in diameter with symbols marked at each of the compass points. Inside the circle was a round table with enough chairs to accommodate all the loups-garous. The lights had been dimmed: a rheostat had turned down the flickering candle-flame light bulbs in the wall sconces. In the center of the table rested a round mirror, perhaps a foot in diameter, with candles in two tall gilt candlesticks on each side. The mirror was set in a wide, circular silver-and-gilt frame, incised with strange symbols. The glass itself was convex, coated on its underside with black pitch, so that its surface reflected the candle flames in mysterious black glints.

"Are we having a séance?" Walt asked. He tried to sound light, but his laugh was shaky.

"You could say so," Apollonius replied. He touched the mirror lightly. "This is a scrying mirror," he explained. "Some believe that, in it, one can see the hidden present, the future, and the past. This one belonged to Dr. John Dee, Queen Elizabeth's magician, the greatest seer of his time."

The werewolves looked at the mirror with great interest.

"How did you get it?" Lucien said, impressed.

"He gave it to me," Apollonius said matter-of-factly.

"Oh," Lucien said, feeling very insignificant all of a sudden.

Only Darryl looked uneasy. "Apollonius, forgive me," Darryl said, "but I was raised a Baptist. Now, you know I ain't very religious, except around election time, but I have a hard time believing in supernatural stuff."

Apollonius looked at him, amused. "Do you believe in werewolves, Darryl?"

Darryl looked puzzled for a few seconds, then thunderstruck.

"You can take your head outta your ass any time now, Darryl," Evangeline said helpfully.

"You've all seen séances in movies," Apollonius said, "and while this isn't the same thing, it's close. We'll all link hands," Apollonius told them. "That's to make our power flow into a circle, where it's strongest for all of us.

The mirror is only a tool: I'll do the scrying and you'll help
me by contributing your own considerable psychic powers.
Now, everyone sit comfortably.''

They all sat in the circle and held hands. The loups-
garous may have been a little spooked, but they were excited. They knew of Apollonius's ancient reputation as a
magician, but they had never seen him do any kind of
magic, other than that which a werewolf always does. This
was a very new experience for all of them, and they knew
they were in the hands of a master.

Apollonius paced slowly around the perimeter of the circle, clockwise. At the north point of the compass, he raised
both hands, palms up.

"I cast this circle to be a bridge between this world and
the next," he intoned. "All those forces and spirits who
come within it shall be perfect and correct for all of us and
for our work, and shall cause no harm. These forces and
spirits I ask to come to us, of your own free will, to join
us in our work of magic."

He waited a moment, then resumed. "From this circle I
banish all those forces and spirits who are not correct for
us and our work, or that may come to do harm. You cannot
enter, and must return to those places that *are* correct for
you. This is our will, and so it must be."

Apollonius took his place at the table. "Now, sit comfortably and hold hands. I'm going to put all of you into a
light trance, just enough to lower your brainwaves so that
your psychic power flows more easily."

They closed their eyes and held hands as Apollonius used
an old Pythagorean method of colors and numbers to induce
trance. The same technique was currently being used by a
modern Witch in Massachusetts, a great teacher, to instruct
her students to access psychic power. Apollonius thought
of this with satisfaction. The old ways endure, he was

thinking with comfort, as long as there are those who respect and use them.

When everyone was ready, Apollonius had them open their eyes.

He gathered his power and gazed steadily into the mirror.

Show me Lycaon and Catherine, he commanded silently. He waited. For Apollonius, it usually took less than two minutes for the images to appear in the mirror. With all the power of the loups-garous, it should take only a few seconds.

But it didn't happen.

He waited. A minute passed, two minutes.

Nothing.

This was impossible. The mirror never failed—*he* had never failed.

Something made him look up, beyond the mirror, beyond the table, to the edge of the circle.

Something was taking shape there.

Sylvie followed Apollonius's gaze and saw the slight column of white vapor forming inside the circle. She gasped, and the others looked.

"It's nothing to be afraid of," Apollonius told them in a hushed voice. "Nothing that could hurt us could get inside the circle."

The apparition continued to take form, growing more solid, until a woman, fully formed and looking very real and alive, stood within the circle.

"Mae," Sylvie breathed

Mae smiled at them. She looked no different than when she'd been alive. Several of the loups-garous turned pale; some, like Zizi and Sylvie, began to cry. But none of them were afraid; how could any of them be anything but glad to see her again?

"Mae," Apollonius said, "you didn't have to come. I

would never have called you from your rest.''

"You called for those spirits who *wanted* to help," Mae replied, "so I'm here, of my own free will." She gave them one of her old sardonic smiles, so like her. "You think I'll leave my old friends without help? Y'all got yourselves in *some* kinda trouble now." Her voice grew more serious. "But be careful what you ask me," she said, "because I can tell only the truth, and sometimes the truth is very hard to hear.

"Listen to me carefully, Apollonius, because I haven't got much time here. Lycaon and Catherine are together right now, at Bayou Goula. And they have Claire with them. They took her from the Marley house an hour ago, while the household was asleep. Her grandparents have no idea she's gone."

Lucien and Sylvie bolted out of their chairs, but Mae held up her hand quickly. "Stop! Don't leave this circle!" she said, as commandingly as she had ever been in her life as Queen of the Voodoos. "You can do nothing. Only Apollonius must go, and one other. Take something silver as a weapon."

"Who should go with me, Mae?"

Mae floated around the circle and stopped behind John Luparo. Putting a hand on his shoulder, she bent slowly and whispered in his ear. No one but John heard her, and he smiled.

Zizi spoke, very softly. "Is someone going to die, Mae?"

"Mother!" Lucien cried. "Don't ask that!"

Mae hesitated. "Yes." She looked at Apollonius. "The adversary must make the sacrifice."

The shock around the table was acute. No one spoke, since there were no words for this horror.

"If it's any comfort," Mae said, "please know that I'll

be waiting here for him, that I'll take his hand and guide him, and be with him until the time comes for him to return to you. We all return," she said soothingly, with a beautiful smile, "and death is never an ending to life. It's just the preparation for a new adventure. Do you understand?"

Zizi nodded her head, but sobs shook her.

"I love you all," Mae said. "And please care for Achille for me."

She started to vanish, dissolving slowly until nothing was left of her except the sweet scent of lemon verbena, her favorite. It filled the room.

Apollonius stood up slowly, moving again to the north compass point, where he lifted his hands as before.

"Spirits and forces who have come to help us in our work, we thank you. Return now to those places that are perfect and correct for you, and if it be agreeable to all, we shall meet again." His voice faltered a little on those last four words, but regained strength. He moved around the circle, counterclockwise this time. "This circle is open, but never shall be broken. So it must be."

He stood motionless for a few minutes. The others, their trance states lifted, were in chaos.

"We'll do exactly as Mae told us," Apollonius said, taking control of the group, knowing that action would calm them. "Giovanni, you're coming with me to Bayou Goula. Sylvie and Lucien, I know it will be hard for you, but stay here with Zizi. With any luck, we'll have Claire back before your parents know she's gone, so don't alarm them now."

He took a key from behind Luna's cash register and opened one of the glass étagère display cases. From this, he removed a small pearl-handled pistol and a set of silver bullets.

While the loups-garous watched, frozen in apprehension,

he loaded the chamber with all six bullets.

Zizi threw her arms around him, then looked into his eyes. "Apollonius," she pleaded, knowing that he wouldn't sway from this task and that she wouldn't really ask it of him. They had had such a short time together, really, when you considered a loup-garou's long life.

"I've been alive a long time, Marie-Thérèse," he said.

"But not with me," she said ruefully. "Every time we come together, something drives us apart."

"Well, my love, we had fifteen entire, uninterrupted years this time. Perhaps the next time around, nothing will part us. We'll be together so long that we'll get on each other's nerves."

She clung to him very tightly, then released him. "I'm not going to make this any harder than it must be," she said with a great effort. "I still believe that you're coming back from this."

He embraced Lucien and Sylvie. He clung to Lucien a long time, while Lucien tried to control his sorrow. There was nothing that Lucien could say, but Apollonius whispered to him, " 'This is my beloved son, in whom I am well pleased.' "

Apollonius embraced each of the loups-garous, some of whom were crying hard. Darryl had to be supported to a chair by his wife.

And then Apollonius and Giovanni were gone.

15

"What's the actual plan, here?" Giovanni asked Apollonius. "Do we have one?"

They had changed and had run with invisible speed through the streets of New Orleans, through Jefferson Parish, through the trees and fields and swamps of the night, toward Bayou Goula. They had sped past animals and humans who, sensing a presence they weren't able to see, shivered momentarily as the quick rush of air of the loupsgarous' passing chilled them.

"You've fought Lycaon before," Apollonius said. "He can't fool you as easily as he could the others. Mae knew that. You're to be my backup, John. If anything goes wrong, use the silver bullets."

"You really think they'll work? Immortality is immortality."

"Mae couldn't lie. She said to take a silver weapon. I think things will become clear to us as we go along."

They ran a little farther, and in a few minutes they arrived on the bayou. Apollonius nudged Giovanni. "There."

Claire was standing with Catherine, quite composed and trusting. Apollonius could tell that Catherine had, quite literally, entranced the girl. There was no sign of Lycaon.

Apollonius reversed his transformation, becoming human again in a few seconds, so as not to frighten Claire.

221

Catherine was kneeling on the ground and talking to Claire, who smiled suddenly. "Yes," Claire said, "I'd like that." And then, with a little apprehension, "Can I tell my mother and father?"

"Oh, no," Catherine admonished her, "it will be our secret. Just yours and mine, and then you can surprise them at the next full moon. Won't that be delicious?"

Apollonius watched as Catherine started her transformation. Her teeth were already lengthened into fangs, her nails rapidly growing into claws. The fangs were all she needed, really, to give Claire the *baiser du loup-garou*, the werewolf's kiss that would make the girl one of them.

Catherine's voice was silky, hypnotic. "And when my friend gets here . . . ," she began.

Apollonius strode into the clearing. "Catherine!" he called angrily.

She looked up, startled. Claire also looked at Apollonius, and at Giovanni waiting a short distance away, and she smiled.

"Is *Apollonius* your friend, Cat?" Claire said with delight. "Why didn't you say you knew Grandfather?"

Catherine tried to recover her shaken poise. "I've known your grandfather for a long time. And your grandmother, too. Isn't that nice?"

"Yes," Claire said, confused. "But . . ."

Apollonius took Claire by the hand and pulled her close to him. He was angrier than he ever thought possible.

"Really, Catherine," he said, his voice tight, "I can't say that I never expected it of you, but I never thought you'd have the nerve to do this."

"Oh, what's your problem, Apollonius? The child is obviously going to be one of us sooner or later, so it might as well be now."

"That isn't your decision, it's her parents' privilege to

do that for her, when and if she's ready. The kiss is a sacred act, Catherine; in your hands it becomes sacrilege. You have no regard for the child's welfare or her feelings; you're only doing this at Lycaon's whim, to cause more trouble. The kiss should be given out of love, and you use it for malice, like everything else you've ever done in your life.''

He looked into Claire's face, and put his hands over her eyes. She was still on her feet, but was instantly hypnotized. "Go over there, to that tree near John. Lie down there, Claire, and go to sleep. When you wake up, you won't remember any of this.''

Claire, following Apollonius's hypnotic suggestion, did as she was told.

"You're a terrible woman, Catherine,'' Apollonius told her, his voice calm with cold anger. "And you're a worse werewolf.''

Catherine seemed unimpressed. "That may be. But I'm still Lycaon's daughter, and my loyalty is with him. And he wants that girl. Don't worry, he'll get her, too. You can't watch her every minute.''

She smiled that terrible smile, repulsive now with her fangs grown out. She moved closer to him, with her old, seductive grace that she used so well.

"You know what Lycaon likes these days, Apollonius?'' she purred. "Little girls. And he particularly likes *that* little girl. He wants her as a loup-garou so that she'll stay ten years old for a very long time. And you know what he's going to do?''

She whispered in his ear.

Apollonius drew back, appalled. With a blinding fury, he struck at Catherine. His blow stunned her, giving him enough time to complete his transformation again. When it was over, he stood over Catherine, tall and fierce, his black pelt shot with silver, his eyes mad with anger.

Catherine shook herself. She finished her own transformation, then jumped to her feet and sprang at Apollonius with a slavering, bloodcurdling snarl.

Catherine was a strong loup-garou, but it was really no contest. With one stunning blow, Apollonius slashed at her throat, almost tearing her head off her body. The blood fountained out of the severed arteries in her neck, and Catherine crumpled toward the ground. She was dead before she got there.

Apollonius, his anger beginning to abate, knelt on the ground beside Catherine. "Oh, Lord," he said wearily. He was glad that Claire was asleep and couldn't see any of this.

Giovanni stood beside him, leaning over to look at the body. "Is she really dead?" he asked. He knew that werewolves recovered from what often looked like fatal wounds; it was part of the moon's gift.

"She is right now," Apollonius said, "but we'd better make sure."

He held out his hand and Giovanni put the pistol into it. Apollonius fired a silver bullet directly into Catherine's heart.

He and Giovanni looked at each other. For a werewolf to kill another was the loups-garous' equivalent of mortal sin, even if the werewolf was as bad as Catherine.

"When I first knew her," Apollonius said, "I thought that there was some hope for her. I tried so hard to teach her the ways of justice, to teach her to live responsibly and happily. But Catherine, I suppose, was too much her father's daughter to change. I can only hope she's found peace now. The poor lost soul." He took her hand briefly. "Sleep well, Catherine."

"You always were too sentimental, Apollonius," a voice sneered.

Lycaon stood a few feet away. Apollonius rose to meet him. "Is that all you can say, Lycaon? Your daughter lies there, dead, and that's your only comment?"

Lycaon regarded Catherine coldly. "She was a splendid companion. But I'll have another." He glanced at Claire, curled on her side under the tree.

"I wouldn't count on that," Apollonius said. "In fact, I don't think you're going to live very much longer. Remember, Lycaon, you exist only because I exist as your adversary. And for me to be your adversary, we must be exact opposites. You kill for blood, I kill for justice, remember? We must be equal. I've just killed for no other reason than anger, and I've killed another werewolf into the bargain. The minute I killed Catherine, I was no longer your adversary. You no longer have one. And so both of us must die."

Apparently, that thought hadn't occurred to Lycaon until just that minute. Apollonius took great satisfaction in the terror in Lycaon's eyes.

"And so, my ancient enemy, I invite you to sit here beside me and wait for death. Surely Dis, the god of the Underworld, has been waiting for us for so long that he'll come for us himself."

"No," Lycaon said, backing away from Apollonius as if, in him, he saw the face of death itself. "Jupiter himself cursed me, I'm Jupiter's creature. He couldn't be finished with me!"

"He was finished with you a long time ago, Lycaon. His curse was his farewell. And now you belong to another."

It seemed to Apollonius that he indeed heard the chariot of Dis, thundering to the surface of the earth from the Underworld, a black-and-gold chariot pulled by six ghostly pale horses.

Lycaon must have heard it, too, because his eyes were stark with terror. He dropped to his knees, shivering.

They waited several minutes, but nothing happened.

More time passed. Nothing.

Lycaon laughed and ran his hands over his body in relief. "It seems that we were both wrong, old friend," Lycaon said. "Perhaps we were adversaries only to provide amusement for ourselves, to make the game interesting. Immortality requires such imagination, doesn't it, or one becomes so bored. So it seems that we still have our game to play. And it looks like, right now, I'm winning."

Apollonius didn't move. Obviously, Lycaon couldn't see what Apollonius saw plainly: the huge chariot of Dis, the six skeletal horses, the commanding driver in a hooded black cape, one strong, spectral hand on the reins, waiting . . . waiting patiently, expectantly.

But for whom? Apollonius was mystified.

"Lycaon!" Giovanni shouted. His voice was so commanding that Lycaon stopped immediately and looked up.

Giovanni stood straight and tall, unafraid. Slowly and deliberately, so that Lycaon could miss nothing, he raised a pistol. Opening the cylinder, he showed Lycaon the circles of silver bullets, each in its own chamber. He snapped the cylinder back in place.

Lycaon laughed. "Silver bullets?" he said derisively. "What do you think this is, a horror movie? Silver bullets won't hurt me . . . *Eminence*," he added with a sneer.

"You made me a werewolf, Lycaon, because you wanted someone equal to you in the same way Apollonius was equal. You wanted someone who believed in the justice of the gods, who never wavered in that belief. And I *am* equal. Unlike Apollonius, I've never killed in my life for any reason except justice."

Lycaon began to understand.

Giovanni. Created in a moment of passion by Lycaon himself, with Lycaon's full intention to create another adversary simply because he wanted the face-to-face challenge that Apollonius, by his silence and absence, had denied him.

The full realization of what he had done and who he had created just dawned on Lycaon. And Apollonius understood what Mae had whispered.

Giovanni smiled. "Apollonius isn't the adversary. *I am!*"

And at that moment, he put the gun in his own mouth, angled it slightly, and pulled the trigger. Lycaon and Apollonius both froze as they watched the back of Giovanni's head splash away.

In the distance, Dis raised his hand, preparing his horses.

Lycaon's hand went slowly to his own head. He brought his hand away covered in blood. His head and face distorted as the wound was duplicated on his own body.

He had time for one startled, ironic laugh before he died.

Apollonius closed his eyes as he heard the beginning sound of hooves racing over the ground. He put his hands over his eyes. This was something that even an immortal man, even a great magician who had lived thousands of years and who would live thousands more, should not witness.

The hooves pounded close to him, shaking the earth. He could feel the cold wind as the chariot drew up, paused to catch up its cargo, then raced off, the smooth rattle of the wheels dying out in the distance as Dis returned home with his booty.

He opened his eyes to quite a different scene. Giovanni, dressed in the splendid scarlet robes of Cardinal Orsini, walking away from the bayou, guided by the Voodoo Queen, also in scarlet, in the dress she wore when performing her own holy offices. Neither one of them looked back.

Mae had always been a woman of her word.

Apollonius gathered up his sleeping granddaughter and started home.

PART
FOUR

✝

The Krewe of Apollonius

16

The day before Lent was one of those days that are not exceptional in New Orleans: they're the rule. Temperate and clear, with a cool breeze and light clouds. Mardi Gras Eve would be a beautiful night, with the southern stars lighting the skies.

That morning, Sylvie and Walt paid a visit to their father and mother. They were determined to end the misunderstandings and soothe hurt feelings, but they were also prepared to state plainly that their lives were their own.

They found Andrew Marley more than willing to listen, though Angela excused herself from the conversation.

"I've got no problems with any of you kids," she said. "It's your father who's always been a tightass."

And Sylvie and Walt were willing to listen as well. With Lycaon's chaotic influences removed, they found that they had much more common ground to agree upon, and Andrew admitted that his anger stemmed from his own fears.

"We aren't asking you to agree with our choice, Dad," Sylvie said. "But we *are* asking you to grant us the dignity of our lives and the respect we deserve. I know you couldn't live as a werewolf, but we can and do. And we're proud of the work we do for justice."

Andrew looked at both his children. "I tried to forget how wonderful it felt, the physical side of it, the compan-

231

ionship. I wanted to wipe the good parts from my mind
because I could see only the killing, and *that* I couldn't
justify. But you've both justified it for yourselves, according to your code of honor and ethics, and I know you're
good people.

"But that was never really the problem," he said. "I just
wanted you both to do more with your lives before you
made that decision. You had so much promise!"

Walt and Sylvie looked at each other, finally understanding.

"Sylvie, you were going to be a doctor, you were going
to save the world through neurobiology, remember? What
happened to that dream of yours? And Walt, with your
mouth you could have been the one honest politician left
in the world. Are either of you happy with your human
lives? And how can you expect me to be happy for you
when you're not content with yourselves?"

They were very quiet for a moment as Andrew's words
struck home with unexpected force.

"I think," Walt said, "that we all have some major life
adjustments to make before we can talk again. But we will
talk again, be sure of it. No more of this silent suffering.
And we'll get Geo on the phone at that horse school she
goes to and make her come home for a few days."

"I wouldn't count on her coming around so fast," Andrew said.

"It'll be a beginning, at least."

Sylvie embraced her father, and he whispered, "You
think I don't remember, but I do. And you think I don't
regret giving it up, but I do. You never forget the call of
the moon and how it feels. Have patience with me. Help
me to understand."

Walt and Sylvie returned to Zizi's house refreshed and

elated. They felt whole again, as if a severed limb had started to grow back.

No one knew what actual words passed that morning between Christian, Gabriel, and Delilah, but all three of them showed up at Zizi's that evening, ready to set the Mardi Gras crowd on its ear. Delilah was her old self, maybe even more outrageous.

"Christian came over to Gabriel's shop," Delilah confided to Zizi, "and he said a lot of things, and we said a lot of things, and you know what we did?" She couldn't contain her excitement, and her voice rose. "Gabriel locked the shop door and pulled the mini-blinds and all three of us *did it*! Together! Right there on the floor of the shop, with all the tourists crowded around the windows looking at the little Mardi Gras displays! If they'd been a little more observant, they'd have a Mardi Gras memory for sure!" She giggled uncontrollably, and Zizi just laughed and shook her head.

"You'll never grow up, Delilah," Apollonius said.

"God, I hope not," Christian said, hugging Delilah.

The loups-garous of Louisiana were gathering again, this time as their joyous tradition demanded, at Zizi's. As of that moment, when they were all assembled, they were no longer simply the loups-garous, they were the Krewe of Apollonius. They took this name only at Mardi Gras, when they would transform publicly into the beautiful, graceful creatures that were their true selves, dancing in the streets, and charming the humans who were fortunate enough to cross their paths.

And few humans could resist them. They would be tall, covered with sleek, shining fur. Their faces would be almost human, but mystical, with elongated, tip-tilted eyes like jewels; brows swept back to the temples; magnificent manes of hair billowing past their shoulders and down their backs. Their hands, tipped with three- or four-inch claws, would move with the hypnotic rhythm of a Chinese mandarin's, carrying huge silver and gold fans. The symbols of the Krewe, a gold howling wolf set against a placid silver full moon with the face of a serene goddess, would shine on their fingers or around their necks. Humans would sense their power and their erotic presence, and would marvel at what they thought were masterful makeup effects, never knowing that they had been embraced by legends.

"Okay, if everyone's accounted for, everybody in the dining room for the Pre–Mardi Gras Pig-Out," Sylvie said. "Uh . . . *is* everybody accounted for?" she asked, counting heads.

"Everybody but Achille," Darryl said softly.

"Shee-it, y'all know there's no accounting for me," Achille said, coming in the door.

No one moved. They were all that surprised.

Achille raised an eyebrow, then looked down at himself. "My fly ain't open, is it? I can see where that'd make everybody speechless, especially the women." He grabbed the nearest woman—it would *have* to be Delilah—and bent her backward with a lascivious, smoldering stare. "Show me how much ya missed me, dawlin'," he growled. "Or," he said, considering, "maybe not. You got two pricks already, you don't need another one."

"Jee-zuz, Achille," Gabriel said, releasing an interested Delilah from Achille's clutches and embracing him. "Don't give her any more ideas."

It became a party for real after that.

The loups-garous had a big meal, a lot of Mardi Gras king cake and lemon sherbet, enough wine to make everyone happy, then all of them prepared for the transformation and the night's festivities.

They transformed together, all but Achille and Apollonius, who promised they'd be along shortly. "Don't you be too long," Zizi teased Apollonius. "I might meet a handsome human who's younger than you."

"Honey, everyone in the world is younger than me," Apollonius said, kissing her.

The loups-garous, shouting, singing, and dancing, pranced out into the raucous streets of the French Quarter.

And suddenly Achille and Apollonius were alone.

Achille's face lost the carefree happiness he'd managed to keep up while the others were there, and Apollonius was sad, but not surprised, to see new lines in his face, a new look in his eyes that told him that Achille had lost his innocence forever.

"I had to do it," Achille said. "I know I should regret it, that I've betrayed everything I've always believed in. But killing him was what I believed in at that moment, Apollonius. I had always protected Mae and, in the end, she deserved that much from me. I couldn't let that monster live for one more minute. I couldn't let the monster in *myself* keep growing. And it would have. I'd never be rid of that obsession for revenge. It would have killed me, or turned me into a man consumed with hate."

"Do you feel hate now, Achille?"

He shook his head. "No. I feel . . . released."

Achille took a deep breath. "I want you to understand, Apollonius: it wasn't Lycaon; it wasn't his influence or his suggestions or his actions. It was me. I wanted to kill Ely. It came from my own soul."

Apollonius did understand. In the past fifteen years, while he had lived with the passionate loups-garous of Louisiana, he had discovered the real world. And in the real world, principles are sometimes stretched and bent by circumstances. He was just sorry that it was Achille who ran afoul of the fallout.

"You shouldn't feel alone," Apollonius told him. "Why did I kill Catherine? Was it really for the good of the were-wolves, or was it my anger and frustration that despite everything, I hadn't been good enough to save her from herself? I don't think I'll ever have the answer to that question."

He embraced Achille and said, "Come on. The Krewe is already out there making mischief."

"You go. I just want to think a few minutes."

"Don't think too long, Achille. To try and find answers for this is useless, and it can only consume you." Achille nodded at him, and Apollonius slipped out the door.

Achille strolled out to the courtyard, where the breeze blew softly and ruffled his hair. The sounds of the Quarter came over the walls, rowdy and mirthful, brewing the fanciful gumbo that would be this year's Mardi Gras.

As he so often did, he touched the little gold hoop in his ear, and thought of the time when Mae took him out to Bayou Goula, when she made him a loup-garou with her Voodoo magic, and gave him his last kiss as a human being.

He became convinced that he could hear her voice in the rustle of the moss in the trees, the delicate splash of water in the fountain. Don't mourn too long, she told him. Make yourself happy, and maybe you'll make another woman as happy as you made me.

That would be just like Mae, he thought. She demanded fidelity while she was alive, and she sure got it. But she'd never want Achille to be alone and bitter. Like she'd always said, the great wheel turns.

It's ironic, he thought, smiling, that after all these years and all the hundreds of years he had left to him, that he had just now learned how painful it was to grow up.

He left the courtyard and went out to join the revelry, to take his place with the Krewe of Apollonius.

. . . And What Came After . . .

Achille was just getting used to his desk at the police department again. He settled into his chair, tilted it back a little, forward, spun around a few times. He opened his drawers and checked the contents. Hmm. He never did get rid of that litter of little paper packages of salt and pepper: now it looked like they'd mated in there and produced more.

He sighed contentedly and started going through his pile of paperwork.

There was a timid tap at the half-opened door. Officer Bayard Holmes poked his head through. "Captain Broussard? Can I talk to you for a minute?"

"Hey, Bayard, where y'at? Good to see ya. What can I do for ya?"

Bayard entered the room and closed the door carefully behind him. When he spoke, it was in an uncertain half-whisper, as if he were acutely embarrassed.

"Well, Captain . . . I have this problem, and . . . uh . . ." He stopped, looking for the words. "Well, my family comes from Addis, y'know? And I got lots of family still out on the bayou . . . and they said that you can . . . y'know . . . *do* stuff, help people?"

From out of nowhere, Achille knew exactly what he was talking about. "Okay," he said quietly and sympathetically, "here's the problem. You love your wife and things been fine up to now. But the last couple of times, you couldn't get it up and you got no idea why. So you heard I might be able to help you, right?"

Bayard looked relieved, then worried. "Man, I sure hope my relatives ain't lied to me, Captain. I feel like a fool already."

"You came to the right man, Bayard, and don't worry: nobody gonna know about this but you, me, and your soon-to-be-ecstatic wife." Achille scrawled an address on a piece of paper and handed it to Bayard. "I'm only in Addis on the weekends and holidays," he said. "Rest of the time, I'm in Mae Charteris's old house in the Quarters. If you don't know where it is, ask anybody around there."

Bayard, looking much less troubled, left Achille's office.

Achille turned, looked out the window, and smiled. So this is the way it's gonna be, he thought. Not a bad deal.

Achille the cop, he was thinking. Achille the Voodoo man. Achille the loup-garou.

He could almost hear Mae now.

You gonna do okay, white boy.

ACKNOWLEDGMENTS

Of the books on the history of the papacy that I used for research, none was more illuminating and horrifying than Malachi Martin's *The Decline and Fall of the Roman Church.*

The fourteenth-century pope in this story, Honorius V, is an invention, but I could never invent a monster as frightening as those men, made insane by unchecked power and arrogance, that the Church produced. That the Church survived them at all says something about Catholicism.

THE
WEREWOLF'S TOUCH
THE VOODOO MOON TRILOGY
Book 2

by Cheri Scotch
ISBN: 0-7434-7483-X

Andrew Marley knew the dark secret that tormented
his family for generations. It had cursed his grandfather, killed his father, drove his mother to madness.
Now, newly sworn into priesthood, Andrew must
face the evil within—a legend born of the Louisiana
bayou.

But temptation calls him from somewhere in the
night, even as the memory of a woman he once loved
stirs Andrew's soul, sets his wildest urges aflame. And
now time is running out—before his true nature is
unveiled by the light of the moon....